TARTARUS

Kieva McLaughlin

FOR SAOIRSE

CONTENTS

CHAPTER 1 - "YOU NEVER SAID ANYTHING ABOUT OTHER PEOPLE."

"James, you got away!" Stevie squealed, embracing him in a hug as his feet landed on Tartarus' hard ground.

"Yes, yes he got away," Grey repeated. "But not for long. I don't doubt our pursuers will be coming out of Big Ben's face any minute now. I know it's still nightfall, but we need to get out of here, and fast."

James smirked, remembering that only moments before he had destroyed one of Torpor's entrances to Tartarus and Arcadius. This ensured The Three World's leader and oppressor's minions could not follow behind him and his two friends, Stevie Miller and Grey Adams. They had just had an unfortunate run-in at The Controller's palace on their hunt to find Stevie that ended badly. "Don't worry mate, nobody will be coming through there from Torpor any time soon," he declared, a rare hint of pride shining through his voice. "Let's just say Torpor's Big Ben portal is out of use for a while."

Stevie shook her head in disbelief. "You never fail to surprise me. Do we even want to know how you did it?"

"Yeah, I think you do. It was pretty cool if I do say so myself, but now is not the time. We should still get out of here and find somewhere safe to lie low. Who knows how far away another entrance into Tartarus is? I am sure this will be the first place they come looking for us when they get here. Grey, lead the way; Tartarus is your territory after all," James instructed, looking around for the first time since arriving in the world and suppressing his shock at the partial wasteland that surrounded him.

"Luckily, I have planned for just this," Grey replied, urging his two new friends to follow his lead.

For the next hour, James and Stevie blindly followed Grey through Tartarus' London. Now that the immediate threat of losing Stevie, and being captured by The Controller's Whiteflyers was over, James could relax a notch and really digest his surroundings. Even though he had been told that Tartarus was the worst of The Three Worlds. A world reserved for the despicable and dishonourable when they died on Earth, nothing could have prepared him for what lay before him. While Torpor, and even the virtuous Arcadius, somewhat resembled the world James had grown up on, Tartarus held few similarities to Earth. The buildings that lined the streets were either halfway demolished or completely burnt to the ground. The roads were covered in potholes and painted with fallen stone. The bright colours of Arcadius were replaced with dull browns and greys and a constant toxic smell of sewage wafted through James' nostrils. These were only to be replaced by char and burning brick when they passed a newly extinguished fire. The grand impressive buildings that were usually associated with London were shells of themselves. Big Ben was the only landmark they had passed so far that had shown any resemblance to earth. However, as it was one of the portals into the other worlds, that was hardly curious as to why the Whiteflyers would leave it untouched.

"I thought I was hearing things at Westminster Palace when I heard my name being screamed," Stevie said to nobody in particular, breaking the eerie night's silence by reflecting on the hours before. "We were summoned by one of the older ladies to deal with intruders. At first, I thought it may have been a group of ignorant citizens wandering through The Controller's palace. I briefly thought I might be able to catch up with them and free them before any of the others found them." Stevie pulled her hand back through her hair as she shook her head. "It wasn't until I saw the frantic look in Darlene's eyes that I realised something a lot more threatening than lost residents was going on. I assume she had already encountered the two of you. I should have known that it had something to do with you by then James. I mean, who else would be crazy enough to break into The Controller's living quarters of all places?"

"Em excuse me, but I did most of the work," Grey announced, his charming smile reappearing on his face for the first time that night.

James rolled his eyes and watched as Stevie embraced Grey from behind. "My hero," she giggled, playfully pinching his sides and laughing as he squirmed. "I suppose you also learnt how to manipulate Earth while I was gone too, did you?" she smiled, well aware that Grey only controlled three of the elemental powers while James had mastered all four.

"James did help a little with the whole rearranged room thing, but it was with my direction of course," Grey insisted.

"I suppose it was with your direction that he destroyed the Big Ben portal as well?"

"Oh yes. You see, I have had your rescue planned for days in advance. Every detail was planned out meticulously. I couldn't have left a mission as important as this one is to chance. James may seem like the impressive one, but on closer inspection you'll see that, in reality, I am the heroic main character of this story and James is merely my trusted steed."

"Ooo, you see that is where you're wrong," Stevie corrected him, using Air to dramatically push a rather large rock out of her way. "James and I have already been through this. We have come to the conclusion that I will always be Batman and James will always be Robin. You're right though, there are three of us now. We will need to find a place for you in our group too. Oh, I know, you can be Catwoman."

James smiled to himself, remembering the conversation Stevie was referring to from a couple of months before. The time they had spent training to become Whiteflyers seemed an age ago now, yet only a few weeks had passed since they had participated in the competition that would decide who would make it. This certainly wasn't where he saw them ending up so soon after becoming Whiteflyers. Tartarus wouldn't be anyone's destination of choice, not for anything more than a visit. However, once he was with Stevie, and as long as she was safe, that was all that mattered.

"I'd have to go with Stevie on this one," James added, joining the conversation. "I've seen the house Stevie lived in on Earth. That has Bruce Wayne written all over it."

Stevie snapped her head back to James, her eyes

squinted and her nostrils flared before she turned back to Grey, "You have officially been upgraded to Robin."

For the next while, James, Grey and Stevie walked on in silence. Each of them growing more tired with every step. Their lack of sleep that night was starting to weigh heavily on their eyelids. Stevie moaned more than once that she would almost risk being seen if it meant they could take to the Air. To make matters worse, the same journey in Torpor would have taken half of the time. The constant redirects due to fallen buildings were taking them on a wild goose chase around the broken city.

"Now I can see why you have never talked about Tartarus before," Stevie yawned, as she moved her head from left to right, taking in her surroundings. "I thought Torpor was bad, but I'd take being bored over living in a burning city any day."

Grey shrugged. "Surprisingly, you get used to it. Not to say it's right that The Controller has left a third of The Three World's population to rot. No prizes for guessing why we decided he needed to be stopped."

James paused, "We?"

"Yes, we," Grey reiterated, throwing his hands up into the air. "You can hardly think that I am the only one who will not sit silently while they are treated like wild animals. They teach us that we did this to ourselves, that all of the ruins here on Tartarus are from rebellions we caused out of greed and lack of respect for The Controller. The fires aren't all old in case you haven't noticed."

"Whiteflyers," Stevie whispered under her breath, looking towards a cloud of black smoke in the far distance.

"Just the culprits. They burn down the buildings looking for possible rebel gatherings, not caring who gets hurt in the process. Luckily for us, the more destruction they cause, the more people they leave eager to join the cause."

"Where are all the people?" Stevie wondered aloud, realising she hadn't seen anyone since arriving at Tartarus.

"Well, it is the middle of the night, but they don't tend to come out too much, even during the day. Not in London anyway. It's safer inside, even if there's a chance you'll be cooked alive. The Whiteflyers don't take kindly to groups of people walking around. Anybody can be blamed for fighting against the system. No proof is necessary."

"Where are you taking us?" James demanded, still hanging on to Grey's first revelation. "What cause?"

"To someone who can help us," Grey replied vaguely, refusing to give in to James' interrogatory tone. "And the cause is the same one that I was under the impression you were working towards. The cause to take down The Controller and his Whiteflyers. Or, now that you've saved Stevie and found out that Liza is still alive, does none of that matter to you anymore?"

"Of course it matters to him, and it matters to me," Stevie answered for them both. "That's always been our end goal. While I didn't think that our chance would come this quickly, if it means our time playing house with the other Whiteflyers is up sooner than later, I'm not complaining."

James shook Stevie's answer off, "You've never said anything about other people. How do I know we can trust them? They could lead us directly to the enemy." James' tone had more than a hint of suspicion running through it.

"Say you, Whiteflyer," an accusatory female's voice came from above. James quickly looked up and positioned himself for attack as a tall dark-skinned woman jumped down from a broken second-story window. Her rough landing told James she was no Whiteflyer.

"Ah, so you were coming to meet us after all? You just thought you'd follow us for some time before you made yourself known," Grey said, feigning appreciation and holding his hand up towards James to let him know the newcomer wasn't an enemy. "James, Stevie, this is Bee. She's a delight, in case you haven't already gathered that."

James carefully surveyed the young woman standing before him. Her choice of black lace-up hunting boots gave off an athletic impression but her dark blue, slim-fit jeans highlighted a feminine side. An oversized denim jacket sat atop a cropped t-shirt with the word McShit written across her chest. Stevie stuck out a friendly hand, but an aloof Bee refused to take it. She chose instead to look past Stevie directly into a defensive James' eyes.

"As I was saying," James said an octave more loudly, meeting Bee's eye contact. "We don't trust outsiders."

"And we don't trust Whiteflyers," Bee replied even louder, running her fingers through her spiked-up short brown hair. "Yet here we are, coerced by Grey to help you out. Although, it seems to me that you don't even want our help, or maybe you just don't think you need it. Grey tells me you are a 'level 4 Whiteflyer' after all."

"You trust me Bee. I am a Whiteflyer too in case you have forgotten," Grey intervened, a small ball of fire appearing on the palms of his hands as he said the word

Whiteflyer.

"Yes, but you were a rebel first and a Whiteflyer second. We know nothing about these two, except what they've fed you. They're not even from Tartarus. They've been living lavishly on Torpor while our people have been left to crumble," Bee replied stubbornly, still staring at James. Her eyes squinted, not daring to blink.

"Well I've been to Torpor, and I certainly would not call it lavish. It is no Arcadius anyway, that's for sure," Grey replied, trying his best to diffuse the tension, "And, in case you have forgotten, the world that people arrive on after Earth is inconsequential. We are all equals. It goes both ways Bee. We can't expect equality if we are not planning to give it in return. Tartarus isn't the only world there are rebels on."

"No need to fight our battle for us Grey, you were wrong for bringing us here. We will be on our way," James said defiantly, taking Stevie gently by the arm and leading her away.

"But..." Stevie gasped, unsure of what to do but allowing herself to be led all the same.

"Now look at what you've done. Do you always have to be so defensive?" Grey moaned at a smirking Bee as he jogged after a steaming James. "Mate, how far do you think you'll get on your own? You've never even been to Tartarus before, and you should be well aware by now how different it is to Torpor. The sun will be up soon and every Whiteflyer in London will be after you, maybe even every Whiteflyer in England. We are hardly inconspicuous wearing the drudge blacks and Stevie is still in her Whiteflyer robes. You don't always have to do everything on your own. You trusted me before, and we got Stevie back. Trust me again."

James faltered, realising Grey was right. This was the second time that night he was questioning Grey's intentions and for no good reason. "Fine, but another accusatory word out of that Wasp and we are out of here faster than her little wings can carry her."

"It's Bee," the muscular woman spat, listening in from a distance.

"Ah even better," James replied, his arms going up in flames as he stared across the road. "You'll be easier to kill."

"And I've officially never been happier that killing isn't possible here," Grey mumbled under his breath.

Before anything more could be said, Grey shuffled back across the road and pulled a growling Bee towards the direction they were walking in before the disturbance. "Let's go! It's getting light."

For the last ten minutes of their journey, Grey let Bee lead the way. They paced down back alleys and over walls, before slowing down at a cul de sac of twenty or so brown-bricked terraced houses. Half of the homes still held strong, some showed signs of minor damage like missing doors and windows, and two or three were completely demolished. Bee turned to Grey and whispered in his ear, before pointing at the worst house of all. Stevie didn't look happy with all the secrecy, but just as she opened her mouth to complain, Grey's rebel friend fled.

"Welcome home!" Grey announced, his arms held high as he walked towards the pile of wood and bricks. "Well at least for the next couple of nights anyway."

CHAPTER 2 - "SCREAMING ALMOST ALWAYS MEANS WHITEFLYERS."

"Well, isn't he just full of surprises today," James shared with Stevie as he watched Grey disappear through a gap in the debris of the fallen house.

"Just come on," Stevie moaned, rolling her eyes. "I don't see you coming up with any better ideas and I need some sleep. I am shattered."

Reluctantly, James followed as Stevie scurried into the same small gap Grey had, mentally preparing himself to spend the day falling in and out of sleep in the cramped and damp pile of bricks that Bee had directed them to. However, the sight of the squashed sleeping quarters he had imagined never came. Instead, the entrance led to a cellar of sorts with wooden stairs leading down into the basement of the fallen house.

"Cool," Stevie gasped, frozen in shock three steps in front of James.

With the top of his head still sticking out of the ground, James nudged her with the end of his foot to get her moving. "Keep it going. I haven't even closed the hatch yet."

Stevie continued down the wooden steps, but her mouth hung open all the same. James followed slowly behind and a similar reaction tingled inside of him. A room as big as the Torpor headquarter's common room lay out in front of him. A voluptuous charcoal grey couch, smothered in cushions, sat on a dark varnished hardwood floor. Paintings, and even photographs, hung on the greeny-blue painted walls to James' left and a filled bookshelf to his right, spanned from one side of the room to the other. A door on the far side of the living area told James that there was more than one room to explore in the hideaway. While the basement, if found at the headquarters, or even at Stevie's old house, would almost look plain, in Tartarus, its contrast to the world above, compelled it to shine.

"Yes James, I am full of surprises today," Grey laughed, looking smugly at his friend's dumbstruck faces.

James smirked and playfully shoved him to the side, accepting defeat. "Well, don't just stand there with that smug look. Show us the rest."

Grey led the way around the other rooms in the hideaway, which were just as warm and comfortable as the first room they had encountered down the hatch. The room through the mystery door proved to be a long but thin and empty hallway complete with three more doors leading off of it. The room immediately to the left was a large bedroom, packed to capacity with six wooden bunk beds. The sight of the fluffy duvets and puffed-up pillows nearly sent James to sleep. "Well that's enough of your tour for me," Stevie yawned, her hands outstretched in the air. "You can show me the rest when I wake up."

"You can stay awake for one minute longer," Grey protested. "We should be safe here, but just in case, I need to show you the emergency exit."

"How about this? If anyone comes barging in the door, I'll completely trust you to lead me to safety," Stevie whispered, already taking her shoes off at the nearest bunk bed, simultaneously peeling the duvet back from the bed.

"Stevie Miller!" James said sternly, pushing his own tiredness to the side. "Don't you dare get into that bed. We might not be there to lead you to safety. They could have taken us out by then."

"Fine!" Stevie moaned, knowing full well that James wouldn't give in. "Hurry up then and show me the rest."

There were two more rooms in the hideaway. This included a small but nicely finished bathroom, with one shower, two sinks and one blocked off toilet, and a second bedroom. This bedroom was slightly smaller than the first but was decorated with more care. While the other room focused on quantity over quality with its bed choices, this room, the master room, only had one centred king sized bed. The walls were painted a dusty rose colour and a long sliding wardrobe ran along the left side of the room.

"So, where is this escape route?" Stevie asked, her eyes closing over.

"Patience Stevie," Grey answered, moving around the room, checking under the beds and then inside the packed wardrobes. "I haven't been here before either. However, all of our emergency exits are in the master bedrooms."

"There," James exclaimed, using up the last of his energy to point into the wardrobe. "Behind the clothes. I think it's a ladder."

"Ding, ding, ding," Grey responded, pulling the mix of white, grey and black robes and regular clothes from their hangers to reveal hidden planks of wood nailed to the back of the closet. "They lead to another hatch."

"Fantastic," Stevie said, a fake smile plastered on her face. "Now, to sleep."

For the first half of the day, Stevie, James and Grey slept in the room with the bunk beds, deciding it was better to stick together than risk being apart for their first night. The hideout proved safe and nobody disturbed them as James dreamt about someone being burnt alive. When the flames died down, he watched helplessly as Stevie lay on the ground unconscious. He woke later that afternoon to the sound of Grey's sporadic snoring to his left. Stretching out, he turned to his right and watched as Stevie, with her mouth wide open, drooled onto her pillow. Thoughts of their first kiss the night before wandered through his brain and his stomach filled with butterflies that fluttered into his chest.

"Staring at her while she sleeps," Grey whispered. "A lot of people would consider that creepy."

James flushed and scrunched his eyes together. "I wasn't staring at anyone. I just woke up, your snoring could wake an elephant."

"It's all of my power, it's just rumbling to get out," Grey chuckled, using air to lift himself a few inches off the bed and shake his body."

"Of course it is. It has nothing to do with that big

snout you call a nose," James teased.

"I'll take that as a compliment. I've often found that those with button noses and chiselled jaws to be rather moody, and after what I've seen this morning, rather creepy," he replied, sitting up and placing his fingers around his eyes and gawking at Stevie.

James threw his pillow into the air and punched it towards Grey, knocking him onto his back. "Shut up. You'll wake her"

"Wake who?" Stevie groaned, rubbing her eyes and sitting up onto the lower bunk bed. "You didn't think I was sleeping through your 'I am prettier than you', 'Well I am funnier than you' tantrum did you?"

James blushed, embarrassed about what she may, or may not, have heard and quickly changed the subject. "Well, it's a good thing that you're up, Grey has a lot of explaining to do." With that James rose from his bed and headed for the bathroom. Before he could find out more about what Grey had involved them in, a hot shower and a change of clothes were in order.

As impressive as the hideout was, the hot shower he had been longing for wasn't up to scratch. While it looked rather modern and pleasant from the outside, it teased him with short bursts of scalding water, followed by even longer bursts of freezing water. There might be a fair share of interior designers and woodworkers amongst the rebels, but they are definitely missing a decent plumber. Nonetheless, any physical reminder of Stevie's rescue had been washed from his pale skin and his mop of dark hair had its first decent clean in days. Afterwards, the master bedroom's stuffed wardrobe came in handy as more than just an emergency exit. James pulled on a dark green jumper and a navy pair of joggers from it. He had toyed with the idea of getting into the white Whiteflyer robes or even the drudge's blacks, but the best diversion he had right now was to blend in with the masses.

Once everyone was clean and dressed, James gathered Stevie and Grey on the couch. "Start from the beginning, Grey. How did you get mixed up in all of this and what exactly is it?" he asked.

"You talk about the rebels and the cause like they're a bad thing. When I met you, I was under the impression that we were on the same side."

"That's still to be determined. I can't be on a side I know nothing about, and you haven't exactly been open about any of this up until now."

Grey frowned. "You were just as, if not more, sceptical of telling me anything. You can't deny that. The only reason you told me everything was because you had no other choice once Stevie was taken to join The Controller's Whiterflyers."

James rolled his eyes. "Okay I get it, but just don't leave anything out."

"Tartarus is nothing like Torpor. Not all of the people here wander the world without purpose. Most of us won't let anyone decide our fate, certainly not The Controller and his followers," Grey began. "When I woke up in Tartarus a couple of years ago, I was almost immediately approached by a group of Whiteflyers claiming they had caught me out after curfew, like I even knew we had one. They burned my legs for ten seconds at a time. Fire, water, fire, water, fire, water. It felt like it went on for hours, I was sure it would never stop. Then I saw it, or maybe I heard it, I'm not sure which came first. There was an explosion only a few streets away. When the Whiteflyers were distracted a woman from the rebels came to me and got me out of there."

James had never seen such a serious side to Grey before, he was usually so carefree and sarcastic. Seemingly, Stevie was just as surprised. She wiped a tear from her eye and leaned forward to rest her hand on his knee, sending a pang of jealousy up James' gut. Not letting it get to him, he brushed it off and focused back on Grey.

"I felt broken, but as the nights passed the rebels put me back together. They explained about The Controller and his followers and how he was the ultimate power on Tartarus and the other worlds. They told me they were a group of people bent on resetting the clock to what it was like before The Controller was born. They explained the need to take him down. Not that they needed to explain that. I was well aware after I was welcomed to Tartarus who was good and who was evil. The Whiteflyers go on and on about the bad people on Tartarus, about how they are righteous in their mission to keep control and order. However, the people here aren't evil. They aren't now and they weren't on Earth. It's just not as black and white as that."

James glanced at Stevie as she nodded along with Grey. He knew she was thinking about her mum. Someone who wasn't given the best chance in life and ended up making all of the wrong decisions.

"I'm with Grey," Stevie piped up after a long silence. "The Controller needs to be stopped, and if that's the rebels' aim, then we should get on board. We've spent endless nights talking about his downfall and now we have the support to turn that dream into a reality."

James wasn't as satisfied. "So, how did you become a Whiteflyer, and why?" he questioned further.

"The more people that the rebels have on the inside the better. Not that I'm on the inside anymore, but at least I still have my powers," Grey explained.

James raised his eyebrows and stared down at his hands, his power source buzzing in his palms. "Yes actually, why do we still have our powers? We were told they were only on loan, that he could and would take them back as he pleased." Turning to Stevie, James directed the next question towards her. "Weren't yours gone as a drudge?"

"Yes they were, but I don't know how. We were unconscious throughout the process. I had to give them a vial of my blood and swallow it again to get them back."

"I think I know how," Grey jumped in. "Well partly anyway. If the rebels are right, it's still through your blood, albeit powers are a lot more complicated to take away than they are to restore. They are yours after all. The story goes that they have to replace every drop of your blood. It cleanses your body of your powers. I've heard rumours that The Controller doesn't need to do any of that though. Apparently, he can steal anyone's powers when they are in his presence. Either way, I vote we don't get close enough to him to test that theory."

James took a deep breath. "I reckon it is most likely scare tactics, but I am with you there."

Grey nodded once and smiled. "And, are you with me when I say I want to take down The Controller? Me and the rebels I mean."

James sighed, "I'm all for taking down The Controller, but it just isn't as simple as that. These rebels, they are mostly citizens, right? How can they go up against the elemental powers?"

"The how isn't important right now. It is the why

you should care about. Even if it takes rescuing one isolated citizen from the Whiteflyer's wrath at a time, that is more than most people can say. Meanwhile, they are gathering intel, waiting for the optimal time to strike," Grey explained, a fiery passion visible in his eyes.

"I don't know. I am still not fully convinced, but I guess it's a start at least," James conceded half-heartedly.

For the rest of the evening, the hideout's new residents made the most of their little home comforts. None of them were sure how long they would be permitted to stay in the basement and their next accommodation may not even have a roof, never mind a living area, bedrooms and a somewhat hot shower.

Tucked up on the large U-shaped couch, James looked around the room. First, his eyes met Grey, stretched out on the opposite side of the couch with a book he had nearly teared up over when he had spotted it a couple of hours before. It was a fiction book, loosely based around a battle that had happened centuries before. While books were bound to be scarce in Tartarus, the holder of this one, amongst others, would be taken and tortured if they were found out. That knowledge, to Grey, brought out a stubborn side in him that demanded it be read. James couldn't help but admire the rebel's small act of defiance. It made him realise the true purpose of the library of books beside him. It was built for a deeper reason than just as a way for the cellar's occupants to pass the time. He began to think more fondly of the rebels than he had since getting to Tartarus.

Next, James' eyes wandered towards the cream rug on the wooden floor, where a childlike Stevie lay stomach down playing cards. Her bent legs flopped up and down in tune with a slight shake of her head. He couldn't help but think back on the moment that they had had the night before and he began to dissect what it all might mean. Stevie hadn't acted any differently with him since she had awoken and was just her normal bubbly self. Was this because she didn't feel the same as he did or maybe because Grey was always with them? *'Maybe she doesn't remember at all,'* James thought a little frantically. *She was unconscious through the first half of the kiss.* James squinted his eyes and glared at Stevie, in an attempt to read her mind. They were usually quite good at knowing how the other was feeling, but on this subject, his best friend was impenetrable. Thinking back, he decided he also hadn't been acting much differently towards her since the night at the Palace. It was possible she was thinking the same and was waiting for him to make a move.

James had never really been the flirting type. Liza had come on to him and jump-started their relationship and he didn't have any other girlfriends before her to compare to his current situation with Stevie. He remembered when he had first told his sister, Jen, that Liza was his girlfriend. She'd snorted and declared that it was about time, as if he had been missing the signs that their friendship was leading somewhere else. He was completely taken aback, he was sure it would have come as a complete surprise. Thinking about Liza, encouraged a fresh wave of relief to wash over James' body. She was alive. He couldn't believe it, all of the months of worry were for nothing. She was safe. He really had been happy with Liza, and she'd always hold a special place within him. However, he could see now that it wasn't the same. It didn't fit in the same way as it did with Stevie. He couldn't explain it, not even to himself.

Pulling himself out of his daydreams, James stretched out on the couch. "Having no clock is even more unsettling when there are no windows," he declared to the room. "I am going to peep my head outside to get a better gauge at what time it is. We were asleep for a lot of the day, so I reckon it's rather late."

"If we're going up there, we have to turn off the lights," Grey warned him. "We can't be too careful when the trap door is open."

James did as he was told before climbing up the near vertical wooden steps. One hand tightly gripped on the bannister and one placed overhead to avoid hitting his head off the trap door on the way up. With a strong push, James threw the door upwards and continued his ascent out of the hole. The space above the hideout wasn't large enough to swing a cat, so James crouched and carefully moved towards the exit. The night was pitch black. Stealing a deep and long breath, James stuck his head out, taking a long look up and down the street before he stepped out of the makeshift wooden debris and into the night. The fresh air felt like home on his skin, and James smiled to himself as he stretched his back out. Ever since mastering all four powers, he had grown an appreciation for the four elements, Air, Fire, Water and Earth. Following behind, Stevie walked through the gap showing no need to duck down and Grey bent only slightly.

"So there are downsides to being tall after all," Grey whispered, watching as James stretched out.

"Don't be so hard on yourself Grey. Your mop of hair has just as much of a chance of knocking over the timber on the way back in," Stevie goaded, sticking her tongue out and moving her eyes towards his nose.

James chuckled and quickly covered his mouth with his hands to avoid being too loud and risk being overheard. Even though it was night and there were no lights around, who knew who could be lurking about.

Then James heard it, a loud deep roar coming from only a street or two away. A man was screaming. Instinctively, James made a start towards the sound of pain, but before he even reached the road a pressure that built up around him dragged him back. After a moment of confusion, he turned towards Grey angrily with a clear understanding of where the Air pull was coming from. "Drop your guard Grey! What do you think you're doing?"

"What do I think I am doing? What do you think you're doing?"

Another roar, this time longer and louder, egged James on. He didn't have time for questions and answers, so with a slight wave of his hand, Grey went flying two metres to the side.

"James Moore," Stevie grunted sternly before he had time to take off again. "If we have learnt anything since arriving at the Three Worlds, and again when we listened to Grey's story, screaming almost always means Whiteflyers. Considering The Controller will have every one of them looking for us by now, it's not a farfetched assumption to think that they are using the screaming to draw us out."

James paused but continued to stare towards the screams, unsure of what to do. Stevie was probably right but it didn't mean he should stand by while an innocent person got tortured.

"They'll come," Grey said, brushing his trousers as he found his feet. "The rebels, that is what they're here for."

21

"Who knows how long that will take?" a frustrated James replied as he turned back into the hideout. "We are minutes away."

"So, it's not just with you then. He always feels he has an incessant need to protect," Grey said quietly when he wrongly thought James was out of earshot.

Back in their hideout, the screams came to a halt. Lying in bed, James considered three reasons they may have stopped, but always landed on the last. The Whiteflyers moved on, the rebels caused a sufficient distraction, or the screaming man became unconscious. Most of the Whiteflyers he knew wouldn't say no to a chance to show off their powers and Grey had said the rebels set off an explosion when they had saved him, yet a bang never came that night.

"I'm just as furious about it as you are," Grey whispered. "Probably even more so. I have experienced it first hand." Too stubborn to reply, and needing something or someone to blame, James turned towards a sleeping Stevie and closed his eyes.

CHAPTER 3 - "WE GET OUT OF LONDON."

The next morning James chose to talk to Grey again. In the end, he had made the decision to ignore the man's screams himself. While it gave him a small comfort to blame Grey the night before, in reality, he wouldn't have been able to have prevented him from leaving if he really believed it was the best thing to do. He still wasn't sure himself what the righteous route was, but blaming others for his own mistake wasn't going to help him. Especially not when he had so few friends and so many enemies.

"So, what is the plan for the day then?" Stevie asked as they all lounged on the couch. "Relaxing yesterday was necessary and all, but I want to go and explore Tartarus."

"Not a chance," Grey snapped back before James had a chance to agree. "We are in a safe house for a reason. Leaving it, especially in the daylight, not only puts us at risk, but the hideout too. The rebels don't have an endless supply of these you know. They weren't exactly willing to let us use this one."

"Hmm, I guess you're right. I don't fancy sleeping

under actual rubble if this place gets compromised," Stevie reluctantly agreed.

Grey added, "Well, destroyed is more accurate. The place is more than likely laced with bombs to protect against intruders."

"What a lovely thought to put me to sleep at night," Stevie rejoiced sarcastically, her head shaking and her eyes wide.

"How did you get them to agree to give us this place anyway?" James wondered, looking around the living room. "And how did they make it?"

"All of the safe houses have been here for decades, if not centuries. It's not like we have a selection of level 4 Whiteflyers on our side to build hideouts for us, well that I know of at least. Maybe we have some in Torpor or Arcadius and they made the foundations on a visit, but I doubt that. It's definitely not made by hand anyway." James had assumed as much, he couldn't imagine a team of diggers and builders would go unnoticed.

"As for how I got them to let us use it, well, I didn't really give them much of a choice," he continued. "After you pulled me aside in Torpor's headquarters and explained your rescue plan, there was no way I wasn't getting involved. I'd spent weeks sucking up to Amos and his possé and had quickly decided that being a Whiteflyer mole was not the job for me. I figured that there was no better way to cushion the blow to the rebels that I was abandoning my post than to recruit two new and powerful members, a level 2 and a level 4, in the process. I figured they may have one less person they can trust inside, but they would have three more people they can use outside." Grey smiled like a Cheshire cat and held his hands out to Stevie and James, almost as if he was presenting them to the rebels himself. "I waited until the very last moment before I sent a message letting them in on the plan, including how we would need access to a safe house in this area when we got away. They of course didn't agree, insisting we'd be caught and captured. However, I went anyway and alas, here we are."

James shook his head. "Well having three new people on the outside is still debatable, but I've got to give it to you, your plan was even more unorganised than mine."

"Yet here we are," Stevie smiled, pulling each of them on either side of her into a hug. "My heroes."

Later that afternoon, while Stevie, Grey and James lay on the floor of the living room playing an old board game, three knocks on the cellar's door announced someone's arrival. Carefully, Grey jumped up with his finger to his lip to check it out. James positioned himself in view of the trap door, ready to fight with force if need be and Stevie ran to the master bedroom to clear the way to the emergency exit if things went badly. Grey had told them the day before that the rebels would knock three times and wait to be let in if they had to stop by, so while they weren't too taken aback by the bangs on the trap door, it was very early days to be expecting a visitor.

"What are you doing here?" Grey whispered as he opened the ceiling's door before James could get a look at who he was talking to. "Surely the hideout isn't needed by someone else already, we haven't even been here two days."

"Not exactly," came the voice James was dreading but half expecting. Bee's lanky legs, followed by her slender body, made their way down the ladder.

As Stevie reentered the room Bee sat herself down

on the couch and began to explain the reason for her arrival. "The news from the headquarters is that The Controller will not stop until you're all found. Our earlier hope that you could wait it out for a few days here and join the main rebels is not going to work. Even from outside the headquarters, it's obvious how seriously he is taking this. People are being attacked all over the city. We don't have the manpower to stop them all."

Grey nodded, remembering the night before. "Yeah, we heard an attack only a street or two away last night."

"I'm not surprised, they've dispersed all over the city. It's only a matter of time before your whereabouts gets out at the rate they're looking for you."

"Gets out?" Stevie asked, confused how a secret hideout's location could be discovered so easily.

"I don't know if Grey has told you yet, but he went pretty rogue on this one," Bee explained, glaring in her comrade's direction. "The operation, if you can even call it that, wasn't able to go as smoothly and secretively as we would like. There wasn't enough time to set up diversions and the hype around what happened caused somewhat of a buzz amongst us. Not all of the rebels are as passionate as we would like them to be. If they torture the wrong one, you might be compromised."

"So, what do we do?" Grey worried, looking from Bee to James as if one of them was bound to have an answer.

"We get out of London," James responded, having made up his mind as soon as he saw Bee emerging down the ladder.

"Out of London?" Stevie replied, a confused and sad tone evident as she spoke. "I haven't brought it up before because the time didn't seem right, but I can't leave London. I have to find mum."

James returned her eye contact as she spoke, a pleading look in her eyes. He knew she'd think he understood, but if the Whiteflyers caught on to what they were doing in London, it would do more damage than the good that reuniting daughter and mother would do. He, however, was not going to be the one to break the news to her.

"As touching as that is," Bee began insincerely. "Grey endangered more than just the three of you when he decided to bring you back here. The place is on lockdown and if getting you out of London will ease the tensions around Tartarus, then that is what we've got to do."

"She's right Stevie," Grey agreed. "You are useless to your mum if you're in the hands of The Controller. You have to think about what she'd want. Bee will look into her whereabouts while we are gone though, won't you Bee?"

Bee stared at Grey for a while, as though she was weighing up her options, before responding, "I'll do what I can. For now, I have been asked to take you to the border of London, you are to head South. Some other rebels have been tasked to make it look like you're headed towards Scotland. The Controller has gathered a task force together to find you, once they are out of London the Tartarus Whiteflyers will hopefully relax on their power display."

"A task force?" James asked, addressing Bee for the first time. "Who is in this task force?"

"How am I to know? Do I look like I am someone who is friendly with the Whiteflyers to you? Like I'd know them all by name, power level and the world they come from just in case you would like an update on your friend's whereabouts?" Bee questioned, her defensiveness from their first meeting still visible.

"Yeah because what use would that be? Finding out more about the people tormenting your city."

Bee scowled and turned back to Grey. "We leave tonight. Be ready."

"Bye Bee," Stevie yelped and waved after her as she fled back up the ladder before turning to a disappointed James. "What? Don't look at me like that. I don't have to hate everyone you do and she's helping me find my mum. It's in my best interest to stay on her good side."

"If she has one that is," James replied with a smirk.

"You should cut her more slack than you do," Grey chimed in. "She's been through a lot."

"We've all been through a lot," James snapped back before Grey had time to finish. "What gives her the right to act so high and mighty?"

"One hundred years of service to the Tartarus Whiteflyers does."

"She was a drudge?" Stevie asked in shock.

"Yes, she signed up to be a Whiteflyer just like we did, but she didn't make it all the way. She only finished her sentence as their slave a couple of years ago" Grey detailed.

Stevie's face went white. She hadn't said much about her short time as a drudge, but what little she did was never positive. James kept quiet, swallowing the lump in his throat and gripping his side as if to contain the guilt that was spilling across his body.

"Well no need for the pity party, just try a bit better to get along," Grey suggested, as he sat back down beside the unfinished card game. "Now, where were we?"

The vigilante Whiteflyers got their last fill of relaxation before Bee came back for them later that night. Thoughts of their first sleep deprived night in Tartarus ensured they took the effort to take a long nap before they gathered in the living area for the last time.

"Has everyone packed a variety of clothes?" Grey asked as he attempted to shove a stolen book into his overspilling backpack.

"I've got some Whiteflyer robes, drudge blacks, two spare tops, jeans and then just the outfit I am wearing now," Stevie said, pointing to her blue baggy jeans, white t-shirt and navy zip-up jumper. "I don't think we will need the recruit's greys, do you?"

"I can't imagine what for, but Grey seems to have packed enough for all of us anyway," James laughed, watching him unpack and repack for the third time. "Do you really need to bring a pillow?"

"Don't come crying to me when we are sleeping under a bridge for the fourth night in a row and your neck has started to cramp up."

CHAPTER 4 - "THE GUTTERS, THEY'RE HUGE."

After four more repacks and three knocks on the trapdoor, James, Grey and Stevie said goodbye to their temporary home to meet Bee above ground. James donned a simple pair of black jeans and the same round-neck green jumper he'd found when he first arrived at the secret hideout. Grey decided to go a bit more covert and wore combat style trousers and a khaki green jacket.

"Of course you're wearing that," Bee chuckled. "Do you want to stop by a muddy field on our way out of London to draw lines on your face too?"

"She jokes," James whispered to Stevie, cupping his mouth as they followed behind.

"Be nice," Stevie demanded, digging him in the side with her elbow before skipping ahead to catch up with Bee and Grey.

"Thanks for taking us partially there Bee. It's not exactly a sociable hour to be traipsing around the city."

Bee looked at Stevie a while before deciding whether or not to engage with her. "Don't worry about it. I'm more of a night owl anyway. If I wasn't here, I am sure I'd be out on some other sort of rebel business."

"Cool! Grey was telling us about some of the work you do. You can put me into action as soon as things settle down."

Bee grinned. "Well it wouldn't be me putting you to work, but I will let Deandra know you are eager to join the cause."

"Deandra?"

"She's our rebel team lead," Grey explained. "I am sure you will meet her soon enough."

"Ah, so there are teams, even better. Will I be on your's?" Stevie queried.

"Hmm, I assume so. They don't like to mix the teams too much, it's better if we know as little about each other as possible in case we are found out and tortured for information. You already know me and Bee, so it seems like the most logical choice."

"Definitely not!" Bee interrupted. "Rebels with powers are scarce, they're not going to group you all together into some sort of superpower task force."

"Well then, I guess they won't be using us at all," James jumped in from behind before a scowl from Stevie reminded him to hold his tone when he was talking to Bee. No matter how hard it was proving to be.

"Anyway, that's hardly relevant now," Grey brushed it off. "What's the plan?"

"I am going to take you out just past the London border. You're on your own after that. Deandra gave me strict instructions to let you pick your end destination yourself. The less we know about your whereabouts the better. Once you're out of view from the city you can take to the air."

"Then what?" Grey asked, expecting a lot more direction.

"Then you don't come back to London for at least a year. Until all of this has died down."

"A year?" Grey yelled louder than he meant to.

"Yes, a year. Weren't you listening to me back at the hideout? The Controller is taking this super seriously. He has no plans to stop looking for you until you're found. A couple of weeks is not going to cut it. He needs to believe you're a lost cause, that you're never coming back and that you have no intention of interfering in any of his plans."

"Well, shouldn't we at least be given a task to do while we are gone? London isn't the only place The Whiteflyers are tormenting the citizens after all. We could go to Cardiff or Edinburgh or even to a smaller town."

"No," Bee snapped. "You can go where you please, but you're not out on rebel business. You have got us all into this mess, so you can get us out of it. You can start by making yourselves invisible."

Grey looked at James for some support. "Aren't you listening to this? We are being exiled, doesn't that bother you?"

James shrugged. "I can't be exiled from something I was never a part of in the first place. A change of scenery sounds nice. Anyway, don't look at me, 'I've to be nice.'" With a grin, James moved ahead, clearing their path of fallen debris to make their exit out of London that much quicker.

As James worked up ahead he could hear Grey and Bee bickering behind him. He had never been a fan of being told what to do, so Bee's revelation that they were free from the grasp of the rebels had been a relief. While he likely wouldn't have gone along with any orders himself, he couldn't be sure of what Stevie would have done, and he wasn't going to leave her again. He had watched too many urban fiction movies to know that relieving one command of power only to replace it with another wasn't ideal. So, until he knew more about these rebels, he wasn't about to lay his blind trust in their regime. None of the Whiteflyers in Torpor had so much as mentioned a rebel group, so they were either really good at pretending to be invisible, or they practically were. In James' opinion, the latter was the most likely.

"So, how long have you been on Tartarus?" Stevie asked Bee while they were walking through the outskirts of London.

"One hundred and twenty-two years, and I have been with the rebels one hundred and eight years," Bee replied, staring at the floor as she walked. "Not much has changed, it's always been the same."

"The rebels, they haven't been able to make any changes in all of that time? Doesn't that worry you that they never will?"

The genuine concern evident in Stevie's voice willed Bee to continue the conversation. "It's not as easy as that. The rebels have been around as long as The Controller has. Where repression lives, the will for freedom will never die. However, sometimes that will is just a lot more active than others. The rebels' history is rich with near takedowns and coups, we are just waiting for the right one to stick. There was one only a couple of years back."

Listening in, James thought back to a history lesson he had a few years previous. The foreign dictator he had been learning about had been in power for more than thirty years. At the time, that seemed like a lifetime to James. He couldn't believe someone so evil could hold power for so long. He then thought about the Three Worlds, a place where people never died, somewhere where time was not relevant. Would that same dictator still be in power on Earth if he too never died?

"This is where I leave you," Bee announced when they'd been walking through less cluttered suburban areas for some time. "Remember, do not come back Grey, not for at least a year anyway, and stay invisible. Don't try to be a hero."

Grey didn't respond and instead walked ahead, filled with an irritation James had never seen in him before.

"Bye Stevie, it's been nice… well it hasn't been horrible getting to know you. Good luck with this one and don't let him get up to any trouble" Bee exclaimed, referencing a moping Grey.

"I will," Stevie promised. "Don't forget about my mum." With a nod, Bee turned and jogged the other way.

"Goodbye to you too," James scowled after her.

Stevie snorted, "You've hardly said a word to her for the whole journey. Was it a farewell hug you were after or maybe it was a kiss?"

With a shake of his head and a slight smile, James turned and followed after Grey. "What are you doing walking mate? Let's take to the sky."

The realisation that they didn't have to walk for any more of the journey brightened Grey's eyes and he shot up into the air. James, harnessing the air around him, pushed himself up after Grey with Stevie following in the rear. He sighed in a huge breath of relief as he swam in the air. As he moved through the sky James closed his eyes and let the moment fully wash over him. He could feel the air move through each strand of hair, down the neck of his jumper and out through his sleeve's cuffs. He could feel his power source buzz alive as it connected with the air through his skin. He hadn't been able to use his powers much since leaving Torpor and he had missed it more than he had realised. While he still hadn't reached his full potential, the longer he was able to manipulate the elements, the more his powers became like second nature to him. It was like speaking or moving his limbs. James went higher and then higher, and then higher again, completely immersed in the energy inside of him. He thought he could hear something, but he pushed it aside and continued upwards, his eyes still closed. Again James heard the same sound. This time it was quieter, but somehow more coherent. By some means, his body knew where, or more accurately who, it was coming from before his mind and a pang of anxiety stung his chest and caught his breath. Stevie, she was screaming for him.

Opening his eyes, James scanned the air around him looking for his best friend, when a separate ball of nerves doubled and then triple folded, filling his whole body. The furthest he had ever flown from Earth was the day of his initiation when he and some other Whiteflyers went building jumping off London's tallest building, The Shard. As James looked down he realised he must be four, if not five or six, times higher than that. He could see the lights of London far off to his left and nothing but the black of the night sky to his right. No wonder Stevie was screaming for him, he was nearly touching the clouds.

A controlled drop brought James swiftly back to the ground, where Stevie and Grey came running to meet him.

"Are you crazy? Have you gone insane?" came

Stevie's voice.

"Ehh sorry," is all James could manage, still a little shocked at how far from the ground he'd been.

"No need to be sorry Moore. That was absolutely deadly," yelped Grey, patting a sitting James on the back. "Show me how you did that. I've tried to see how far I could go before, but the higher I go, the weaker my power source's connection is."

"Don't encourage him," Stevie yelled, her eyes still wide from fear. "I was screaming for you to stop, but you just kept rising. Did you weaken at all?"

"I don't think so," James answered, taking himself back to the minutes before. "I don't know what happened, it consumed me."

"Well, no surprise that you're a level 4 mate," Grey continued, his face still full of awe. "I wonder what else you can do. I reckon now that we have nothing else to do we should spend a lot of time testing our limits, namely yours."

Stevie shook her head, "We won't be testing anything else tonight. My nerves have had just about enough. Let's plan a destination and then we can find somewhere to sleep."

"I say we head towards the sea. I want to see what James can do with Water," Grey excitedly decided.

James had only half registered what he had just done but was already yearning for more. "Yeah, let's head to the sea. Let's have some fun with Water."

"That's my boy," Grey yelped as he helped James up to standing. "South it is."

James, Stevie, and Grey headed towards Brighton but kept on the lookout for an abandoned flat or a house where they could get a few hours of sleep before making the bulk of their journey the following day. Now that they weren't in the city they could travel by day. However, finding somewhere to stay proved a lot harder than James had originally presumed it would be and as they lay amongst a grove of trees, he stared at Grey and his pillow in envy.

"I did warn you," Grey said smugly, his eyes shut. I don't know what it was like in Torpor, but most of the accommodations here have been called for, they do have to fit a third of the people that die on Earth here after all. I suppose if you're willing to spoon I can make a little bit of headspace for you Stevie, but James I am afraid your mead won't fit."

"Mead?" James asked, slightly disgruntled at the thought of Stevie and Grey spooning for the night.

"Your mega-head, your mead."

Stevie laughed but rejected Grey's offer. Instead, she pulled her Whiteflyer robes out of her bag and rested them under her head. James threw a stick at Grey's torso and followed Stevie's lead. "Just as comfortable," he boasted, raising the ground slightly under his makeshift pillow and softening and manipulating the hard mud he lay in to fit perfectly around his body.

"Hey, that's cheating," Grey squeaked. "What about us?"

"Oh sorry, where are my manners?" James answered back, swiftly doing the same for Stevie before closing his eyes and drifting off to sleep with a smile.

For the first half of the night, James' dreams were tormented with images of The Controller. He somehow had his family and was torturing them until James gave himself up. Matthew was with them, laughing as his mum screamed and his sister Jen cried out for his help.

When James finally woke up he could feel very real anger bursting to break free from his skin. A look around at a sleeping Stevie and Grey settled him and sent him back to sleep. This time, however, James' mind went elsewhere. It went to his granny's house in Ireland, she was telling him a story about her grandad when he was younger. He had commandeered a courthouse from the British for five days and nights, demanding they restore the law to the Irish people. His granny was very passionate about filling James and Jen's heads with Irish history and customs as much as she could. She didn't want them to lose their heritage.

"Time to wake up," his granny told them. James looked at her confused, her voice was a lot deeper than he had remembered it to be. "Wake up Sleeping Beauty," came again, but this time it wasn't his granny talking, it was Grey.

"What are you waking me up for," James moaned as he opened his eyes, realising what was actually happening.

"We have been sleeping all night, it's daytime. It's time to make a move. It would be ideal if we could make it to the seaside before nightfall. I'm sure you had a comfortable sleep on your Earth made bed, but some of us didn't have that privilege. I would quite like it if I could sleep on a mattress tonight, or at least inside."

Silently agreeing, James stretched out and took in his surroundings. It was his first time out in the daylight in Tartarus, and it only served to highlight the chaos around him.

"This place really is a dump," James shared, looking at the fallen down trees to his left and the brown patchy grass straight ahead. "It makes even nature look sad."

"Yes, yes my world is a dump and Torpor is a King's playground."

"I'm hardly saying that, but there's not so much as a healthy shard of grass in sight. I thought once we got out of the city it would clean up a bit better," James explained.

"If you think this is bad, wait until we pass a gutter."

"A gutter?"

"Where did you think all those people being relocated out of London were going to?" Grey asked.

Stevie nodded knowingly. "I heard about this while I was at The Controller's palace. It's like a slum of sorts. Well not just one, it sounded like there were hundreds around the UK."

"Thousands," Grey corrected. "I saw a couple of them when I first got to Tartarus. They ain't pretty."

"When we found you there, at the Palace, you said you went looking for information and that you found out some of his secrets," James remembered. "Was this what you were talking about?"

"Yes, well some of it anyway," Stevie answered. "A lot of it didn't make sense at the time or it only did in parts, but the more I am learning from Grey, the more sense they're all making."

"Well, if there's anything you think could be useful, don't refrain from telling us," Grey stated. "Even seemingly inconsequential things can mean something if it's paired with something else."

Once they were packed up, Grey led the way toward the seaside. They used Air to propel them there faster, but made sure to only fly a few metres off the ground. The closer they were to the ground the less energy they used up and after James' excursion into the clouds the night before, Stevie demanded he stayed close by. James feigned annoyance at her request, but in reality, her protectiveness sent a warm feeling throughout his body.

"Why aren't there any cars in Tartarus actually?" Stevie asked Grey, realising that it would be a far faster journey if they could drive.

"There are, just very few. I guess The Controller wasn't feeling generous enough to populate the country with them when he made Tartarus. I suppose we are 'too evil' to be afforded such luxuries. Some of the top Whiteflyers have them though. Either way, I can't imagine it would be very inconspicuous for us to be speeding through the countryside. We are supposed to be invisible after all."

"I would hardly call this the countryside," James commented, looking down at the rows of houses below him. "It is way more built-up than I remember the journey on Earth to be." James had been to Brighton a fair few times when he was younger. His dad would rent a house near the sea for some of the sunnier long weekends and as Brighton was close to some great fishing spots it would often make the cut. James fondly remembered one year when his dad borrowed a friend's old yellow convertible to make their holiday extra special. Jen complained the whole way there that her hair was being messed up and demanded the roof be pulled up. When their dad pulled over to concede to her demands and manually roll up the roof, he pulled one of the spokes that was keeping it attached to the car free. He refused to touch it again and cursed her for forcing his hand for the next twenty minutes. Nobody dared say a word when the rain came down on top of them until their dad broke the silence to ask Jen, with a loud laugh, 'how her hair had been holding up now'. The rest of the journey was spent in a fit of drowned giggles.

"I told you, they need to make room for all of the people. If we take a slight detour left we should come up to one of the gutters shortly. What do you say?" Grey asked.

"Lead the way."

After less than fifteen minutes of air time, James saw it. Half a mile away, over a dozen grey buildings sandwiched together. They were all as high, if not higher, than London's tallest skyscrapers. James couldn't help but scowl at the collection of buildings that stood before him. The closer he got to the gutter the harder the blocks of stone appeared on the eye. What first seemed like glass windows spanning almost the width of the towers, revealed itself to be holes in the walls. Even the highest floor held no protection from the drop to the hard cold ground. With no need for roads, there was less than two metres of space between each building.

Stevie gasped from beside him. "The gutters, they're huge."

As they got closer, the thousands of people inhabiting this space became visible. Every hole in every building was filled with hundreds of sunken faces. Walking around Torpor, he had thought it couldn't get worse, watching the people as they aimlessly went about their day. However, here the people didn't just seem nonchalant and uncontent with their lives, they were downright miserable and even worse, they looked terrified.

"We need to get back to ground," Grey announced, watching James and Stevie's reaction as they came up to the gutter. "There aren't usually around these areas, but there may be Whiteflyers on patrol. Three flying people not wearing white robes will give us away quicker than we can say Tartarus."

"This place," Stevie gasped, as she followed Grey's instruction. "It's worse than I imagined. Worse than I ever could."

"Why do they stay here?" James asked, refusing to believe anyone would want to live here by choice. While the rest of Tartarus was a burnt wasteland, anything was better than this.

"You'll see why soon enough."

As they walked toward the gutter Grey kept his eyes firmly concentrated on the ground, moving more slowly the closer they got. The ground was made of stone from a quarter of a mile out from the nearest building. There was not even a lost patch of brown grass or an undernourished tree to break up the sameness, so James couldn't imagine what he was looking out for. Then he felt it, moments before Grey shouted for them to stop. He would have felt it as soon as he landed if he was looking out for it, but his concentration was thrown towards the makeshift city that stood before him. As a level four Whiteflyer he was always in tune with the materials around him, subconsciously separating them out in case it came in handy. Two metres ahead, where the ground looked slightly lighter, his power source had come to a halt. It wasn't a walkway at all, it was something James had used less than a week beforehand to hold off the Palace Whiteflyers. There was a hole in the ground, four metres wide, entirely circling the gutter, with a thin layer of concrete hiding its whereabouts.

"We don't know how deep it is, but we do know whoever goes down, never comes back up," Grey gulped, staring at a knowing James. "You look shocked! I presumed that's where you got the idea from The Controller's Palace?"

James shook his head, unsure of what to say. He had thought just like him, just like The Controller did.

"How deep what goes? What are you looking at?" Stevie enquired, looking from one friend to the other.

Grey stopped staring at James, sensing his discomfort. "There's a hole, two metres away. If you look carefully you can see where the ground's colour lightens. The best way I can describe it is like a thin layer of ice over the deepest part of the sea. We need to fly over it, just don't go too high."

"So, there are people down there?" Stevie gasped. "Alive people?"

"Yeah, but not that many. When newcomers arrive they are forewarned of the dangers of trying to leave the gutter, but some people think the risk of getting out is worth the potential fall."

James closed his eyes, and concentrated on the ground below him, sending his power source in a direction he hadn't tried before. As it sored down, he passed all 23 materials over and over again, sending it off to the side every now and again to test the hole's limits.

"I'm no distance expert, but it's super deep. It seems like it goes more than a mile down," James explained when his power source finally reached out to no hole.

"Well then, that is a relief at least. There won't be anyone conscious down there. The pressure will be too much to handle," Grey observed and made his way a foot into the air before moving towards the cluster of buildings.

Stevie and James followed, but both stared at the floor as they did, hoping to get a glimpse through the thin earth to the abyss below.

"You won't see anything," came Grey from ahead. "It's just one more thing to add to the list of reasons why we need to take back the system and overthrow The Controller."

James' eyes lit up, an idea coming to mind, "I could build a bridge, give them an escape route."

Grey shook his head. "They will know we have been here, we can't leave a trace. The rebels have diverted the Whiteflyers that are tasked to find us up North. We need it to stay like that or leaving London will have been for nothing," Grey noted, tearing the smug look off James' face. "I am not sure about this gutter, but some of them have been here for over two hundred years. They will have to last a bit longer, or maybe a lot longer. It all depends on how long it takes to take down The Controller."

James shook his head, understanding, but annoyed at Grey's reasoning. "Yeah, because it's not like the rebels have got anywhere in hundreds of years."

As they walked through the buildings, the residents of Tartarus silently stared at their visitors. Their freshly washed bodies and clothes highlighted them as newcomers and James noted a few were eyeing up his rucksack. He moved closer to Stevie, keeping a firm eye on anyone that seemed to dare get closer to her. The people here seemed almost diseased, with their filthy cut faces. Their ungroomed hair reached their waistline, and engulfed the male's faces. Few even wore shoes and while he felt for them, he was well aware of the lengths people were willing to go when they were desperate. When you have nothing to lose, you have everything to gain.

Grey wasn't shocked by the residents like the other two were. Instead, eyes forward, he moved onwards, a predetermined destination in his mind. James wasn't sure where Grey was taking them but he obediently followed. He was putting all of his trust in him that they would come out of the gutter in the same state that they had gone in. Thousands of watching eyes later they arrived at the only open area James had seen so far. It was a square, roughly 40 metres long and wide. People clustered here, some sitting and some lying on the hard stone ground. It reminded James of the town square he had visited in Spain, without the grand clock, the plethora of restaurants and bars, and certainly without the happy and lively buzz in the air. Some stared into space, others had their eyes closed, but just like everyone else they had passed, most had their eyes on the new arrivals.

"This is the centre of the gutter," Grey explained. "The gutters that are made up of tower blocks can often be dangerous. People fight for territory and try to overrun buildings for themselves and their cronies. As a result, some choose to live here, out in the open. Rain or shine, they don't leave."

"Why is everyone staring at us?" Stevie whispered quietly, so only James and Grey could hear.

"Word travels fast here, the only benefit of being so close together. People don't leave and they certainly don't arrive in small groups of three. If they come, they come in their dozens, sometimes in their hundreds. Hauled in from all over the United Kingdom."

"And there are thousands of these gutters around the place?" James asked, looking up at the high buildings surrounding him.

"Yes and in almost every country. They are in Torpor and Arcadius too, but as you can imagine, Tartarus is home to the worst. There are too many people in the Three Worlds and not enough land."

"Why are they separated? Why doesn't he put them all together?"

"I guess because it's easier to transport the people to them this way."

Stevie shook her head, a tear dropping from her eye as she stared down at an old lady dressed in rags sleeping a few metres from her feet, "We told Anne to go with them if they come to take her. Who knows how long it will be before they move her. Tracey too. Let's go, I don't want to see anymore."

CHAPTER 5 - "IT'S LIKE OUR OWN SECRET HOLIDAY HOME."

That evening, James, Stevie and Grey had reached Brighton. Invisible in the dark, they took advantage of their bird's eye view as they stared down at the partially lit seaside city from up above. Usually known for its great food, enchanting seafront, museums, Ferris wheel and pier, the three friends were all deflated to find one of the UK's most popular summer destinations in such a state. While not completely surprised after their journey through Tartarus' London and the South of England, they had all the same been hoping for better. Even Grey, who hadn't visited the seaside since arriving in Tartarus, was dispirited. There was certainly no food in Tartarus, not any that the residents could have anyway, and the once magical seafront was covered in waste. Old clothes and useless items littered the beach and a smell of rotten eggs reached James' nostrils from five metres high. Impressive buildings that housed the museums had all partially collapsed, or had the windows knocked out of them, and while the infamous Ferris wheel was still there, it had been carelessly pulled to the ground. The people here were also a lot more visible than those in London, especially considering nightfall had just arrived. They were roaming the streets and scurrying through the rubbish laid out on the beach's sand.

"Are they not scared?" James asked, watching two women to his left fight over a pair of boots on the half collapsed pier.

"There are no rebel groups stationed here, so I imagine the Whiteflyers aren't as strict," Grey guessed. "This isn't what I had in mind though when I suggested we take some time to test our power's limits. It's not exactly covert and the sea is filthy. It's not inviting to even go for a swim."

James stared at the familiar, yet very different, city below him. "I have a better idea. We should never have come to such a populated area. What we need is somewhere quiet, somewhere super secluded. Luckily my dad brought me and my family here enough, so I know just the spot."

Three-quarters of an hour later, James turned back to signal to Stevie and Grey to land. While his mum always loved staying central on their weekend breaks, his dad sometimes got his way and rented somewhere more rural, close to the country's good fishing spots. The small yellow brick cabin with a traditional thatched roof in front of him was one of those places. James was unsure if it would be in a similar state to how it looked on Earth, however, from the outside anyway, it was nearly the same. Surrounded on three sides by trees and a small garden on the fourth side that led out to the sea. It was the closest thing to a postcard any of them had seen on Tartarus and even on Torpor so far.

"So, not everything in this world has turned to dust after all," Grey smiled, his feet coming to a light landing between two oak trees.

"You wouldn't even know it's here if you weren't coming from the sky. The surrounding forest must have kept it protected from too many intruders," James replied. "Not to say it's not already occupied. A previous owner or even a Whiteflyer could be inside. Get behind me. I will go first."

Stevie and Grey did as they were told, both aware that James was their best bet if they came across trouble, and the three of them slowly walked the remaining few feet into the little cottage.

"Is anybody there?" James shouted into the dark cottage, as he gently pushed open the dark wood door. "We mean no harm, we're just looking for shelter." When nobody answered, he stepped inside, signalling for Stevie and Grey to wait outside the entrance.

The small house drove a warm fuzzy feeling through James' body. Although without furniture, it was just as he remembered. As he slowly checked each of the five rooms for occupants, memories came swimming back to him. The first room to the left of the hall door was the smaller bedroom where he and Jen fought each night for the top bunk. There were no sides to keep the sleeper from falling out of bed during the night which made it all the more fun and adventurous. The next room was the living room, still with the fireplace where they gathered around to play board games. Jen always cheated, and they would usually end in tears, but on this particular holiday, he remembered nothing but laughter. The small kitchen in the front of the house was filled with wooden presses and looked out onto the ocean. He could almost smell his mum's apple pancakes that she only made on holidays. The last two rooms were a small bathroom and the room his parents used to sleep in, both as empty as the rest of the house. Free from people and household items.

"Pity we don't have sleeping bags," Stevie's voice came from behind him.

James whipped his head around, "I told you to wait outside."

"You were taking too long, and anyway, since when do you get to tell me what to do?"

"Or me?" came Grey as he followed in after Stevie.

James smiled and shook his head. "Well, there's nobody here anyway. We are in the clear, and as far as I can tell nobody has been here before. Not for a long time anyway. There's no furniture anywhere."

"This place is cool all the same. It's like our own secret holiday home," Stevie smiled, walking out of the bedroom and peering down the hall into the kitchen.

"It's just as I remember it. Now, let's get some sleep and suss out our surroundings in the morning," James suggested.

"Let's hope the sea isn't as nasty as it was in Brighton," Grey chimed in, stretching out his muscles with a yawn. "A morning swim is exactly what I need after a day of flying."

That night, as James heard Grey's loud snores, and watched him cuddle into his pillow, he swore he would fish out his own bedclothes, and maybe even furniture, from the local town the next day. If he remembered correctly, there was one a ten or fifteen minutes walk away in the opposite direction to Brighton. While he would go back to the city if needed, the dense population and the wreckage of streets didn't seem like a promising place to find anything half decent. He turned over to get comfortable and found Stevie wide-eyed staring back at him.

"Well hello Ms Miller," James whispered. "Wishing you had brought a pillow too?"

"Yeah, we didn't think that through, did we?" she replied quietly, hugging the spare jumper that was wrapped around her that much tighter.

Looking into Stevie's big brown eyes, James had a sudden urge to pull her closer to him. However, aware that he had no idea where they stood since their first kiss, he reluctantly refrained. "It feels like we haven't talked since leaving Torpor. Not properly anyway."

"Yeah, I suppose we were so used to it being just us. It feels different now Grey is here."

"Different good, or different bad?" James asked, nerves bubbling into his chest.

"Just different," Stevie smiled gently. "But, I do like having him here. He's fun to have around."

Even though James had to partially agree, he had been hoping for a different answer. He had spent numerous nights, since getting to Tartarus, fantasising about what it would be like if he could get Stevie alone. He always imagined she would be just as enthusiastic as he was. "I don't know if you remember, but just after we took you from the Controller's Palace...well I... we kinda kissed. Well, I suppose more accurately, I kissed you."

Stevie stared at James for a while before answering, her face unreadable. "Of course I remember, and it felt good." James' heart sped up twofold, and for one second he debated leaning in for a second kiss before Stevie continued, "However, I've been thinking about it and it wasn't a good idea. Not with everything going on anyway."

James' heart sank. He urged himself to speak, to say anything, but it was as if he had swallowed his tongue, no words came out. Instead, he settled on an agreeing nod and turned back to face Grey. He couldn't believe what he had just heard, she didn't like him. How could he be so stupid? He had let himself get too carried away.

That night, James turned in and out of sleep, Stevie tumbling in and out of his dreams. He woke that morning before anyone else and decided to get up and get moving. Sitting and thinking about the night before would do no good. He had set himself a mission to find a more suitable sleeping arrangement the night before and he wasn't going to come back until he found it. Rushing, before anyone else had the chance to wake up, he unlocked the back door using Air and flew into the sky. If he squinted he could see the village he had visited as a kid in the distance, so onwards he went, all thoughts of Stevie left back at the house.

While James' visit to the village wasn't completely useless, he didn't stumble upon the goldmine he had expected. It was a lot less populated than Brighton had been and after knocking on a few already inhabited doors, he found one house down a lane that was at least temporarily vacant. A half an hour later, he emerged from the small cottage, a single blanket richer. Not wanting to return home, and very aware that he had not yet completed his goal of getting bedding for both him and Stevie, he took to the sky again heading slightly inland. In the hopes of spotting more houses, or maybe even another village, he kept his eyes peeled for any sign of life.

After only around ten minutes of airtime James'

wish was answered and he eyed a rather large farmhouse surrounded by brown earth. He could only imagine it would be filled with fresh green grass, flowers, and maybe even animals if it was on Arcadius. However, as James went to land, he spotted a stout older man through the window. Staring at him, his face filled with fear, James realised almost immediately what the resident saw, a Whiteflyer. Deciding to keep the man from any further panic, and knowing there would be no spare bedding in an occupied house, he continued on his way.

House after house, James gradually began to gather a rather large loot. So much so that he had to make a makeshift bag, in addition to his backpack, out of one of the larger blankets. Still, he continued on his travels throughout the morning and into the afternoon, refusing to acknowledge the real reason he was reluctant to return to the cottage. He repeated to himself over and over that he would make one more house call and head on back. Eventually, as the sun began to shy away, James finally decided it was time to face the music.

As James flew back to the seaside cottage, he thought of his family and friends, and even a bit of Liza. Anything to keep his mind off the person he was refusing to let consume him, but as their new accommodation came into sight, all of the fences he had been building all day came crashing down. His anxiety began to consume him. He made a quick decision to let it take over, but only until the count of five.

He whispered, "Five...four...three...two...one..."

"Stevie, he's back!"

As James landed in the back garden beside Grey, a furious Stevie ran out to meet him. "Where in the Three Worlds have you been?" she scolded.

While he was in one mind to ask her why she even cared, Stevie's clenched fists told him it wasn't the time to dive deeper into her bad side. "I was out exploring, gathering us some supplies." When he didn't get an immediate reply, James nudged his head toward the floating blanket full of pillows and cushions to further prove his point.

Stevie didn't look in the blanket's direction and kept her eyes on James'. "And you didn't think to bring us along, or to even let us know you were leaving? It's now nightfall and you have been gone since before we woke up."

James started to get angry, he didn't deserve Stevie's wrath. She had told him exactly how she felt about him the night before, or rather that she didn't feel anything for him at all, so why should he feel guilty for getting away? "You're not my mum Stevie, and you're certainly not my girlfriend, that was Liza, so I shouldn't have to tell YOU anything. If I want to go off on my own, I have every right to." Stevie's scrunched-up face fell limp and she released her tensed-up hands. She took one last look at James before turning around and making her way back inside.

James turned to Grey for reassurance, but his shocked face told him immediately that he wasn't going to find it with him. Instead, he dropped the blankets to the ground and headed toward the sea.

An hour later, after James had finished his swim, he sat on one of the bigger rocks on the water's edge. He had wanted to run after Stevie and apologise to her as soon as the words about Liza came tumbling out of his mouth, but his incessant stubbornness refused to let him move.

"Are you going to stay out here all night then mate?" came Grey's voice from behind him, before he took a seat on a rock next to him. "More blankets for us I guess."

James smiled slightly and continued to throw the small pebbles he had gathered in his hands into the sea.

"I don't know what happened between you two last night, but she's been freaking out all day. She didn't even know if you were coming back. A note would have been nice," Grey suggested.

James breathed heavily. "Of course I was coming back. I just needed some space and I brought us back bedding, didn't I? Not that you'll be getting any. That stupid pillow of yours has been mocking me for days."

Grey laughed, "Well then, in that case, you better get inside. I've already taken the big knitted blue blanket and if you're not inside in the next five minutes who knows what I'll do to it? I've got to mark my territory." Grey got up, patting James on the shoulder before turning back towards the cottage. James glanced back after him just in time to see a panicked Stevie, who had been evidently spying on them, leave the room.

James took one last deep breath, before dropping the small stones out of his hands and making his way towards the back door.

Grey smiled as he saw James come into the kitchen and signalled with a head nod that Stevie was in the bedroom. James pulled at his sleeves, but followed his friend's direction. While he wasn't entirely sure that he owed her an apology for taking off without telling her where he was going, he was sure he owed her one for his comment about Liza. As he walked into the front room, Stevie, who was knelt in the far corner of the room folding her clothes, didn't look up, but noticeably tensed up as the floorboard creaked under James' step.

"I didn't mean what I said earlier. I was angry and taken aback by your reaction to my leaving. I didn't think you'd care if I left."

Stevie turned to her right, her red hair falling out from behind her ear and in front of her face. "Exactly, you didn't think. How would you feel if you woke up one morning and I was gone? No sign of where I was. Especially here, especially now."

James gulped. "It's not the same, I.. and you.."

"It's exactly the same," Stevie interrupted. "You are my best friend, probably the best friend I've ever had. You can't just get up and leave everytime we get into a disagreement. You didn't even let me explain what I meant last night."

James pierced his lips. "There's nothing to explain. I don't want to talk about yesterday. I want to talk about today."

Stevie raised her eyebrows and took a step towards the door. "Well then let's talk."

James stared at her for a moment, realising for the first time how red her eyes were. She had been crying. "I am sorry. I should have woken you up or even left a note. It won't happen again."

The corners of Stevie's eyes began to rise and she took three more steps to close the gap between them. "You bet it won't happen again. Or else." Her arms opened and she embraced him in a hug.

"Or else what?" James joked, as his body filled with a warmth you can only find from human connection. "Is the mighty Stevie Miller going to get me?"

"You can be sure of that," Stevie answered, pulling

away from their embrace and tensing her arm muscles.

"Amazing, you've made up," remarked Grey from the hallway. "Is this something I've to look forward to frequently or can we all stay friends from here on out?"

Stevie narrowed her eyes and pointed from Grey to James. "That depends on whether either of you plan on getting on my bad side again."

Grey held up his hands in submission. "Not me anyway."

"Nor me," James quickly added, shaking his head faster and for longer than was needed.

"Good," Stevie smiled. "Now, down to business. I bags the blue knitted blanket."

"I've already bagsed it," Grey jumped in. "Don't you even try."

James laughed, "There are enough blankets and pillows for everyone. In case you didn't notice, I've been gone all day looking for them.."

Stevie raised her eyebrow. "Too soon for jokes Moore."

The next morning, James' eyes opened to a pressure on his bare shoulders and a smiling face with curly, sandy blonde hair and blue beady eyes staring down at him. "Wakey, wakey, shaky shaky." The end of Grey's rhyme came with a rather harsh shake of the shoulders he was grabbing a hold of. James, never a jolly morning person, brought his power source to his shoulders, and concentrated on heating his skin to the point just before Fire would appear.

"Ah, what the Tartarus?" Grey roared, jumping up and shaking his hands. "Are you trying to burn me?"

"No," James huffed quietly as he turned to face the window and closed his eyes again. "Just helping you to get up faster."

"Ah, but it's morning. The sun is out. You were gone for the whole day yesterday and Stevie refused to have any fun until you came back. I thought we came here to practise our powers and we can't do that if you're sleeping?"

James grunted, "I was flying all day yesterday and I hardly slept the night before. Give me a couple of hours uninterrupted and I'm yours."

Grey didn't push it further but the loud bang on his way out told James he wasn't happy about the arrangement. James shuffled around for another while in the empty room trying to get back to sleep, but he couldn't connect his overworking mind to his body's desire. The sounds of Stevie's laugh from the kitchen finally urged him to get up and start the day.

Grey's eyes brightened as James walked in to join them. "Oh look who this is. I thought Prince Charming needed his beauty sleep?"

"We live forever and you still won't get enough beauty sleep to turn your froggy face into a handsome prince," James smirked. Stevie swung her head back and laughed loudly, not trying to conceal the continuous snorts that escaped.

Grey beamed in her direction and ran towards her snorting himself. "Rather a frog than a pig," he told her, squeezing her sides to heighten her laughter. James' eyes narrowed and he couldn't help but stare at where Grey pinched her waist. However, quickly realising his jealousy was uncalled for, and not even his to have anymore, he plastered a smile on his face and joined in on the laughter.

"So, what power do you want to practice with first?" James asked as they all stood in the kitchen dressed and ready for the day. James hadn't brought many clothes options but had found a clean dark grey hoodie on his travels the day before, so he'd thrown it on with his jeans. Stevie, who had packed slightly more clothes than him, wore tight light blue jeans and a blue oversized flannel shirt. The colour made her already huge blue eyes glow even stronger. Grey, who evidently didn't think there was a need to discuss what powers they were going to begin the day training with, wore his white Whiteflyer underwear which doubled as a bathing suit.

Grey pointed towards the sea and shook his head as if that was a stupid question, "Where do I want to begin? Well, considering there's a sea of water only steps from where we stand, I think that would be with Water."

Stevie rolled her eyes, "I am only a level 2 Whiteflyer. I can't manipulate water like you two can. Can't we do something we can all have fun with?"

Grey, with nothing to come back with, looked at a nonchalant James for support before stamping his foot and walking back into the room to get changed. "Fine, if we must. Let's start with Fire then. However, do not think it will even be up for debate in the morning, tomorrow we take to the sea."

As the three friends stood in the garden, Grey began the light show that was to ensue for the rest of the morning and late into the afternoon. Channelling his power source, a small ball of fire appeared on the tip of his finger and slowly, for effect, ran up his arms, down his chest, and onto his legs. He then moved two steps to the left, leaving a fire shaped man of identical proportions standing in his wake. "Cool," Stevie yelped, admiring how well he kept his shape.

"I thought so myself. I did it during the free style

of the competition," Grey smiled back. "Have you got it in you to challenge me, Miller?"

Stevie grinned from ear to ear and stepped forward. She shot a small ball of fire onto the gravel beside her. As it rolled through the brown grass and towards the sea, another bigger ball followed, and then another, and another. Just as the first ball extinguished when it touched the water, the tenth, and last, ball came tumbling out of Stevie, this one nearly as tall as her hips. James watched as the remainder of the balls made their way down to the waterfront and couldn't help but feel excited thinking about how far she had come. Only a few months before, he wasn't sure she'd make it far enough to keep her powers and now here they were, perfecting them.

"Hmm, I will give you points for control but mine still wins on creativity," Grey decided with a cheeky grin and a raised eyebrow. "You're up next Mr Moore, show us why they stepped past us and made you a level 4."

James thought for only a second before facing Stevie and Grey, his back to the sea. He held his hands out and smiled at his two person audience, as they intently glared back in anticipation. Suddenly, a ball appeared on James' left hand. He looked down at it quickly with an open mouth, feigning surprise. Next, another ball flashed onto his right hand, James moved his shocked face to follow, this time taking a slight jump back for dramatics. James shook his hands to rid them of their newest companions but the fireballs dared not move. So, James did as anyone would do if their hands were holding red hot flames and he threw them high into the air. Instead of moving away from the returning balls of fire, James conjured two more and threw them up as his first ones dropped back into his hands. Up they went, two and three circling the air as the others were passed from hand to hand and then shot straight back up.

"You can juggle!" Stevie stated obviously, whistling and clapping as James added the fifth and final ball to the mix.

"Boring," Grey yawned before chanting "We want more! We want more!"

James picked up the pace, using Air to move the balls along faster, eventually removing the need to catch them at all. James moved his arms out for effect and the circle of flames expanded. Slowly, he moved them back towards his chest and the balls followed, gathering together a metre from the ground. Quickly James shot his arms and fingers into the air and all of the flaming balls followed, zooming upwards further than the eye could see.

Stevie and Grey's eyes came back down to Earth and they stared unblinking at James. He could tell they knew more was coming and he wasn't prepared to disappoint. He moved his power source into the Earth and willed the ground to tremble. He closed his eyes and encouraged the vibrations to speed up, to get faster and more violent.

Stevie screamed and pointed at the sky, "IT'S A DRAGON! It's coming for us."

Grey yelped with joy as the flying flaming creature, created from the fireballs, swooped down towards them, more fire breathing out from its mouth. Stevie knelt onto the floor and closed her eyes to embrace its impact, but there was no need. A few metres from its target it burst into a firework display, before disappearing altogether.

Grey took a deep breath and pushed the sweat

from his forehead back into his hair before taking three swift strides towards James. "That was…. INCREDIBLE!!"

Stevie, whose legs were still too weak to stand, opened her eyes wide and shook her head. "You never fail to surprise me."

James laughed, "So, I guess I get points for difficulty and creativity then."

Grey squeezed his shoulder and nodded. "You definitely do and you'll get even more points once you teach me exactly how that was done."

James winked. "A magician never tells their tricks."

CHAPTER 6 - "I WAS NEVER A FIGHTER, BUT I AM AS TRUSTWORTHY AS THEY COME."

The following afternoon, James, Stevie and Grey all lined up in the garden in their white bathing suits.

"Ready, set, go," Grey shouted before they all sprinted towards the sea. James, of course, got their first but Stevie was surprisingly only a metre or so away from beating him by the time they hit the water. Grey, who had been the one to suggest the race, had stopped running when he had got to the rocks and chose to hobble the last three metres instead.

"I do wonder about you a lot," James goaded him. "Would you stop being such a wimp and get in here?"

"It's hurting my feet," Grey yelped as he used Air to jump the last couple of feet to avoid walking on the pebbles. "What's wrong with both of your feet? You're aliens, my skin must just be too soft."

"It's not your skin that's too soft," Stevie joked as

she splashed him with water.

"Oh, is that how you want to play it then?" he gasped, submerging himself in the sea and swimming towards her with a devilish look in his eyes.

"Don't you..." Stevie began, but never managed to get the rest of her sentence out because she was plunged into the sea. James chuckled and ran for Grey, lifting him up by the legs and sending him under after her. He had less than a minute to bask in his glory before the two drowned rats emerged and pulled his head under the salty waves with them.

After half an hour or so of messing around, James began the call for power practice. He decided, because she was unable to take part, that Stevie would be the judge for the day. It was up to them to use Water in any way that they could to impress her. Whoever she decided was worthy enough to take home the metaphorical trophy for the day was allowed to use the highly sought-after blue blanket that night.

"Deal, but you're going first," Grey told James. "You had too much time to think yesterday, which is the only reason you got the better of us. Today, let's see how you do under pressure."

James smirked and turned to face away from Stevie and Grey. He didn't need time to think. In order to beat Grey, he needed nothing more than to show his sheer abilities. No sparkles were necessary.

James concentrated on the water directly in front of him, to make sure that the sea surrounding him and his friends was not affected by his plans and remained still. He then expanded his reach to outside the safe zone and willed the water to move. The waves began to grow, each bigger and more powerful than the next. Within seconds, they were twice the height of James. Then three times, and then four.

Stevie gasped as they came crashing down on the seafront. "You'll drown the house," she protested. However, James had already thought of this and just before the water hit the grass it came rushing back to meet the sea. When he had finished with the waves, James immediately set up a whirlpool, and the water a dozen feet in front of them went swarming in circles. Faster and faster it went like a washing machine spun out of control. He let his power slip slightly into their direct circle to wash Grey and Stevie around in slow circles. Stevie let out a little yelp that sent a pang of joy all over James' body.

"Is that it? A few manmade natural disasters," Grey yawned as he spun around before James had brought his performance to a close. "I was expecting more than that mate. What a snore."

James blushed and slowed down his whirlpool before turning back to Grey. "I wasn't finished."

Grey extended out his arms into a stretch. "No need, we get the gist."

"Let's see what you've got for us then," James said defensively.

"Stand together my hunnies," Grey began, pulling James' arm towards himself and Stevie to nudge him closer. "Hold onto your swimming togs, because I am about to bring you on the adventure of a lifetime."

James rolled his eyes but did as he was asked and moved into a huddle.

The water in the small circle surrounding them, that had been previously used in James' trick, began to drop. James realised instantly what Grey was doing. He was creating a cylinder of air for them to stand in; somewhere that they could watch directly into the sea, as if in an aquarium.

Grey motioned for them to follow him as he moved deeper into the sea, the water-free zone following behind. The water walls had to be doubled to twice their height within a minute as they wandered deeper into the ocean. James mimicked Stevie as she reached her hand out to skim the water on her left side. Under the sea wasn't as spectacular as some movies had made it out to be, namely a comic book he loved based majorly underwater, but it was beautiful all the same. Tartarus was filthy, and while he couldn't speak for the whole ocean, this small patch of water they had outside their small cottage was almost untouched. He almost expected to see a fish or two swim by before remembering that there were no animals on Tartarus or Torpor. He made a note to himself that he would have to try this same trick when they were next in Arcadius, if they ever got the chance to go back there.

As they slowed down, it was obvious as to where Grey was taking them. An abandoned sunken black and white boat lay ahead of them. It was at least seven metres long and three metres wide. Made from a mix of wood and steel, the boat was in pretty good shape considering its age. The bottom of the boat had three intact yet rusty cannons popping out from holes on the right side that reminded James of the old war films his grandad used to watch.

"Freedom," Stevie read aloud in an awe-struck voice, referencing the chipped gold encrusted name written along the side of the bow. "Where did it come from? I didn't think The Controller would have copied this much detail when he mimicked Earth."

"It's an old rebel boat. I think it's nearly two hundred years old if I am judging correctly," Grey explained. "It must have belonged to one of the big coups that attempted to defeat the Controller and his Whiteflyers, the rebels had a fleet of boats just like this back in the day. They each had an inspirational name like Freedom or Hope."

Just staring at it inspired James. He never imagined the rebels would be big enough to even have one boat, nevermind a whole fleet of them. "How do you know all of this and how did you know this was even here?"

Grey shrugged. "I know most of it from the books I have found around various rebel strongholds and meeting points. The Whiteflyers aren't the only ones with a history you know. As for how I found this boat, I went swimming the day after we got here. You were off moping around England and Stevie refused to leave the house until you came back."

Stevie blushed. "I hardly refused. I just wasn't in the mood to go swimming that day. We had a long journey the day before."

"Well either way you weren't joining in on any of my plans, so I was left to my own devices," Grey replied. "Anyway, let's get closer to the boat. I didn't get a chance to explore inside it the last time I was here. I thought I'd wait until we were all here to do it together."

"Was someone too scared to board the pirate ship alone?" Stevie goaded, which was followed by a not so gentle shove from Grey.

As they moved next to the boat, Grey expanded their air source to cover the abandoned vessel. James took hold of the side of the boat tilted nearest the seafloor and hauled himself up. He then took hold of Stevie's outstretched arms and pulled her up after him. "Need help up princess?" he asked Grey, who was trying his best to reach the side of the boat.

"Nope, no need," Grey said cheerfully and rose into the air. "You shouldn't be standing on it either. It's centuries old and has been living underwater. I am sure it's not very stable. I am surprised it's even holding your hefty weight."

"Well then let's fix that," James smiled, simultaneously releasing his power source into the boat to feel it out. First, he drove the water out from the woodwork, before tightening the pieces that could be saved and replacing those that could not. He could feel the metal work was rusted, dented, and worn but from the look on Grey's face when he saw the water drip out of the boat James decided he was best off leaving as much of the boat's character as he could.

"Or do that." Grey rolled his eyes, joining the others on the deck. "It's not like every nook and cranny of this boat is a piece of history."

"Oh, give it over. I just gave it a slight makeover so we could explore it without fear of falling through the floorboards. I even left the blast marks on the left side of the basement, where the cannons used to go, untouched. I guess their enemies had cannons too."

"It's called an underside," Grey corrected him, as he walked towards the boat's stairs wide-eyed to get a look at the holes in the boat James was referring to.

"Cannons did this?" Stevie asked, looking through the huge hole in the boat out into the waterless sea. The black scorch marks were a reminder that this boat didn't live out its days in peace.

"I don't know, I just figured that if this boat has cannons, the one that took it down probably did too."

"Wrong you are," Grey corrected him. "You need to remember who they were up against. The Whiteflyers don't need cannons to fight their battles. I am sure these holes were made using powers alone."

James nodded, realising how stupid his comment had been. "Brain fog."

The rest of the boat was just as interesting as the scorched side was. It was littered with old broken weapons, and even had a small bedroom in it with remnants of the boat's captain and a couple of crew members. Pieces of cloth and a fork, two spoons and an old pot lay on the floor. James could picture people just like Grey fighting for their freedom on this boat. He wondered where they were now, considering nobody could die on the Three Worlds they would have to be somewhere. He then remembered the mote around the gutter and decided that in the meantime, while he couldn't do anything about it, he would selfishly rather not know their whereabouts.

"So, who wins?" a gleeful Grey asked as they walked back to the house a few hours later, their minds full of battles past.

Predicting the result before it was announced, James' competitive side came flying out. "It wasn't a fair fight, you've been planning this for days. You specifically told me I wasn't allowed to plan it, knowing you'd sought out that boat days before. "

"Excuse me, I will decide what is and isn't a fair fight," Stevie interrupted him before he had more time to influence her decision. "And I decide that the winner is…

drumroll please."

Grey obeyed and even acted out the playing of drums.

"The one and only... MR GREY ADAMS."

James bared his teeth in jest and hissed at his competitor. "It's on tomorrow."

"Yes it is!" Stevie answered. "Tomorrow we take to the air."

That night, when everyone had got into bed, or more accurately, into their blanketed spot on the floor, Stevie asked Grey a question that James had been wondering since he had met him. "So, who was Grey on Earth? I know we've established that the people on Tartarus aren't evil, but some have done some... well like my mum, they have done some questionable things on Earth. Was that you?"

While Grey's response seemed defensive, his tone showed he was more reflective than anything. "Haven't we all done some questionable things? I don't regret anything I did, even if it led me here. Anything I did, I did for my family."

James and Stevie gave him room to continue and after a couple of quiet minutes, he did. "I haven't seen my dad since I was three and my younger brother has never even met him. He ran out on my mum and me when she was five months pregnant with Lucas. He told her he had met someone younger in Scotland on a business trip the previous month, and that he needed a fresh start. He said kids were never in his plans and that he didn't know how to be a father. Luckily for me and my brother, my mum was enough of a parent to fill in for both of them. We grew up with everything we needed. Probably with more than we needed, which maybe is why things started to go downhill.

"Four years ago, my mum came home a mess, she told me her hairdressing store was gone, it was being repossessed. It was that or our home, so she had no choice. I saw her go into a downward spiral from then on. Some days she'd barely get out of bed. So, I did what anybody in my position would do. I got up, got out, and brought home some money. She'd made enough in her lifetime for us, the least I could do was give some of it back when she needed it most."

"You couldn't have been older than 16 or 17, you were still only a kid," Stevie replied during a moment of silence.

"In the eyes of the law I was yes. Which I guess is why nobody would hire me or maybe it was my lack of experience. So, I went to the only other people in my area that I knew who would help me. I did some bad things, but for a couple of years I fed my family. My mum never asked where I got the money from, so I never told her. I figured it wasn't so bad, and that I'd get out as soon as I left college, once I was able to get a proper job. However, I never made it that far.

One night, I was told to wait for one of our regulars with a package a few streets away from my house. I arrived early and heard something behind me. When I was half turned around I got a brief look at two men in black ski masks running at me. They'd pummelled my head with the handle of their knife before I even had time to register the situation. I was never a fighter, but I am as trustworthy as they come. If I say I'll wait for a customer to hand over a package, you better believe it when I say nobody is getting my sticky hands off it. They used their fists for most of it, but when they realised I wasn't giving it up, they moved onto their blades. I blacked out and when I woke they were gone and I was here. Little did I know there was worse about to come. They were soon to be replaced by Whiteflyers."

James didn't ask what exactly Grey had been involved in, and who the people who helped him out were, there was no need. He knew the kind of trouble he'd get into if his family needed it and he knew the kind of people in his area that he'd go looking for. "You did what you had to do," James told him. "You stepped up."

"But wasn't there another way?" Stevie whispered, her voice hesitant.

Grey took a deep breath. "At the time I didn't think so, but in hindsight maybe there was."

That night, James dreamt of his grandparents, he'd been dreaming about them a lot since arriving in Tartarus. He was remembering a beach day from one summer he'd spent in Donegal with his sister. His granny sat on their tartan picnic blanket looking as royal as ever as she unpacked their lunch. She always brought the same thing, but it never failed to hit the hunger spot. Leftover chicken sandwiches from their roast dinner the night before, with homemade jelly for dessert. There was nothing as satisfying as a tasty meal after a long swim and run on the sand. Grandad Jim, short for James' namesake, looked out of place as always. He saw no point in changing out of his golfing attire, cord trousers and a polo t-shirt, because he never got in for a swim. If James and his sister Jen badgered him enough, he'd sometimes take off his shoes and socks, roll up his trousers and get into the sea up to his knees for a splash. One summer they'd pulled him under the water, but the roar he'd let out made sure that they never did it again.

James woke up smiling and stretched out his body. It was slightly achy from the night before. He wiped his eyes open and dared to take a glance at Stevie while she still slept. His face immediately dropped and his eyebrows arched. Her hand was outstretched and she was gently latching on to Grey's equally extended arm. He coughed loudly, not wanting their small measure of affection to go on any longer. A sleepy Stevie opened her eyes and quickly pulled her hand away when she saw James sitting up staring at them.

"Time to wake up," James said when Grey didn't stir, a couple octaves louder and more cheerful than was necessary. "We've got training to do."

Oblivious to any awkwardness, Grey chimed in just as cheery as he stretched out. "That's the spirit. I see my Water showcase yesterday has brought out an even more competitive side to you. Looking to get back on top is it?"

"No, I think Stevie is the only one looking to get back on top today," James smiled as Stevie turned bright red and hurriedly made her way to the bathroom to freshen up. James swore he could see a tear fall from her eyes as she took her last step out of the room and felt immediately ashamed for his actions.

"What was that about?" Grey asked innocently.

James shrugged. "No idea."

For the next few weeks the three runaways spent their days harnessing their powers, bathing in the sea and scouting for supplies. They had turned the abandoned cottage into a fully furnished home in no time at all. The kitchen was equipped with a varnished wooden table and mismatched chairs and they had two mattresses and a couch in the room they slept in. While Grey and Stevie hadn't been openly affectionate with each other since the morning he caught them sort of holding hands, James could see their connection growing stronger. He hated how he couldn't let it go and he tried to spin his thoughts to be happy that his two closest friend's relationship was evolving, but he just couldn't shake his own feelings for Stevie away. He'd never experienced such strong affection for someone before, not even Liza, and it wasn't turning off overnight.

"It's hard to believe how much better we've become in just over ten weeks," Stevie smiled proudly on their way back into their new home after a long day in the sky. "It makes me wonder how much more I would have progressed with Water and Earth if they had only given us a longer shot. I could be a level 4 by now for sure. I just know it.

"I've been thinking that myself," Grey acknowledged. "I wasn't even that far from mastering Earth. I easily had two thirds of the materials down. Another couple of weeks and I'd even have given James a run for his money."

Stevie chortled, "Ha, I wouldn't go that far. James has progressed even faster than we have. He built a house last week in barely any time at all."

James had to silently agree, he was even surprising himself these days at some of the things he could do. He imagined how different his life would have been on Earth if he had the ability to give his mum the house, or multiple houses, of her dreams. He could even have made his dad his very own private lake to go fishing in in the back garden.

James drifted off to sleep that night dreaming about what his life could have been like. He imagined his family living in a house not dissimilar to Stevie's uncle's house and holidaying in a country resort of their own. He was out golfing with his dad when something woke him. There was whispering coming from behind him, but the blanket was bunched over the side of his face and he couldn't make it out at first. Slowly, and as quietly as he could, James pulled his ear free from the clasps of the most sought after blue knit.

"You should tell him," came Grey's voice.

"What's the point? We haven't talked about the kiss we had in months. It's over," Stevie whispered back.

"Speaking as a man and his friend, I still think he should know," Grey replied. "I would want to if I was him."

"It's not up for discussion," Stevie snapped back a little louder than their hushed tones had been before.

"Alright, alright, I guess he will just continue to stay in the dark until you think the time is right. Now, get some sleep, will you? The sun will be up before we know it."

James scrunched his face, before taking a deep breath in an attempt to regulate his breathing. He knew there was something between Grey and Stevie, but for Stevie to so blatantly refuse to let him know stung deep. He didn't care if it was months since they had kissed, if she thought what they were doing was right, she wouldn't feel the need to keep it so secret.

The next morning, James got up early to shower and pack, and by the time Stevie and Grey had awoken he was ready to leave. "What are you doing?" Stevie enquired as she opened her eyes. "Are you packed?"

"Yes, we're going back to London, well I am anyway. I refuse to play house anymore," James replied, trying his best to bury his anger.

"House? Is that what you think we are doing?" Stevie asked, surprised by the abruptness of it all. "We've been training and we have got a ton better."

James couldn't help his harsh tone. "Yes, well some of us have been anyway, but regardless, it's time. You talked about it yourself yesterday, about how far we've come. I don't see the use of staying here anymore."

Grey rose out of bed. "You heard what Bee said, we can't go back."

James' anger heightened. "I don't care what she said, we don't even know her. I can do whatever I want to do and Stevie, so can you. What happened to finding your mum? Do you think we are going to find her in a local village or maybe swimming in the sea? No, she's in London, so that is where I think you will be happiest too."

Grey shook his head disappointed and Stevie's eyes glossed over. As soon as he'd calmed down, James knew it wasn't a fair thing to say. He shouldn't guilt trip her into doing what he wanted for selfish reasons. It had to be her choice. "I'm sorry. That's not what I really feel. I know you'd run to her now if you had any clue where she is and I know you didn't want to leave London in the first place. I just think now it's time to go back."

"No you are right," Stevie said, swiftly flicking a fallen tear from under her eye. "I'll leave with you tonight, once the sun goes down."

CHAPTER 7 -
"YOU ARE HIM,
AREN'T YOU?"

As soon as the night fell, James, Stevie and a reluctant Grey took to the sky. It had taken more convincing from Stevie than James had thought it would to get Grey to agree to go back to London. However, once he was confident that if he stayed, he stayed alone, he started to pack up his few belongings. He claimed that the reason he didn't want to leave was because it was against his orders, but from the way he reacted to Bee's revelation that they weren't to return for years convinced James that there was an ulterior motive for Grey's hesitance, and it wasn't a bad guess that it had something to do with his growing relationship with Stevie.

"So, what's the plan when we get there?" Grey asked, turning to James after an hour of silent flying.

James hesitated before answering. He'd decided to leave so quickly that he hadn't really thought of what they'd do once they had arrived back in London. He had thought that day that maybe they could go back to the safe house, but thinking again, Bee was pretty adamant that they'd be found if they stayed there so it probably wasn't an option anymore. He opened his mouth to ask if there were any other rebel hideouts Grey knew about, but was silenced by Stevie. "We're going to my mum's dad's old house, my grandad's. We didn't stay in places very often, but that was our most consistent home."

James nodded and smiled gently before glancing over at an unresponsive Grey. He had his eyes shut and was taking a deep breath. "Come clean Grey, why are you so weird about going back?"

Grey immediately went on the defence. "Give it a rest Moore. I've told you ten times that it's against my orders. Ask me to tell you for an eleventh, I dare you."

The way back to the city seemed a lot longer than the way there. The way there was filled with new revelations about Tartarus. Regardless of their depressive nature, they piqued James' interest. However, the way back to London just highlighted how depressing the third and most rundown world could be when they were outside their bubble that had been the cottage by the sea. The slightly different route took them near two gutters, neither of which they had visited on their way to Brighton. The first they came upon after a couple of hours of travelling. It was dark and completely silent, and if it wasn't for Grey pointing it out, James would have missed it completely. He could hardly believe that so many people piled into one small area could be so quiet. They didn't go close enough to see inside, so James hoped the emptiness was the result of a lack of people and not a lack of energy.

In contrast, the second gutter burned bright and could be seen from miles away. Smoke painted the air around it and roars of freedom made their way to the three travellers' ears as they flew closer.

"What's going on in there?" Stevie asked. "Does the

fire mean there are Whiteflyers about? Why is the place burning?"

"Maybe it means Whiteflyers," Grey replied. "Or maybe the people inside are taking a stand. Either way we should probably lay low, get back to hard ground. Whiteflyers will be showing up soon if they're not the cause already."

"If they are taking a stand, maybe we should join them?" James said, his heart filled with pride for thousands of people he had never met.

"How can we find my mum if we are captured?" Stevie argued. "We are only a couple of hours away from London now anyway and the sun is about to come. Let's get some rest. That cluster of buildings up ahead might have somewhere we can hide out for a few hours."

"Sorry, you're right. We should find your mum, the gutters can wait," James agreed, before he and Grey did as Stevie suggested. They found a one roomed abandoned office to sleep in in what proved to be a small local village that James imagined to be quite quaint and picturesque once upon a time ago.

Until the hustle and bustle of the nearby gutter calmed down, the best they could do was fill up on sleep. However, even though they were over a mile away from the fires, a strong scent of burning wafted through the large hole in the side of the room and filled their nostrils as they tried to doze off. James, stubborn as he knew it to be, curled up on a spot on the hard grey floor that would make any touching impossible between his two friends.

"Are you awake?" Stevie asked James just as he was about to fall into a slumber.

"I sure am," he replied, not wanting to miss the chance for some alone time with Stevie while Grey snored nearby.

"Do you ever wonder what the others are doing?" Stevie asked quietly. "Marcus and Richie, but also Annabelle and the other Whiteflyers from Torpor."

"Marcus, Richie and the other drudges, almost everyday. However, Annabelle knows what those people were and she chose to stand by them. She made excuses and turned a blind eye when you needed her most, so no, she doesn't concern me. I am sure she is living it up with Matthew, Tim and Roe. Doing what Vask and Catherine ask her to, no matter the consequences."

Stevie sighed, "She was still my friend. She's just easier to manipulate than us. If she knew what we knew, if she had seen what we've seen, the gutters and this whole world, I am sure she would feel differently."

"Maybe," James whispered back. "Or maybe she'd fall in line and close her eyes just a little tighter."

After another silence, Stevie smiled. "I reckon Matthew is fuming you got away. Oh to be a fly on the wall when Hatt told them all what happened. I can picture him putting on a show now,' 'I knew he was a traitor from the start but nobody listened to me. He's been a coward from the get-go.'"

James chuckled at Stevie's impression. "I'd say he's partially relieved, after all, he doesn't have to compete for his dear Catherine's approval anymore."

"Catherine will be cursing at Vask for agreeing to let me become a Whitelflyer after Tessa was taken," Stevie added, reminding James of the tension between his best friend and Matthew's great aunt. He was sure she wouldn't rest until she found Stevie and put her back 'where she belonged', just as The Controller wouldn't stop until James was found. He imagined they'd both be sentenced to a lifetime as drudges or even worse, to a lifetime in the gutters. He then corrected his train of thought and decided that as long as they were put in the same gutter it wouldn't be that bad.

"You know, even though he is one of The Controller's most loyal followers, I couldn't help but always respect Vask. He was like one of those teachers in school that was terrifying but fair. He knew you deserved a spot to become a Whiteflyer and he wasn't going to let Catherine's prejudices stand in the way of that."

Stevie nodded. "Yeah I think I do too, just a little."

"However, that's not to say that if I was to see him today I wouldn't let all of Tartarus let loose on him, but you know what I mean," James added.

Stevie's eyes twinkled. "I don't doubt that you would for a second James Moore. My hero."

James smiled, this was the first time in a while that himself and Stevie fell asleep talking, and it gave him a warm comfort to know that no matter what happened with her and Grey they'd at least always stay best friends. Clutching a small orange cushion he packed for the journey, James fell into a deep dreamless sleep.

Hours later, James woke up and gently shook Stevie and Grey until their eyes peeled open. The sun was low in the sky and the low buzz they'd gone asleep to had died down.

"I am going to take to the sky and confirm that the gutter has calmed and then I think we should make a move. I want to make it to London by nightfall."

"No," Stevie protested, as James opened the door out onto the other derelict grey buildings. "I can see shadows out there. They could be Whiteflyers for all we know. I don't think we should make any rash decisions."

"Of course there are shadows out there, ordinary people live here. I am not wasting the next two hours sitting in this little room, if you can even call it that," James replied and continued on his way. "I'll be careful," he added as Stevie's worried face flashed in his direction as he finished closing the door behind him.

Taking his word seriously, James pulled the green hood on his jumper up to cover his distinct brown fluffy hair and tied the drawstrings around his neck to close the rough material in on his face. He eyed his surroundings and spotted an older woman and younger man a few metres to his right. Dressed in drab charcoal and browns, he knew immediately that they weren't a threat. They huddled together in a manic whisper and paid him no attention. Whether that was down to their oblivion to his existence or because they didn't see the use in acknowledging his presence, James didn't know or care. Quickly, he brought his gaze to the other side of the road where a young dark haired boy dressed relatively clean and composed walked passed. He met his wide eyes for a second before the skinny boy quickly looked away and continued his path down the broken street. *He must be fairly new to Tartarus,* James thought, wishing he could take him with him, or at least promise him that he was going to make sure things got better. However, he knew enough about the Three Worlds by now to know that that was one promise he would find extremely hard to keep.

After passing a handful or more of the strange and mysterious residents that called Tartarus their home, James made his way towards the tallest building in the so-called village, an old church tower. He didn't think it would be smart to take to the air in front of so many bystanders while the sun was still out, but once inside, with the absence of stairs, he flew upwards to peer out of the open roof. Confident that the four surrounding brick walls were covering any sign of his powers from the outside, he popped his head over the wall and stared out at the area that the fires were coming from the night before. He nodded a confirmation to himself that the commotion in the gutters had died down and lowered himself back to the ground to turn and make his return to Stevie and Grey. He was immediately forced back in fright at the sight of the young boy who he had seen across the street not so long ago.

"You are him, aren't you?" the boy asked, a hopeful twinkle in his eyes.

"I am who?" James replied, oblivious to what the boy was referring to. "How much did you see just now? How long have you been standing there for?"

"You are the one the Whiteflyers are looking for. It must be you. You can fly but you aren't dressed like them and I saw a girl and a boy in the building you came out of. I bet they have powers too."

"Slow down," James interrupted as the boy took a deep breath. "Start from the start. Where did you hear about me and my friends?"

"I don't know how long ago, time does not exactly move the same way here as it did at home, but a while back anyway, a group of Whiteflyers came by. They were being nice for the first time in... well ever, or for as long as I've been here anyway. Not that that's been super long, well, I don't think so anyway. They went door to door asking if anyone had seen you. They described you as a dangerous rogue Whiteflyer that was on the loose. They said you might be dressed differently to them but that you could fly and use Fire, Air, Earth, and Water like they could. They said you were very dangerous and that they were looking for you for our own good, for our protection. However, they didn't fool me, not for one breath. I knew immediately that any enemy of theirs would be a friend of mine. They mentioned your friends too and that they had some of the abilities you do, but the focus was on you for the most part."

James stared at him blankly for a while, not knowing what to do or say. The Whiteflyers must have got a clue to the fact that they didn't go North after all and if they had started going from village to village, they must be desperate to find him. Why the Controller cared so much about three missing Whiteflyers, James still didn't know.

"So, is it you?" the boy nudged.

James bent down to the boy's level and decided, seeing the hope in his eyes, to tell the truth. "It is me, but you can't say you've seen me here to anyone, especially not to the Whiteflyers if they come back, and you are right I am not the bad guy. Can you promise me that?"

The boy smiled sincerely for the first time since James had set eyes on him. "You must have really pissed them off,"

"I sure did," James smiled back. "And I plan to piss them off even further."

"Are you going to get us out of this mess?"

James' face turned serious. He didn't want to make any promises that he couldn't keep, but he also couldn't stand to disappoint the boy. "I can't promise I will be able to do that, but I promise I'll do everything I can to try."

The boy flashed a toothy grin and did something unexpected, he took a step towards James and wrapped his arms around his waist, before turning back around and running out of the church tower and out of sight.

When James got back to his previous night's accommodation, he told Stevie and Grey about the encounter with the young boy and they wondered together what it all meant.

"He really did hate you, The Controller that is, but to go to such lengths to find you. It just doesn't make sense," Stevie voiced.

"It makes perfect sense," Grey debated. "Think about it, a rebel with level 4 Whiteflyer powers and then if you add me and Stevie in there a level 3 and a level 2, we will be unstoppable."

James rolled his eyes. "I am not a rebel and neither is Stevie and even if I was, The Controller would hardly know that.."

"Excuse me, I will say what I am or aren't," Stevie bit back. "However, yeah I am not a rebel either, Grey. It seemed cool before, but I have been going over our options for the last few weeks and they haven't exactly made us feel super welcome so far. I mean, they banished us before we could even commit to the cause. We never even got to see their headquarters or meet anyone but Bee."

"I haven't even seen their headquarters. Either way, rebels or not, we are all on the same side, and The Controller knows that. He needs to set an example and I am sure if they find us, that example will be very public now that the word of our disappearance seems to be spreading."

"It's spreading by his own doing," James clarified.

"Not necessarily, it is possible that the rebels were the first to spread the word. The Controller might have just decided to use it to his advantage to try and control the narrative."

Stevie smirked. "Well if that is the case, it's not working. That boy didn't believe a word of it from the sounds of things."

For the rest of their journey back to London, while the sun was still out, James, Stevie and Grey travelled by foot, avoiding main roads and staying away from towns and villages or anywhere they could bump into The Controller's followers. While the boy had decided that James was no threat, that couldn't be assumed for the rest of Tartarus. Judging by the number of people that applied to be a Whiteflyer every year, it wouldn't be surprising if some even attempted to gain sympathy with the Whiteflyers by feeding them information about their whereabouts.

"So, what's your plan when we get there?" James asked Stevie as they saw their first signs of London up ahead. "Are we just going to go up and knock on the door? You need to keep in mind that we don't know what kind of state she will be in if we find her. She may not be the mum that you remember, during the good times I mean. You know how Torpor can change a person, and from what we've seen from Tartarus, I am sure it does an even better job of it."

Stevie shook her head and wriggled out her shoulders. "She may not be there at all. I just need to concentrate on finding her, I can deal with the rest after. It's too overwhelming to think through the different possibilities now. She's my mum. I am sure I will know what to do when the time comes."

Grey stared at Stevie for a while and just as James thought he was going to say something he turned his head to face the other way and continued to walk towards the broken city. A city James found very hard to believe was modelled on his home on Earth.

CHAPTER 8 - "YOU ARE AN AVERY, YOU HAVE A NAME TO LIVE UP TO."

The night was dark and eerily quiet as Stevie directed James and Grey to her grandfather's home. They took the side roads and stayed away from any areas that were too built up or that Grey knew to be associated with Whiteflyers at one time or another.

Grandad Miller's house was on the West side of the city near a shopping centre James used to visit before he died. When they were a couple of years younger he used to hang around there with Liza, his girlfriend on Earth, sneaking into movies at the cinema and eating sugared jellies until the few pounds his dad gave him every Monday ran out. As they got older, their trips to the shopping centre became more concentrated on Liza dragging him around the stores as she tried on clothes for one of the many parties she'd be going to on the weekends or getting piercings in a local arcade. He regretted now how much of a fuss he used to make if she'd spend more than fifteen minutes in each shop. It was little memories from his life like that that he missed the most since he arrived in the Three Worlds. Everyday things that almost seemed meaningless at the time. What he would do to spend a day roaming the streets of London, eating junk food and laughing with his friends. While he didn't see Liza in a romantic way anymore, he would always see her as the first real friend he'd ever had.

"It's just up here," Stevie directed, pointing at a clustered group of four terraced houses up ahead. The buildings were painted in chipped burgundy paint and the tiles on the roof were one and far between.

The house closest was almost non-existent, reduced to a couple of lone standing walls and a pile of rubble. Through the window of the adjoining building, stacks of useless gadgets and clutter caught James' eye. He had no doubt the house was claimed by a resident that must have been on Tartarus for quite some time. It seemed to be mostly junk from what could be seen through the window, a half burnt mattress, piles of dirty cloth and rusty metals. It reminded James of the littered seafront in Brighton.

The house to the left of that had nothing to show in the way of things, but seven sleeping lumps on the ground highlighted its occupancy.

"It's this house," Stevie whispered, aware they weren't alone, as she stopped in front of the fourth and final house. James had no idea if there was anyone living there as the windows were covered in a thick layer of dirt that could only be rubbed off from the inside. However, the crowdedness of the houses next door only pointed to one obvious answer.

"Let me go in first," James asked. "Wait here and I will call you in once I know it's safe."

"I know you're only trying to help, but I should be

the first to see her if she's in there," Stevie replied. "We can tell that no Whiteflyers live here, they'd never live in such filth and I sure as Tartarus can protect myself from the residents here. Even if I am not as powerful as you, I am still able to take care of myself."

James mulled over what she said for a minute before nodding. She was right, she'd been through enough to prove that she could look after herself and even if she couldn't, who was he to tell her what she could and couldn't do? "We will be right outside. Scream if you need anything and I will be standing beside you before you even have time to blink."

James watched as Stevie knocked on the door multiple times before using Air to undo the lock. It was something she had shown him how to do when they were back training on Torpor. It was the beginning of their first adventure together and probably the moment he would pin point to them becoming inseparable. It was when Stevie had first opened up to him about her mum and her life back on Earth.

She looked back and smiled reassuringly before pushing open the dark green door and stepping inside. James could only see the hallway from where he stood and it was dark, so it didn't reveal much. He thought he could make out a lone chair in the shadows or maybe it was a small table.

James turned to look at Grey for the first time since they arrived. "Why are you so quiet?"

Grey was staring at the ground, seemingly not bothered about what was going on inside the house. "I am not being so quiet. I just don't think she will be in there, is all. Nobody came to the door when she knocked."

"That doesn't mean anything, she could be asleep."

"Or she could be anywhere else in this whole entire world. Stevie is just setting herself up for disappointment and you've been encouraging her to do so just so you could go back to London," Grey bit back with a snappy edge to his tone that didn't suit his usual upbeat personality.

Guilt flooded James' face. "This isn't about me and you know it. You've been off since we left the cottage. You're just annoyed that you can't continue whatever it was you've been doing with Stevie for the last few weeks," he deflected

Grey looked genuinely shocked. "Doing with Stevie? What is that supposed to mean?"

James nearly blurted out everything that had been consuming his thoughts since he caught them whispering, but a bang inside the house diverted his attention.

"Stevie," both of them said at the same time before running towards the house.

Without saying anything Grey took downstairs and James upstairs.

"Stevie, where are you?" James shouted as his feet touched down on the grimy carpeted landing.

"In here," Stevie shouted back from the bedroom furthest away.

James entered to see a floating man a metre from the floor, his eyes wide with terror.

"He attacked me," she said, very offended but with no fear. "Well he tried to attack me, hence the situation he forced me to put him in."

The man looked like someone they'd find in the gutter, his pale skin clung to his hollow bones. He wore patchy clothes and had only one shoe. His second foot was dressed in a woollen sock with his big toe peeping through. His long brown hair was unwashed and his face unshaven. "If I put you down, are you going to be more reasonable?" Stevie asked firmly, as if she was talking to a misbehaving child.

The man nodded, either too scared or just uninclined to speak. "Now, why did you try to grab me? You mumbled something about Catherine while you did it. Are you talking about Catherine Avery?"

The man nodded again but once again remained mute.

Grey had joined them by now and was glaring intently at the guy. "He's been put here, he's keeping watch. We need to leave," he decided.

James glanced from Grey to the man and then to Stevie. "He's right, let's go and now, it is clear that your mum's not here."

"No," the man yelled, before covering his mouth quickly with his hand.

Stevie took a step closer to him. "You can tell me. What did Catherine do? Why are you so reluctant to tell us anything?"

The man hesitated, but when James pulled Stevie's sleeve towards the door he spoke. "She's taken my sister. She said she'd give her back if I brought you to her. She was quite certain that you might show up here. She described you as a red haired girl travelling with two other males. She told me to wait until you did and bring back any news, she missed the part that you were a Whiteflyer too."

"Catherine?" Stevie asked. "When did she come here?"

"Months ago now, but a rather fat Whiteflyer

shows up every now and again to ask for updates. I haven't left the house since."

"Let's go!" Grey said more urgently than the first time. "We have walked right into a trap."

James pulled on Stevie's sleeve once more and this time she followed.

"You can't leave," the man pleaded, but didn't come any closer. "Who knows what they are doing to her?"

"I'm sorry," Stevie whispered, before running down the stairs and out of the front door with Grey and James.

They spilled onto the street and followed Grey away from the house. They went down alleyway after alleyway and hopped over more walls than James had fingers before Stevie finally stopped.

"Enough," she shouted up to Grey out of breath, taking a seat on a roadside kerb in the middle of five to ten high blocks of flats. Nearly every area in London contained accommodation that looked just like them, well every area bar maybe near where Stevie's uncles house resided. Grey concrete buildings, twenty or sometimes more stories high, complete with windows framed in a white plastic material that went a yellow colour over time.

James came to a stop and looked up at his surroundings. "I don't like this, there are too many eyes. Who knows who lives here?"

Stevie sighed, "It's dark, nobody can see us down here, and anyway I need to catch my breath. We have been running, well jogging, for nearly an hour. Do we even have a plan?"

"We tried our best Stevie, they'll have people watching out for us wherever we go to look for your mum. I reckon we get back out of London and come back when everything dies down," Grey suggested.

Stevie's eyes went wide before a rare wrinkle appeared between her eyebrows. "Out of London, are you mad? Did you not hear that man? They're threatening people to try and find us."

"This Catherine lady was well aware that that man would not have been able to bring you in, she was never intending to give him his sister back. Who knows where she could be by now? She needed someone to give word if they saw you," Grey told her logically. "

"They could easily have my mum. I am not leaving London and for a matter of fact, I know where I want to go next. I am going to Tartarus' Whiteflyer headquarters. I don't expect either of you to come, or to even understand, but that's where I will be."

Without waiting for a reply Stevie abruptly stood up and headed in the general way of Trafalgar Square.

"Stevie wait," James implored, a million thoughts running through his mind. He was the one that pushed her to come to London, he was the one that was leading her right into The Controller's hand. Grey wasn't being weird or suspicious, he was just doing what James should have been doing this whole time, he was looking out for Stevie. "Your uncle's," he blurted out, realising that if he was in her same position it was the only logical reason he'd hold off on going into the Lion's nest. "That's where she'd go. That's where she'd wait for you. That was your home growing up, she knows that. Let's at least check there before we don't have the chance to anymore."

Stevie slowed her step. "Fine. First my uncle's, then the headquarters."

"You do realise her uncle's is going to be just as

bad as her grandfathers, if not worse?" Grey whispered to James as Stevie marched ahead.

"Yes I realise that, but I also realise that it's unlikely to be covered in hundreds, if not thousands of Whiteflyers, maybe even The Controller himself. One or two rogues I can take. It's better than where she was headed."

"And when her mum is nowhere to be seen?" Grey pushed.

James ran his hands through his hair and down the back of his neck. "I don't know. Let's just deal with one crisis at a time. How far is it to Chelsea from here?"

"Walking? Maybe another hour. You better get your thinking cap on."

When they got within a few streets of Stevie's uncle's house, Stevie finally agreed to take a breather and figure out their plan of action. They had made record time getting to the house and James couldn't think of one feasible reason why they shouldn't go to the headquarters once they'd searched the house.

"So, what's your plan Stevie?" Grey asked her abruptly as they hunkered down in the laneway of a rundown house.

Stevie looked to James with an intriguing yet hopeful look in her eye. It was obvious she hadn't made much progress on planning either.

"Look, it's very possible that there are Whiteflyers waiting for us inside your house. Vask is very aware of how you see that house as home and I am sure he has let it be known to whoever they have sent looking for us. That is if he is not looking for us himself," James rationalised. "I know you want to be the first to see her, but it's too dangerous. Let me go inside and have a look around. I'll make myself scarce. If I see your mum, I won't go near her. I'll leave you to go back in. If I see anyone else, I'll make a run for it."

Stevie looked over James' shoulder in thought. He could see two conflicting thoughts running over her face. She was one of the bravest people he knew, but she was also one of the smartest. She was very aware that she was no match for a level 4 Whiteflyer if there was one inside, or even a level 3.

"Fine," she conceded. "But I want to be in view of the house. If you need help, blow air through the window panes to smash them.

James agreed but knew deep down that he wouldn't openly invite Stevie to a Whiteflyer fight. Not after what happened to her before in Torpor.

"And I go with you," Grey chimed in, very matter of factly.

"Out of the question," James replied quickly. "Stealth is hardly your specialty. If I am to go in unnoticed, I need to be alone."

After some back and forth, Grey agreed to stay behind with Stevie and all three of them moved towards a house across the street from the one Stevie grew up in. There was nobody inside of it when they arrived which didn't scream good news to James. He could think of one big reason that the residents of an overpopulated Tartarus wouldn't want to occupy such a big house

"Remember, we are right here, don't forget about the glass if you come into trouble," Stevie whispered as she opened the window in the bottom room of the house, hoping to hear any going ons better.

James squeezed her shoulder, "I know, I know, but it won't come to that. I'll be in and out before you know it, no matter what I find inside."

Luckily the dark night was still on James' side. He pulled up his hood and floated a couple of inches off the floor as he went across the street. He certainly wasn't going to let something as silly as creaking floorboards give him away. The front door was too risky to open, so he went through the house next door and out into their back garden. It was a long enough empty space, complete with a brown tall fence that blocked off his destination. Slowly he made his way to the very back, and using Earth, buried the last metre of fence beneath the soil at his feet before stepping into the garden.

The house was just as dark and quiet from the back as it was from the front, with no sign of life behind the thick, expensive walls. James was sure that if there was anyone inside, they would be under strict instructions to not scare any of them away and to stay unnoticed from the outside, so he didn't rule out anyone being inside yet.

Staying close to the fence, hidden in the shadows, he slowly pushed himself to float towards the sliding back door. He could see no movement inside so gently tugged on the handle to pull it open. Like most places in the Three Worlds, the lock was undone, in line with The Controller's rule that nobody was allowed to own anything and that all property was shared between the residents. This, of course, did not hold true when James and Stevie first arrived at Torpor and visited this same house. It was slightly less run down on Torpor as it was on Tartarus, but the body remained the same and compared to some other buildings he had seen, it didn't show much damage. The white paint was chipped in places and the gardens weren't as well kept but the integrity of the building remained intact.

James stuck his head inside the large empty kitchen and looked from side to side. While it looked similar to Torpor's version it gave off an eerily empty vibe. When he saw nobody, he hovered inside, his guard up completely.

When downstairs was covered and discovered to be vacant, James hesitantly moved up the wooden stairs to the impressive second floor. He had a brief thought of leaving it there, pretending to Stevie that there was nobody at home, but then his realisation that she'd only demand to go straight to the headquarters willed him further. He sped up the process, and finished examining the second floor in half the time as the first. There was only one floor left, this one consisting of two bedrooms and an ensuite.

As soon as he got halfway up the stairs, James froze. He could hear a faint sound for the first time since entering the house. When he realised it wasn't coming from outside, but from one of the bedrooms up above, he turned to leave. Two men were talking quietly to one another which confirmed what he knew since entering the property, Stevie's mum Monica was not there. Just as he began his descent to get out of there and break the news to Stevie that it was a dead end, something stopped him, one of the voices was very familiar. Actually, they both were. It was Matthew and Tim.

James cursed himself, of course they were here. They'd revel being in the thick of trying to find Stevie and him, Grey would just be a bonus. He couldn't help but want to move closer to the door, to listen to what they were saying, so against his better judgement, he moved back up the stairs and perched himself outside the slightly ajar door they were talking behind.

"Why do we always get stuck with this shift? We know him better than any of the other Whiteflyers, maybe bar Annabelle, but I can't imagine she'd give them away, no matter what side she claims to be on," Matthew said in muffled tones. "We should be out in the thick of it, searching the villages and interrogating the residents."

"Can't you talk to Catherine, get her to see our value? She is part of your family after all," Tim asked.

Matthew grunted, "You know I can't. She's as rotten as the rest of them." His voice then switched to an alarmingly accurate version of Catherine Avery's, "'Why am I hearing reports that James is doing better than you?' 'Level 3 isn't good enough.' 'You are an Avery, you have a name to live up to.' 'If you're not going to come first, I don't see why you bother taking part in it to begin with.', 'Are you going to sit on the bench for the whole season, because I have more important places to be if so?'"

James realised that Matthew was no longer mimicking Catherine and was thinking back to a former life.

"She's just like my father, down to her pointy nose and yellow teeth. I am sick of people telling me what I can and can't do. They have been looking for Moore and his little posse for weeks, and they haven't so much as found a missing sock since they found that rebel house he'd been hiding in. I had to listen to Catherine ramble on about how pathetic it was that I couldn't beat him in training for weeks yet here she and the others are, completely lost on how to track him down. I didn't live up to my true potential on Earth because of certain family members and their arrogant ways but I am not going to let the same thing happen here. This is my fresh start and I am going to make a name for myself."

James didn't dare to make a noise. He was shocked to hear the anger coming through Matthews's tone when he talked about his distant aunt. He had been nothing but boastful about his connection to her while they were in training. He had guessed their relationship was far from a loving one, but he didn't expect Matthew to be so vocal about it with Tim, or with anyone for that matter.

"Do you know, when I first woke up on Torpor and realised I now lived in a world without my father, I was actually happy? I missed my mum a little I guess, but in the end her whole personality could be summed up in one measly little word, weak. If she could stand by while her husband dominated her, and refused to build up the courage to pack her bags, to remove her only kid from his clutches, why should I pine for her? Why should I feel bad that she was left alone with him? It was her fault we were stuck with him in the first place."

Tim mumbled something James couldn't make out, but he could sense from Matthew's tone it wasn't something he agreed with. "Of course it was her fault, you don't even know her. No wonder I never talk to you about anything worth a damn. You've nothing going on up there. I thought you'd know better than to believe a social media post or a television ad you read one day about the dangers of victim blaming. Then again how can I really blame you? Your family was perfectly normal."

Tim grunted, "I wasn't saying I thought that. I was just saying some people did. Obviously I don't agree."

James wasn't so sure that Tim didn't agree, or that he was even smart enough to have an opinion on the matter either way, but he wasn't at all surprised that he didn't let Matthew know that.

"Anyway, we are getting off the point. I say we

wait here until sunrise and then go back to Torpor and convince Vask of our real value. He's been organising this search from the start. Ignore Catherine, he's the one that has the power to put us out on the field looking for..."

Just as Matthew was finishing his sentence, a high pitched voice came from the bottom of the stairs. "Well, well, well, what do we have here?"

James froze in place, he knew from the first word that it was Roe. He should have known the lap dog wouldn't be far from her master.

"Who's out there?" Matthew asked, whispering no longer.

James quickly turned to the stairs as he heard their footsteps coming towards the landing. One level 2 Whiteflyer was better than one level 2 and a level 3.

"It's him," Rowena yelled back. "Don't let him get away."

James placed his feet on the ground for the first time since entering the house and jumped halfway down the stairs. He felt a feeble attempt of Air coming at him with the aim to knock him off his feet, so he sent it back twofold and knocked Roe on to her back.

"Don't even think about moving Moore," came Matthew's voice from behind.

Roe was already getting back on her feet ahead, so James jumped sideways, over the bannister and onto the hardwood landing of the second floor.

He heard Matthew curse as his footsteps moved forward. He attempted a step onto the ground floor stairs but a fireball beat him to it, flying towards his feet to block his path. He looked up to see Matthew in the spot he had just landed on. He threw one back but Matthew was too fast with a gust of wind that extinguished it before it had even flown half the distance to meet him. James didn't wait a heartbeat before summoning a gust of air of his own. He spun it in violent circles towards his pursuers. It took some energy but Matthew pushed it behind him. Unluckily, it fell into Tim who screamed loud enough to wake the whole road. James afforded him a quick glance and could vaguely make out his right arm pushed out awkwardly as if broken inside the mini twister. Roe was up by now and working to stop the gruesome scene, she was pushing the wind in the opposite direction in order to slow it down enough for Tim to get out.

James blew the fire on the stairs out and continued his retreat from the house. However, as he came onto the hallway, another Whiteflyer came running up to meet him. It was someone he had never met before, probably from a different world than Torpor. He was a big guy with mousy brown hair that was thinning in parts and he had a stubby pig-like nose that sat under little beady eyes. A stream of water came flying in from behind him, revealing him to James as a level 3. James knew all of the level 4 Whiteflyers to see after Catherine's history lessons during his training days, and luckily this was not one of them.

Before James had time to think the large Whiteflyer directed a mass of water his way. James grew stiff as the icy water enclosed his skin. He could feel it filling his lungs while he desperately gasped for air. Just as he thought it was all over, that he was going to pass out, air entered his lungs. His arms were no longer desperately swimming out in front but heavy. He dropped to the ground coughing, managing a short glance behind him to someone the Whiteflyer was staring at.

"I was hoping to find you here Grey," the man smirked, little bits of spit flying from his lisp.

"I can see you are still doing Amos's bidding Glaze," James' saviour replied.

The man clenched his fists as his skin glowed red. "Don't call me that. My name is Robbie!" He went to throw a fireball in Grey's direction but Stevie, who was just behind him, beat the man to it. James felt the heat as it passed over his head and watched as the Whiteflyer went up in flames. He ran towards the toilet, hopelessly looking to reach an open water source. He did not have the energy to reach the liquid from the pipes he had attacked James with before collapsing on the ground. Stevie then directed her attention at the stairs where three wide eyed familiar faces were appearing and she blew a big gust of wind in their direction. It wouldn't stop them, but it certainly seemed to be slowing them down.

"Into the garden," James coughed as he rose from the ground. Grey and Stevie blindly obeyed effortlessly lining up in formation. They were facing the door Matthew, Tim, and Roe were a heartbeat away from leaving; James in the middle, Stevie to his right and Grey to his left.

Tim was the first to enter, showing once again that he was all muscle and no brain. Angry because of his broken arm, he threw himself in James' direction. Tim's fists were raised as spit flew from his roaring mouth. James smiled to harden the blow, simultaneously moving the Earth under his feet enough to trip him up. He lost his footing and crashed backwards. Dust rose from the hard mud beneath him and a thin crack appeared from under his shoulders. James was no longer on the defence. He had

had just about enough of these people since he had signed up to become a Whiteflyer.

Matthew was next to enter the garden, with Roe slightly in the rear. They weren't, however, as reckless and thoughtless as Tim and came in with their guns blazing. Simultaneously, Matthew pushed a gust of wind at James and Roe threw a fireball at Stevie. James ducked just in time, but Stevie lost her footing slightly. Grey noticed and stepped in with fire of his own. He opted for a stream instead of the usual ball, and it reminded James of a particularly brutal weapon in a war movie he had seen once upon a time. Matthew pushed himself up into the air to dodge it, and instantly everyone else followed the lead. They were taking the fight to the sky.

For one moment, they all stared directly at each other, nobody making a move or a sound until Roe, with a taunting evil grin on her lips, spoke. "Your mum says hello Miller."

James could see the anger swarm over Stevie's whole body as she considered the best way to attack. However, Grey, who was the first to sense the water the rogue Whiteflyer had used in the house, was the first to react. Water burst through the pipes under the concrete to the front of the garden and shot into the air directly under Roe and Matthew, chunks of cement and metal went flying under the pressure of the water. Matthew moved upwards to avoid being hit but Roe wasn't as smooth and was hit violently on her right leg. She screamed as she fell crashing to the floor. Matthew, being the kind of friend James always knew him to be, ignored her and instead used the water to his own advantage. He summoned it towards its first master, and held Grey in a similar bubble of water that James had just been rescued from. Grey couldn't hold consciousness for long enough for James to help him and he fell to the ground.

"I'll get him," Stevie screamed, giving James the go ahead to finish things with Matthew. It was getting light and they had been making enough noise to attract some more unwanted attention. The other Whiteflyers would be here before long. James floated back down to earth, coming in contact with the only power Matthew was defenceless against. Matthew, knowing what was coming, flew upwards, but it was too late. As soon as James' first toe touched the ground, the earth exploded upwards. He moulded the elements in a long stream of endless soil that reached out for Matthew. James could see the terror on his face but he didn't care, it just willed him on further. The almost snake-like mud creature caught the end of its target's foot around fifteen metres from the ground. It quickly enclosed itself around Matthew's whole body from the bottom up, pulling him downwards as it did. By the time it was back to the ground only a few hairs on the top of his head were visible.

Without giving his work another thought, using Air, James turned and picked up a motionless Grey from the ground where Stevie sat with him. "We need to get out of here. Quickly."

CHAPTER 9 - "IF WE ARE GOING TO DO IT, IT'S GOING TO BE MY WAY."

Stevie and James brought Grey to a big empty garage at the edge of what looked to be an old garden centre while he came back to his senses. It was around four metres in length and height and housed nothing at all. Even though it wasn't far from the scene of the battle, with so many Whiteflyers about, it was the best they could do until they were all up and moving and until the sun was down again. Within ten minutes Grey was already showing slight signs of movement and within twenty, he was sitting up.

"What happened?" Grey asked, his memory failing him.

"Matthew Avery happened," James replied, sitting against the concrete wall opposite him. "He got you back with your water explosion. I finished him off, but I am sure they've been rescued by some of the other Whiteflyers by now."

Grey grinned, "That Matthew seems like such a pleasant young man. I can't see any possible reason that you two wouldn't get along. Let's not even start on the rhino and the snotty witch that he pretends are his friends. "

James smiled and rolled his eyes. "Even now you joke."

Grey shuffled his head in Stevie's direction. "There's no better time." Stevie was staring wide-eyed at the floor, chewing her nails into non-existence.

James knew what she was thinking about, it had been stuck in his mind too. "Don't listen to her, Stevie, she was just trying to get at you. You know what she's like," he sympathised.

Stevie looked up sharply. "I don't care about her reasons, I care about what she said. They've captured my mum. Who knows how long they've had her for or what they've been doing to her? Even though they'd probably know she'd have no information, they would torture her for the fun of it. How could she know anything about us? I haven't seen her since I was a child."

"We don't know that they have her for sure. They know you'd be looking for her, it could be a hoax to get us to come in." James didn't believe it himself, Roe's grin was too self-assured, but he couldn't risk Stevie letting her win by running straight into the palm of her hand.

"I know it for sure," Stevie replied before lying down to face the wall. "And I am going to go and get her back once the sun goes down, whether you want to come with me or not."

James took a deep breath, there was no choice to make, of course he would go with her.

James drifted off to sleep an hour or two after arriving at the garage. In his dream, James was standing outside a house not too different from his family home on Earth. The door was ajar and he could hear screaming coming from the inside, so he stepped in. He called out but nobody answered, so he followed the sound. It was coming from the kitchen. James entered a light yellow room with white presses. It had a daisy covered table cloth in the centre and freshly cut flowers decorated the window. It was in complete contrast to the situation set out in front of him. A dark haired man of a medium to tall build was roaring at a slender woman with thinning fair hair. He was obviously drunk and seemed to be building himself into an aggressive state. James moved to step in front of him, to get him out of the crying woman's slightly wrinkled face, however, he instantly felt too heavy and his body wouldn't allow him to move forward. He could do nothing but watch.

"You're as worthless as your useless son," the man shouted, his index finger pointing an inch from her face, spit landing on her pale skin. "I would never have married you if I'd known just how pathetic you are. Your good looks only lasted so long, and then your true colours really came out." The woman didn't respond but moved her hand to her face instinctively, she knew what was coming before it happened. The man grabbed her arm away with his left hand and followed it with his right closed fist. It connected with her nose and James swore he could hear a crack.

For the first time, James noticed a little boy under the kitchen table, hugging his legs while silent tears streamed down his face. He looked like someone he knew, but he didn't think he knew many children. When his mum fell to the ground, he ran to her, blocking her from the violent pursuer. The man picked him up by his navy striped t-shirt, as if he weighed nothing, and threw him to the side.

Just then, James opened his eyes, he was back in the garage. It was only then that he realised why the little boy in his dreams was familiar to him. It had been Matthew. James shook his body. He didn't want to feel anything but anger and hatred towards him, but in that moment he couldn't help but feel a mix of pity and sorrow. The rant Matthew had had with Tim while he listened at the door had clearly had an impact on his dreams. While he knew that that exact situation may never have occurred, he had a very strong suspicion that it wasn't far from reality. While it may explain why Matthew was the way he was, it definitely did not excuse it, so James pushed the dream from his head and continued to hate him.

James tried to fall back asleep, but was unable to. He was afraid to return to his vivid dream, so he sat up and rooted in his bag for something to distract him.

"Can't sleep either?" a quiet voice came from behind him. "I've been up all night worrying about my mum. I just can't get Roe's smug little face out of my head."

Grey who had evidently been asleep stretched awake.

"I'll go and find her with you Stevie. I know you'd do the same for me. However, you need to know that we might not make it that far, actually we probably won't make it that far. You need to be prepared to get caught, possibly even taken back to The Controller's Palace. Can you handle that?"

Stevie shuddered, "I can. Who knows? If they catch me they might even bring me to her themselves. However, I know I can't ask you both to take the same risk."

"Leaving you to go alone is out of the question, so let's make a plan."

James glanced at Grey to gauge if he was in agreement. "You in?" He had already been staring at James with squinted eyes when he looked over. He didn't respond to James' question but he shook his head ever so slightly when Stevie wasn't looking. He was trying to tell him something, but didn't want to announce it to the room. James was unsure of how to talk to him in private while Stevie was around, so pushed it from his mind and engaged back with Stevie.

"We aren't too far from the Whiteflyer's headquarters, maybe an hour on foot, or half that time if we take to the air," Stevie observed.

James shook his head. "No, it's still a bit light out and we don't know who is in the neighbourhood from last night. We can't risk using our powers, we need to blend in. If this mission has any chance of working out we need to be as covert as possible. You know where the drudges are kept, so we will start there. If your mum is nowhere to be seen, we can move from room to room until we find her. If she is there at all, that is."

James didn't go into detail on where else she could be, but he knew it wasn't necessary. Stevie was with him when he first went into the gutters. She knew just as well as he did that if she wasn't in the headquarters, she was likely to be in one of them.

Grey stood up. "I can see there's no talking you out of this, but if we are going to do it, it's going to be my way. This plan of yours has way too many holes in it. We have no idea if Stevie knows where the drudge's living quarters are, they don't necessarily stay in the same part here as they do in Torpor. We can scope out the building once it gets dark, monitor how many people are coming and going and go from there. We need to take this slowly."

James was taken aback, Grey hadn't shown any interest in looking for Stevie's mum since they had left the beach house and had shown the very opposite, only minutes before, yet here he was taking the lead. This plan was better than his but a lot slower, so he was unsure whether it would be enough to satisfy Stevie's needs. He said nothing and instead looked to her for reassurance and when she didn't argue he nodded sharply.

Over the next couple of hours, Grey took Stevie and James through the layout of the Tartarus headquarters, the parts he knew anyway, and gave them a rundown of who was who. The building seemed quite different to Torpor's headquarters and now that James thought about it he was hardly surprised. A lot of the rooms had been manipulated by the level 4 Whiteflyers, making them longer or wider. This was similar to what was done in the Torpor headquarters. Some had even been created entirely new, so the likelihood of the buildings being identical was slim to none. Grey drew a map of all the areas he had been in (which had been a lot) and gave a detailed description of what they were used for.

When it came to the people, it turned out that the man he had called Glaze was a particularly rotten egg that would do anything to get on top. Grey liked to call Robbie Glaze because when he exercised with no top on, his sweaty belly hung over the top of his trousers and looked uncannily like a glazed doughnut. This stuck with a lot of the other Whiteflyers and Robbie Hick, had a vendetta against him since.

Amos, whom James already knew, was of course the Hatt of Tartarus. Grey described him as a quiet observant character who you did not want to cross. Grey had once seen him skin a recruit alive with a floating piece of gravel, because he was still practising Air by the time most of the others had moved onto Water. It reminded James of when Rebecca was set on fire in his own training camp and he couldn't help but feel a wave of guilt for all of the drudges he had left back on Torpor. Images of Richie and Marcus flashed into his brain, but he quickly moved them aside.

"Another one to watch out for is Rosie Bartley. I suppose you could describe her as my Matthew of Tartarus. She never goes anywhere without Danica Alinsky and Corinne Jones. They are pure poison and Rosie is the teeth of the snake that unleashes it," Grey explained. "Don't let her good looks fool you, if you underestimate her you will regret it."

Stevie scoffed, "Of course you have to warn him about her good looks. Boys are so predictable. If any of you thought with your brain, you'd know that a girl is only as interesting as her personality."

Grey let out a forced loud 'Ha', "So, you are telling me that when you first saw James you didn't swoon at his perfectly imperfect hair and his strong and tall stature?"

Stevie rolled her eyes but James was happy to see she couldn't hide the blush rising on her cheeks. "I most certainly did not, and I would hardly call that untidy mop that sits atop his head 'perfectly imperfect hair'."

Grey grinned to himself but continued with his lesson on the unsavoury characters that may be lurking around Tartarus' headquarters. Overall, James felt a lot more prepared and was happy he chose to go with Grey's plan over his own. In retrospect, his not so covert idea to break into the building and walk around aimlessly until they may or may not have run into Stevie's mum was really not a well thought out plan at all. They really would not have lasted long before bumping into another Whiteflyer, and whether he'd be able to get Stevie out of there was not very likely.

"So, is everyone prepared?" Grey asked, staring directly at Stevie as they walked towards the headquarters. The air smelt more like smoke than usual. James imagined the tarnish the Whiteflyers would be causing around the city after realising that himself and his friends had escaped unscathed, apart from Grey's momentary unconsciousness, once again. Matthew would have got into a whole lot of trouble from Catherine of course, and maybe even from The Controller himself. However, the younger Avery had never been a match for James, so why he was put in charge of Stevie's uncle's house he didn't know. It was a likely place they'd visit while in Tartarus, considering they'd visited the same place in Torpor before starting their training. Then again, maybe Vask didn't think they'd be so stupid after their first encounter or maybe he thought too highly of Matthew. How wrong he was.

"Yes, yes I am ready," Stevie replied. "Stay hidden in the building opposite it and keep watch."

"And.." Grey nudged.

"And we don't leave the building unless our position is compromised."

Grey stared at her as if he needed more.

Stevie rolled her eyes and sighed. "And if I see my mum, I don't follow her."

"You need to promise me Stevie. This is a stake

out, not a rescue mission. We will deal with it once we have the proper information," Grey said, his tone uncompromising.

Grey had gone over this point again and again before they left the garage. James didn't know why he was being so adamant about it. He didn't imagine they'd even see her. After all, why would she be outside the headquarters or strolling past the windows and not locked up inside a dungeon or wherever they locked their prisoners? However, Grey knew Tartarus best so if he thought it was important, it must be. He had never been the overly organised controlling type that would include pointless information for the sake of it.

It was an hour before sunrise when they reached the back of the building Grey had flagged as having one of the best viewpoints of the headquarters. He had used it multiple times himself before he had signed up to be a Whiteflyer. He had come there with the rebels to scope out the enemy he was about to befriend. To learn as much about them as possible before entering the lion's den.

They flew into the small yard, careful not to float above the building's height and blow their cover before they'd even begun. They then entered through the back door. The room was small and narrow and James pictured it as a small coffee shop or a newsagent back on Earth. It didn't have much in the way of furniture, apart from a few wooden chairs and a broken console table. The left of the room had a broken staircase leading to another small room that was likely used for extra seating or a small office. The window of this room had a good view of the headquarters and wasn't covered in the black paint that the one below had been. All the same, it was not as great as James had pictured when Grey had sold them the idea.

"Is this it?" Stevie asked, reading James' mind.

Grey smiled and walked over to the back left corner of the beige room. "Nope, this is it." He jumped into the air and grabbed hold of a dangling piece of string that James hadn't noticed before. As he came down with the string, so did a metal ladder.

James was first up the ladder followed by Stevie and then Grey, who brought the entrance back up with him.

The attic of the building was a lot more airy than the rooms below them had been. It was decorated in exposed brick with a wooden floor, as opposed to the neutral colours below. There were no windows in the empty room, but there was a small passageway that led to ten narrow but sturdy stone steps that continued onto the roof of the property.

"That's more like it," James praised Grey, patting him on the back as he looked over the wall lined roof, out onto a complete aerial view of the headquarters. He could see everything from the grand entrance into the building to the training grounds out the back.

The sun was setting and for one split second, if James didn't focus on anything in particular, Tartarus actually looked beautiful. However, black smoke rising from the corner of his right eye in the distance brought him back to reality.

"How did you find this?" Stevie asked, hope filling her face as she peered out onto the headquarters.

Grey smiled, content with a job well done. "I told you. I've been here before with the rebels."

"What if they come up here?" James asked.

"Nah, they won't, they haven't used it in a while, but even if they did, I've told you before, they are on our side."

James still didn't know enough about the rebels to consider himself on their side. However, they did get them out of London, so he had to admit they weren't all bad. Even if he couldn't stand the sight of Bee.

"So, now what?" Stevie asked, hyped to begin the mission.

Grey took his bag off his back and took a seat on the ground. He fiddled with one of the stones on the wall overlooking the headquarters until it came loose, leaving a birds eye view of their target. "Now, we wait."

For the next hour, there wasn't much movement coming from the headquarters. A few lights went on and off inside the building, but nobody left or entered. Just when James noticed Stevie growing irritable, they got their first sighting of their enemies.

A rather large group of Whiteflyers walked up to the building from their left. They looked tired and fed up and their white outfits were smeared with mud and charcoal. James didn't recognise any of them.

"Coming back from a shift looking for us I would bet," Grey snarled, staring at a young blonde woman who was leading the pack. "Typical that she made sure she was in charge of Tartarus' effort to find us."

James looked at the girl closer and figured it must be Rosie. While he wasn't close enough to get a good look at her individual features, even from a distance she looked as beautiful as Grey warned. Her long dirty blonde hair swayed down her back, complimenting her sallow skin. Even the way she held herself intrigued James further.

The rest of the people surrounding Rosie, both boys and girls, seemed just as taken with her as James had been. Their eyes followed her hand as she swirled her hair or brushed it off her upper thigh. When she talked they no longer broke out into smaller groups but came together to listen.

"Emmm, everything okay there?" Stevie asked, noticeably annoyed by James' goggled eyes.

James shook his head and came out of his trance, embarrassed he'd been so obvious.

Grey narrowed his eyes as he glared at Rosie. "What did I tell you? The devil dressed as an angel," he remarked.

"She can't be that bad," James replied, subconsciously looking back at her as she walked further away, up the headquarter's stairs and into the building.

Grey snorted, "Yeah, come to think of it, The Controller isn't bad looking himself, so I don't know why we are even running from him."

James smirked, "Point taken."

He had imagined Grey had tried it on with Rosie while he was living in the Tartarus headquarters. She wasn't at the recruits first meeting with The Controller so she must not have trained with Grey, but he was the friendly, sociable type so it wasn't a difficult task for James to picture him chatting up the more experienced Whiteflyers, maybe even while he was still training.

Another while had passed before there was any more movement around the headquarters. They noticed the odd civilian quickly scurry by but nobody of value to their mission. The sun went and came back, and was high in the sky when the next batch of Whiteflyers came stumbling home after a long night out.

"It's Matthew, Roe, Tim and that Glaze man," Stevie snarled. She refused to lose eye contact with them as they sullenly made their way back to bed.

They were obviously wrecked and Glaze, or Robbie as he insisted he be called, even fell on his way up the stairs. Tim of course let out a loud chuckle that would have startled anyone nearby. Roe also let out a small laugh, but Matthew just stared at the hefty man in disgust before stepping over his leg and continuing on his way into the headquarters as if nothing concerning him had just happened.

"No surprises there," Grey laughed. "As clumsy as ever. I would have loved to be in his training group. If he can pass the competition, anyone can. It's a wonder he made it to level 3."

James smiled thinking of Matthew's reaction. It wasn't like him to turn down laughing at someone else's expense. "He must have been out all night looking for us. I'd say he's raging that we got away."

The rest of the day went similarly to the night. People came and went from the headquarters but after Matthew and his posse, none were familiar to James or Stevie. Grey seemed to know most of them and gave a running commentary to make their stake out worthwhile, but also to fill the time. He was a marvellous storyteller, so even the dreariest of run ins he had had with these people, seemed like an adventure in itself. They took turns taking naps so as not to miss anything, but as it turned out there really was not much point. There was no sign of Monica Miller.

James was conscious that Stevie's irritation was growing the longer the day went on. She was a lot more quiet than usual and he couldn't blame her. They were getting nowhere closer to finding her mum.

As the sun came down, Stevie voiced what James

was fearing she would all day, "I am going in. Tonight."

Grey sat up alert. "It was one day Stevie, just give it a couple more, and then I promise James and I will be by your side when we go inside to find her."

Stevie turned to James ignoring Grey's pleas. "If the tables were turned, I wouldn't ask for a few more days with you. I would be by your side no matter what."

James nodded. "You are right. We are going in tonight."

Grey panicked, looking for words that would convince them otherwise. Instantly, hope filled his face. "Tomorrow morning is the weekly announcement. We should at least wait for that. We could get invaluable information from it. We need to know what they're saying to the public about us, if anything at all. That boy that James met on our way back to London was told to look out for us, so now that they know we are back in London, I'd imagine the same information will be spread here. We don't even have to wait until nightfall to go into the headquarters after that. As soon as it's over, I'll ram the door myself."

James stared at Grey confused, he didn't understand why he was so reluctant to go in at night when most people were out on a mission or in bed asleep, yet he was willing to scour the building in full sight the following afternoon.

He looked to Stevie for guidance, she was wide eyed in deep thought. "Tomorrow then, but I won't wait another minute. Once the square clears, I am going in to find her."

CHAPTER 10 - "I THINK IT'S TIME WE TOOK A TRIP."

James lay awake in the room under the rooftop wondering what Grey's plan was for the following day. It was very obvious that whatever he had up his sleeve he wasn't willing to share with Stevie, so James tried to get him alone with no success. He couldn't believe that he was eager to storm the headquarters in daylight, but now that he had told Stevie he would, there was no way out of it, for any of them.

When James finally fell asleep, he dreamt about his own mum. She was trapped in a cage in The Controller's palace and was being repeatedly tortured for information about James' whereabouts. She screamed ignorance but nothing she said satisfied The Controller's need for vengeance. He ran for her but was stopped when he heard a scream to the right of the now glass room he was in. His mum had been moved and was now tied to a doctor's bed with Catherine operating on her body while she was still awake. The glass between them was impenetrable. She was staring at the ceiling screaming. He woke up in a sweat and for one split second was charged and ready to do whatever was needed to save his mum. When he realised that it wasn't his mum in danger, but Stevie's, a pang of guilt made its way to his stomach and tightened his chest. He wasn't doing enough to help Stevie, he hadn't really been doing anything at all. His sole concern up until now had been her safety. It was time he started paying more attention to her sanity. She would follow him around the Three Worlds without the need for him to even ask.

James shook Stevie awake in a panic. "I'm sorry. I'll do more"

She rubbed her eyes and whispered back in a croaky voice, "Thank you, that's all I need, your best."

James, Stevie and Grey got ready on the rooftop as the sun came up. They were in a prime position to see whatever display the Whiteflyers were going to put on this week. Grey told them them that a similar voice enhancing trick was used in Tartarus as it was in Torpor, so they would have no problem hearing what was going on.

When they were settled, they watched as scattered groups of nervous people made their way towards the square from all angles. There were substantially less people here than James had ever witnessed at Torpor's weekly meeting and they all looked lost and afraid.

"It's less of a turn out than usual," Grey told them. "They must really be reigning hell and fire down on the city. It seems that only the desperate and the hopeful have made a show."

James remembered the feeling of loneliness and confusion he had experienced when he had first arrived on Torpor. He understood why some people would show up regardless of how the Whiteflyers had been treating them. Some were probably too new to have experienced their wrath at all just yet. Others, like Anne, would do anything to find out news about the newly dead if it meant that they had a chance to be reunited with their loved ones.

When the doors of the headquarters opened, those closest to the entrance took a step back. Whiteflyers came flooding out of the building, and just like they had in Torpor, they were all desperate to prove themselves to the crowd below.

Fire balls and streams coloured the sky as those beneath the flames cowered to the floor. Whiteflyers rose high into the sky and then came swooping back down as if they were superheroes, and a few took from the fountains in Trafalgar Square, to make it rain.

Amos came through the doors to read off a list of those who had died and arrived at Tartarus that week, but began his speech with an over-rehearsed paragraph about why they deserved to be there. He categorised the group as murderers, cheats and cowards. He screamed that they were pathetic excuses for humans before ending on a message of hope and redemption if they would just get on the right path, if they would join the cause for justice and righteousness.

Just as Amos began to read the list of newcomers, James noticed a woman to his left, with shimmering shoulder length red hair. Her skin was sallow and her eyes were a deep brown colour that was further highlighted by the whites of her Whiteflyer robes. She was completely familiar, but James was also aware that he had never met this woman before. It was Stevie in twenty years time. There was no question that needed answering, it had to be her mother. Roe wasn't telling Stevie that they had captured her mum, she was letting her know that she was one of them.

James cocked his head quickly to his left where Stevie sat, her eyes wide and wet and her mouth slightly open. She was in shock. It wasn't how she expected to find her mum. She was up and well, smiling brightly with her hands in the air. She was one of them.

"No, it can't be," Stevie whispered, after what seemed like forever in silence. "She would never. She's good. I know she is. She is my mum."

James went to move towards her, to hold her.

Stevie put her arm out to stop him. "No! Don't touch me," she insisted.

She looked past him and so James turned to follow her line of sight. Grey was sitting behind him staring at her with a mix of pity and knowing. He trained in Tartarus, he'd lived here for years. James had guessed who this woman was within seconds of seeing her, there was no denying that Grey had known who she was all this time.

"It was the only way Stevie. You wouldn't have believed me otherwise," he protested before Stevie had even gathered her words together.

"You knew," Stevie shouted, louder than was safe. James quickly put up a sound proof air wall around them so they'd continue to go unnoticed and so that the Whiteflyer's announcement didn't reach their ears. Stevie didn't need to hear anymore.

"You know you wouldn't have. You needed to see it for yourself."

"If I needed to see it for myself, then why did you not want to leave the beachhouse? Why did we leave London at all?" Stevie fought back, her voice breaking.

Grey hesitated, "I... I wanted to protect you."

James couldn't help but feel sympathy for him, he didn't know what he would do in the same situation, but he couldn't rule out total denial if it would save Stevie from the hurt she was quite clearly experiencing now.

Tears streamed down her face as she turned to look back out at the woman she thought she knew. "Maybe it's, maybe it's all an act. Maybe she doesn't know I am here."

Grey took a deep breath. "They're lovers Stevie, her and Amos. It's not an act. They have been together since I woke up here and for who knows how long beforehand."

Stevie fell back to sit against the wall surrounding the roof and put her head in her hands. "And Bee, she must have known too. I'd say you both got a real laugh out of pretending she was going to find her for me."

Grey took a step towards her. "I am sorry Stevie, if I didn't go about it in the right way, or if there was more I could have done, but I didn't know how to break the news to you in a way that wouldn't force you right into their hands. I've been thinking about it since I realised who you were. This was the best I could do."

James thought back to every moment over the last few weeks when he had wondered about Grey's intentions and everything clicked into place. Grey really had been holding onto this for a long time. It explained everything from why he didn't want to leave the beach house up until last night when he asked Stevie to wait one more morning before storming into the Whiteflyer's headquarters. She was never going to get the answers she wanted, so they would have been doomed from the second they entered the building.

After a long moment, Stevie lifted her head from her hands and turned to face the announcement once more. "Let me hear."

James hesitated, he wasn't sure if she was ready, but when she stared at him with her 'do what I say or else' look he complied and removed the dense air bubble he had placed there to block out their words. Amos had finished his list of people who had arrived at Tartarus and was just finishing off listing the rules of the world. He was letting them know that, just like Torpor, nobody could own anything in the world for themselves.

"Now that we have all of that out of the way," Amos announced. "We have a very different topic to discuss than usual."

Grey leaned forward, as if to get a closer look. "Here we go."

"There are two young men and a young woman on the loose in Tartarus. They were last seen in this very city. The leader is of tall stature, with pale skin and dark hair. He is very dangerous and should not be trusted under any circumstances. He will not hesitate to destroy · anyone who gets in his way. He is travelling with a young man from Tartarus who is of small build with fair hair. He is also extremely dangerous. The girl with them has long red hair and brown eyes." Amos then looked at Stevie's mum before adding, "We believe that she may be accompanying them under duress."

James glanced at Stevie just in time to see her purse her lips, scrunch her nose, and shake her head. She no longer looked like the sad innocent Stevie from just minutes before. She was angry.

Amos continued, "These people may come to you under false pretences. They may even look like one of us, like a Whiteflyer who is there to protect you and serve The Controller. This couldn't be further from the truth.

They are a danger to anyone they come across and aim to release destruction on this place we call home. Anyone with any information on their whereabouts is urged to come straight to the headquarters. You will be rewarded for their recovery."

The crowd began to murmur and James couldn't tell whether it was in their favour or not. Just because the little boy in the village believed in his innocence did not mean these people would too. While adults pride themselves on their intelligence, when it comes to good and evil, it is usually the young and the innocent that can best tell them apart.

"What a load of baloney," Grey snorted. "Surely they won't believe any of that."

James grunted, "It's likely to be a mix. There always is when it comes to political beliefs."

Grey scoffed, "Political beliefs. What a way to sugar coat the mess that is the hierarchy of the Three Worlds. What do you think Stevie, will they believe it?"

Without replying, or even looking in Grey's direction, Stevie turned to go back inside.

James took a step towards Grey and patted him on the back as he watched her leave. "Give her some time. She will come around. It wasn't that long ago that she wasn't talking to me."

Grey took a deep breath. "That was just a small bit different."

For the rest of the day, James, Stevie and Grey stayed inside the building opposite the headquarters. The Whiteflyers had just put out an alert about them only metres away so they figured it was best to wait until night fell before they moved location. James couldn't get them all together for long enough to find out what that location would be, but he knew that they couldn't stay there they were. Every time Grey came into the room, Stevie would leave, resulting in a rather awkward day for James. He didn't want to take sides. He wasn't completely sure that he wouldn't have kept the information from Stevie himself. However, he could also see how upset Stevie was about the situation, so he didn't want to make light of it or appear to be unsympathetic towards what she must be going through. He couldn't even imagine what he'd do if that was his mum out there. He thought he was confident it never would be, but Stevie hadn't entertained the idea that her mum would be against them either, so who really knew. She had at least tried to influence Amos regarding Stevie's willingness to go up against the Whiteflyers, but Vask, and certainly Catherine, would never believe or ignorantly go along with that story, so it was extremely doubtful that The Controller would either.

While Stevie didn't leave the room when James walked into it, she didn't want to talk about the situation either. She avoided any conversation about what happened that morning or any talk at all for that matter, so it wasn't until they all got settled for the last nap before they left the building, and when they could hear Grey's gentle snores, that she opened up at all.

"None of this makes sense, I know she was never the best mum growing up, but she's sober now. I always thought she was a great person underneath all of her problems," she confided.

"She can still be a great person and be with the Whiteflyers Stevie. We don't know what she's been told, maybe she is just going along with it until she finds you. We signed up to be Whiteflyers too after all."

Stevie shook her head. "You don't really believe

that James. I think you forget how well I know you by now. We signed up to find the ones we loved. I signed up for her. I was alive when she applied to be a Whiteflyer, so that cannot be her excuse."

James hated seeing her lose the hope she'd held onto since he found her on the hospital bed in Torpor. "What about Annabelle? It wasn't too long ago that you said you believed she was still a good person, so why is it different with your mum?"

"And it wasn't too long ago that you told me she was just as bad as the rest of them." Stevie stared at James as he tried to think of a believable response. "I can see what you're trying to do, but it's not going to work. My mum wasn't the person I remember. I have to come to terms with that."

"And Grey?" James wondered.

"I'll forgive him eventually, but for now can't I just be mad at him? I need to take it out on someone and seeing as my mum isn't here, he is the next best thing."

James smiled. "Of course you can. I will even be mad at him with you if you want."

Stevie forced a feeble smile. "I wouldn't give you the satisfaction."

"Well then, I guess I will just have to think of my own reason to be annoyed at him," James replied, before falling into a short but necessary sleep.

It turned out that James' reason to be annoyed at Grey didn't take much energy to think up after all. When he had risen from his nap, his friend was already awake and packed. "I've been thinking, and I think it's time we took a trip to visit one of the rebel bases. They will know we are back by now and it is probably the safest place we could be at the moment."

James shook his head. "Absolutely not. They sent us off with Bee last time we went to them for help. If they give us shelter now it will be to take advantage of our powers alone."

Grey huffed loudly, "Stevie I know you're not talking to me right now, but you know this is the right thing to do. James has a weird grudge against the rebels that he refuses to shake off, but you can see my plan for what it's worth."

Stevie glared at Grey for a while before answering, "I am doing whatever James is doing."

Grey shook his head before readdressing James, "Moore, you are thinking about it all wrong. It's not what you can do for them, but rather what they can do for you. You are a proud person, but you need to know when to throw in the towel and ask for help. We have no other moves."

James hated to admit it, but Grey was right, he didn't know what else to do from here. He had no idea where they should even sleep for the next few nights, never mind how they were going to dissolve the whole system and stop The Controller. The longer he waited to do something, the more people that would be piled into the gutters. His thoughts shifted to Ann following the Whiteflyers to the countryside because of a promise she had made to him, and his heart ached. "Fine, but I need them to be very clear on the fact that I am not one of them. We can use each other. They can take advantage of my powers while I use their accommodations and knowledge, but that is as far as our relationship goes. I am my own person and I will definitely not just do as they say like some lap dog."

Grey flashed a toothy grin. "That's all I am asking,

but if you really gave them a chance you'd realise that they're not bad."

"If Bee is anything to go by, I beg to differ."

Grey looked to Stevie to make sure she was on board and with a silent agreement they made their way back out of the building and through the streets of Tartarus once more.

"So, how far are we?" James asked Grey when they'd been walking for quite some time.

"There's not very long to go now. There were some smaller shelters close by, but I reckon they would have sent us this way if we'd gone knocking so best to save the time and effort and go straight to our base camp. Deandra will be there."

"Want to fill us in on anything before we get here?"

Grey thought for a minute. "Well I have already told you that we are broken into groups, so you won't meet everyone here, but you'll meet some of my team anyway. There's half a dozen of us at the moment, and you two will make eight."

James glared at Grey and he quickly corrected himself in a somewhat sarcastic tone, "There are six of us and the two of you are completely separate."

"Much better," Stevie chimed in.

"It wasn't so long ago that you couldn't wait to be part of the team," Grey sighed.

"It wasn't so long ago that you betrayed me about my mother's whereabouts and true intentions," Stevie snarled back.

James could sense the situation heating up so jumped in to put the conversation back on track. "So these people, are they your friends? Can they all be trusted? When we were leaving London you mentioned that our whereabouts could get leaked."

"These things can happen James. Just like we convert some of the Whiteflyers to our cause, they can do the same with us."

James mumbled under his breath, "Not turning out to be a very stable plan."

Grey snapped, "And neither is roaming the streets until we find The Controller and he locks us up and takes away our powers. We are nearly there, so get with it James or we turn around now. "

"Fine, fine, I am with it. For now anyway."

Grey came to a stop a few streets later. He stood in front of, what looked like, the place a block of flats would use for bin storage. There were four brick walls with no roof and only a small entrance. They walked through the gap to an empty two by two area, that was empty apart from a rather large grate on the ground.

"Surely it's not down there?" James asked, thinking back to the last hideout that appeared to be a burnt down building from the outside and turned out to be a pretty swanky underground home from the inside.

Grey smiled. "It sure is and we better get a move on before anyone comes along. We usually aren't allowed to enter in groups, but seeing as you two have never been here before and don't know your way around, we don't exactly have any other option."

The entrance to the rebel's base led to an underground grey cement tunnel. It was quite dark with nothing but the entrance to light it and a faint glow up ahead. Grey summoned a small fire just above the palm of his hand. The tunnel was perfectly square and James would have put money on it that it was made using a Whiteflyer's powers. There were no imperfections, not even wear and tear.

"Who made this?" James inquired, brushing his hand off the left wall as they strolled towards the light ahead.

Grey shrugged. "How am I to know? They're very secretive around here if you haven't gathered yet from my stories. I haven't been on Tartarus for that long really. This was here when I arrived."

"Well, it wasn't made using a couple of shovels, that's for sure. Maybe I am not the only level 4 Whiteflyer that has gone rogue. All of your hideouts are looking very professional," James suggested, a gleam of hope telling him that the rebels might not be a big joke after all. Maybe they had a chance.

"Let's not jump to conclusions, maybe it was made years ago when there were still those with powers. It could have even been created by a Whiteflyer rebel who was captured. If there were level 4 Whiteflyers on our side now, I am sure they would have told me when they positioned me to become one. Such a powerful ally would have been more than useful."

Stevie joined in, "Yeah I don't know James. That is a bit of a jump, just because you think the tunnel was made well."

James lowered his voice, "Anyway, we are coming up closer, let's not tell these people anything we don't have to."

Grey laughed, "These people are my people, and I hope one day they are your people too. Both of you."

Stevie scoffed, still obviously annoyed with Grey. James smirked to himself, delighted that her joining the rebels was one less thing he had to worry about.

The light turned out to be a small white room

with a single bulb hanging from the ceiling. It was very clinical and didn't have any furniture, but had a double door to the right of it, which Grey jumped towards to dramatically open, "Welcome my friends, to my humble abode."

James wasn't sure what he expected when Grey had suggested bringing them here. On the way here, he had toyed with the idea that it was a whole underground city, but he pulled back his expectations to something like the safe house they'd arrived at when they first came to Tartarus. The reality of the base camp was somewhere in between.

The rather large room leading from the tunnel was in contrast to the clinical area just outside the doors. It had the same low ceilings and concrete walls but it was nothing like a hospital or a state run primary school. The walls and floors donned colourful graffiti and told a story all of their own. It was a story of freedom and expression. Couches were sprawled across the space and hammocks hung on the adjacent wall, giving the room a sociable vibe even though it accommodated nobody. A couple of doors told James that there was more to the building than just this room, so there was still a good chance that they weren't alone.

"So, where are they all? No grand entrance, nobody to roll out the red carpet for us?" James asked.

Grey huffed, "Let me remind you that they don't even know we are coming and that it is the middle of the night. They're most likely in bed or out roaming Tartaturus on missions."

James raised his eyebrows. "Well, either way, security isn't exactly tight around here, is it? We just strolled in without even as much as a locked door or an alarm going off."

Grey didn't answer but instead, an older female's voice from behind him did, "Or maybe that is exactly why nobody is here, because security is tight."

CHAPTER 11 - "A SPRINKLE OF HOPE CAN LIGHT A FIRE TOO BRIGHT TO PUT OUT."

James turned to see a group of three women and two men standing behind them. He cursed himself for not noticing their arrival before they had announced themselves. The woman at the front of the group looked to be in her late 40s when she died. It was evident from her demeanour that she was the one that Grey called Deandra. She had long blonde hair, almost white it was so light, with two streaks of brown framing her face. Her tight jeans and white t-shirt showed off her well kept long and lean figure. She had a serious but gentle face that reminded James of the woman who owned the local gardening shop back on Earth.

The man to her left looked a good bit older than her, but James couldn't tell if that was only down to the big bush of unbrushed grey hair on his head. He was small but stocky and watched the woman who had spoken like a hawk. James took a small step forward to test his boundaries and he immediately responded by moving toward James himself. He couldn't tell if his protectiveness over this woman was because she was his leader or because they had a romantic connection. He later introduced himself as Denis McGee or 'Mack' for short.

Josh, the younger man, was dark and lanky. He smiled a goofy grin at the three of them and eagerly waved at Grey who responded in kind. He wasn't much older than James and seemed like a cheery guy who couldn't cause any harm. James made a mental note not to take him at face value though and to spend more time with him before trusting him with anything important.

The girl next to Josh, Emmy, seemed small and timid. She had mousy hair and blue eyes. She was wringing her hands anxiously for the majority of their first meeting. She didn't say a word, and didn't take her eyes off Grey. James wondered if something had happened between the two but if it did, Grey hadn't mentioned it and had seemed to have moved on pretty quickly with Stevie.

The last person was someone James was sure would be here, but was disappointed all the same to meet again. It was Bee. She stood staring at him with a scowl that would frighten a bear back into hibernation. She wore her usual chunky boots, with khaki trousers and a black long sleeved jumper.

"So, you've made your way back to us after all Grey?" Deandra noted.

Bee jumped in before anyone had the time to respond, "Despite my warning to get lost."

James scoffed, "Not that anyone would take your warnings seriously, least of all me."

"Relax Bee, let's hear Grey out," Deandra ordered.

"We couldn't do nothing for any longer. The fight is here, so this is where we need to be."

"And Stevie's mum is here," Bee chimed in again. "Don't think we didn't hear about what happened the other night."

It was now Stevie's turn to scowl. "Leave her out of this, don't think I am ignorant enough to believe that you didn't know who she was all this time. This was a mistake James, let's go. I can tell when we are not wanted somewhere, not that I imagine Bee would ever make anyone feel welcome."

Grey grabbed her arm to stop her from leaving before turning to Deandra. "You could use us. You know it."

Deandra stayed silent in thought before taking a long sigh. "I suppose you are right, and you are here now so there is not much point in letting your powers go to waste," she conceded.

"I hope you are only talking about Grey's powers there," James questioned. "Mine aren't up for grabs."

"And neither are mine," Stevie chimed in.

"Then neither is our base camp," Bee snapped back.

Deandra turned her head towards James' adversary. "I say what is and what isn't up for grabs Bee and if you interrupt us once again, the only person this base camp won't be accommodating is you."

"Let me rephrase that James. Of course your powers are yours and yours alone, but if we are on the same side, like I think we are, your powers will be of use in the fight to take down The Controller, in whatever way you feel that it is necessary to use them."

James looked at Stevie and when she nodded, he followed suit.

Deandra rubbed her hands together. "Right, well before we get down to discussing both of our last few weeks, you all look like you could do with a hot shower and some down-time to settle. Josh, show them where they will be staying while they are here with us, will you?"

As all three of them went to follow Josh out one of the doors, Deandra called Grey back, "Let's have a chat just me and you first, shall we?" Grey obeyed and they left through the other door. To James' frustration, they were having their conversation out of earshot and he would just have to wait until Grey came back to find out what was being said.

Through the door that Stevie and James were brought through, there was a long hall with multiple bedrooms, each complete with its own bathroom off of it. They were somehow all identical but completely different. Each bedroom held the same set of furniture, one bunk bed, one wardrobe and a desk. However, every bedroom they passed gave off a different vibe. The first was painted bright pink and had old posters of Hollywood movie stars on the wall from magazines that James was certain didn't come from Tartarus. Another room was a mix of orange and green and had comic books laid out on the floor and an unmade bed. Then there was another, that James would have put money on it being Bees. It wasn't decorated at all. Only the bare essentials could be seen. The room that Josh brought Stevie and James to didn't hold much either, but it was painted a warm blue and had burnt orange sheets that gave off some comfort.

James looked at the bunk bed in front of him. "Is

Grey not staying with us? We'd rather stick together."

Josh shrugged. "Grey used to live here, he shares with me. We are in the orange and green room two doors down."

James couldn't argue with that further, so let Josh go back to the common room. He wasn't even sure where Grey would prefer to sleep himself. He didn't look at these people as a potential threat like James did. He trusted them.

"Well, what do you think?" Stevie asked as she sat down on the lower bunk bed, bouncing gently up and down to test the springs.

"I don't know. It's too early to tell, their quarters are pretty sweet though," James replied, taking her lead and sitting down on the swinging office chair. "What do you suppose Grey and Deandra are talking about?"

"How am I to know? I don't bet on Grey telling us the truth either. He's more than happy to keep secrets when it benefits him."

James knew Stevie was still hurt over her mum so he didn't fight the point, but he didn't agree with it either. Grey had proved his loyalty on more than one occasion over the last couple of months and while he'd gone through phases of being annoyed at him for his actions with Stevie, deep down he knew he was a true friend. "Well, either way, I'd rather we all sleep in the same room. I suppose Grey will have to decide for himself when he comes back."

James took a long hot shower and thought back on the last hectic few days. While it was his decision to come back to London, he couldn't help but think it had been the wrong one. It had achieved his desired end goal and put a rift between Stevie and Grey, but in hindsight, it wasn't really what he wanted. He loved their little friendship group, he just had a moment or two of jealousy that spiralled out of control. He'd also risked their safety quite a bit by coming back into contact with the headquarters. He then thought of the gutters and the little boy that had faith in him to make a change, and he realised that while it wasn't the most comfortable decision, it was the only one. Not for his superficial reasons, but for the reasons he had promised himself in bed in the headquarters during his time training. It was time to make a change.

When James got out of the shower, his questions about where Grey would stay were answered. He was clumsily colliding through the door with a single mattress he'd evidently taken from his original bedroom. "Room for one more?" he asked as he knocked the chair over and fell to the ground, the mattress on top of him. Stevie giggled before catching herself and turning away.

"We always have room for you," James confirmed, staring down at the lump on the ground, then looking over at Stevie who was trying to control her laughter. He certainly wasn't where he thought he would be a year ago but he wouldn't trade it for anything. He would change it alright, and he planned to, but he wouldn't swap Stevie and Grey for anyone. They were some of the best friends he had ever had.

James' mind shifted to Liza as he had these thoughts and he wondered what she'd be doing now that some time had passed since James' death. He was sure she'd have a new boyfriend, she had never gone long without one before they started dating, so he was confident that trend would continue. He then thought of his parents, and his stomach twisted with anxiety. His mum would still be mourning, his dad too. Hopefully, his sister Jen would have moved past it somewhat by now. He'd see them all again, even if they didn't know that just yet, and when he did the Three Worlds would be one. Travel unrestricted and powers restored.

James came out of his thoughts. Grey had got out from under the mattress and was sitting on the floor in the centre of the room smiling up at Stevie. She rolled her eyes and grinned slightly. Grey's face turned more serious. "I am sorry Stevie and I will keep saying it until you forgive me. I went about it in the wrong way, but at the time I really didn't know what else to do. I should have told you from the moment I realised who Monica was. It wasn't my secret to keep. I know that now, but you must at least believe that I did it for all the right reasons."

Stevie nodded. "I do, but it needs to stop." Stevie then stared at James, "Both of you, I can see that you are always trying to prove your 'manhood' with a bizarre need to protect me. I am more than able to look after myself. I've been doing it for my whole life and now that I am a Whiteflyer I am even more capable of taking care of myself."

James looked down at his hands. He was aware that he worried too much about her, but it had nothing to do with his manhood and everything to do with his feelings towards her.

Grey smiled and nodded eagerly, happy to accept any terms if it meant Stevie would forgive him. "Oh I know you can protect yourself. You hold your own like no other. You're the last person I'd dare cross again."

Stevie held out her arms for a hug and Grey skipped into it. James came up the rear and wrapped his arms around both of them, lifting them into an embrace.

Soon after that, James, Stevie and Grey fell into

their beds and drifted off to sleep. It had been a long few days. James dreamt about Matthew as a child again, but this time he was older. He was nearly a teenager and at school. He was surrounded by friends, picking on a younger boy. He woke up in a sweat and wished more than anything he could throw Matthew from his mind. He thought about him enough during the day without the presumptions of his childhood haunting him at night.

He stretched out and realised Grey and Stevie were both awake. James turned over in his bed to face Grey, who was lying on his mattress on the floor. He had been dying to know what was said between him and Deandra, but didn't want to ruin Stevie's moment the night before by prying on it too soon. "What did your leader want last night? Is she fine with us being here?" he queried.

Grey turned his head out of the comic he was reading. "Yeah she is more than fine. She wasn't exactly chuffed that I broke her orders and came back to London, but she couldn't deny that we are more valuable here than we are out in the middle of nowhere. She didn't go into too much detail about what happened while we were gone, she said she would go through some of it when we were together. I told her about where we stayed, but nothing about the journey home and what happened with Matthew and the others. It's better if it comes from all of us together. I wasn't even there for some of it, like the boy in the village and when you first got to Stevie's uncle's house."

"And when will that be?" James asked.

"A few hours I'd say, maybe even tomorrow. Knowing her she will want the two of you to feel comfortable before she talks to you."

Stevie pulled her blankets off her and stood up. "Well then, let's get comfortable. Introduce us to those friends of yours."

Grey jumped up gleefully. "My pleasure. If they're awake, they'll be in the common room I'd imagine."

The common room was the same as it had been the night before, but this time three people sprawled out on the couches. When James, Stevie and Grey came in they all looked up and went silent. It was obvious that the newcomers were the topic of conversation moments before.

"Well, what kind of welcome is this?" Grey asked, throwing his arms in the air and playfully scoffing when nobody said anything or walked over.

Grey's old roommate Josh jumped up first. "He's back," he cheered, punching the air in exaggeration.

Grey winked and moved towards him. "That's more like it."

James and Stevie followed, and they all took a seat in the middle of the room, pulling a couch over to accommodate them comfortably.

"Tell us everything," Josh urged his friend. "Where have you been the last few months?"

"Lounging on the beach, drinking mojitos, skinnydipping and getting a golden tan," Grey teased.

Bee coughed loudly. "You are paler than when you left."

James bit his lip in an effort to not give her the satisfaction of a laugh.

"Well the first part is partially true," Stevie confirmed. "We did stay on a beach, but I'll have to deny the rest. Well, I only speak for myself when I say we weren't skinny dipping, who knows what James and Grey were up to when I wasn't around."

James laughed and threw his hands into the air. "There was absolutely no skinny dipping over this way."

The third person, Emmy, didn't say anything but glared at Stevie when she started talking and had not taken her eyes off since. Grey seemed to notice, but decided ignorance was his best course of action and instead told a partial recap of the real story. "Yes I may have been exaggerating a bit, but as Stevie said we did stay by the sea and we got a crazy amount of practice in with our powers. You should see what James can do. I may have learnt even more with him than I did at training."

"Well I am glad you were off enjoying yourself," Bee interjected, never happy with keeping the mood positive for too long. "In the meantime, we have been here trying to clean up your mess."

Josh interrupted, "What a load to put on them Bee. They've only just arrived."

"That doesn't make it any less true. The Whiteflyers have got twice as bad, and their surveillance has gone up triple fold around the city, probably the country, looking for these nuisances."

Josh gave a face of knowing, and James knew it to be true.

Grey nodded once. "Well, we are back now and we are not going anywhere. In case you forgot, we didn't choose to leave, we were told to and you weren't exactly happy to see us again Bee, so you can get off that high horse you love to sit on."

"Yes, you were made to leave, because you went chasing this one around The Controller's Palace," Bee argued, motioning at Stevie.

James went to jump in and defend her, but

remembered his promise from the previous night.

Stevie pointed at herself. "This one has a name and she isn't the right person to be antagonising right now. I've had a lot to deal with over the last few days, and I sure as Tartarus won't let you act like this whole thing is my fault. I'd like to see any of you last a day in the Controller's palace."

James raised his chin and grunted in solidarity with Stevie.

"Enough, enough," Josh intervened before the room got too tense. "Let's stay positive. We're all going through a lot, we don't need to turn on each other too."

"Yeah chill Bee, I know you don't get on very well with James, but Stevie too?" Josh asked. Bee rolled her eyes and sat back on the sofa.

"So, what's actually been happening while we have been gone? It is really bad, is it?" Grey asked once everyone had simmered down.

"They've been doing raids on houses all over London and I've heard word that they've even been travelling to the towns outside," Josh told his eager listeners.

"I can confirm that," Grey said. "We passed through a town on the way back from Brighton. The Whiteflyers had been there looking for us. They haven't exactly been painting us in the best light either."

"I am sure they haven't," Josh noted. "They've also been rounding off more and more people to send to the gutters. I don't know whether that has anything to do with you though, I know you said they were planning that before. It is truck loads at a time. Eight huge lorries passed here only yesterday. The cries coming from inside were unbearable."

Stevie leaned forward. "Well, the gutters aren't taking it lightly. There was a riot in one of them. They are trying to rebel."

James took a deep breath and shook his head. He couldn't stand listening to people talk about the gutters as if there was nothing that could be done about it, as if they should be left to their own devices. "They can try to fight back all they want. They won't get out, not without powers or help from the outside. We need to be that help. What are the rebels doing to try and save them?"

Josh's face turned pink and he turned to Grey, who answered for the group.

"I've told you James, we need to look at the bigger picture. We need to take down The Controller. The rebels can't save every gutter, one at a time. We free one, all that will happen is that two more will pop up."

"Well then, what are the rebels doing to take down The Controller?" Josh turned to Grey to answer once more, but Bee jumped in this time.

"What are you doing to take down The Controller peabrain? You come in here demanding answers as if you've done your time in Tartarus. You are new to the Three Worlds, you don't know anything about our past, and what we have gone through to exist, to make our whereabouts a secret."

"Being here in secret isn't helping anyone, but yes you're right I haven't done much either, but I am ready and now is the time we fight back."

"You and what army?" Bee pushed back, leaning forward and clenching her fists. "You think you are all mighty and powerful because you are a level 4 Whiteflyer. You are nothing in comparison to him."

"You say that as if you admire his powers," James

spat. "Don't forget that he is the reason that you don't have any. That none of you do. Who knows how long I will have mine for?"

"Or mine," Stevie tagged on. "I'm with James. Let's get to work, use us while you can."

"Well I wouldn't say use us, work with us is more accurate."

Josh's eyes were bright and wide and a smile grew on his face as James spoke. "I'm in too. I am tired of sitting around, going out on small missions when we preach that he is the only mission. Let's take him down."

Emmy cleared her throat and spoke for the first time. She had a quiet squeaky voice that matched her timid appearance, "That is all being worked on, I am sure. Deandra and the other leaders know what they are doing. Let's trust the process and they will get us there. We have to have faith in their vision. If it was easy enough to take him down it would have been done by now."

"And you're fine with being kept in the dark?" Stevie questioned, slightly more aggressively than James would have addressed Emmy.

She bit her top lip and stared from Stevie to Grey before whispering two words and sitting back. "It's confidential."

"Screw confidential. You are involved in this just as much as they are. Who knows they are even doing anything?"

Josh, Emmy and Bee turned to face the door, so James, Grey, and Stevie followed. Deandra and her shadow Mack were standing there. "I see you've made yourselves at home," Deandra observed with a frown and a forced grin.

Stevie stuttered, "I just.. Ehh I just meant, if there

is anything we can be doing to help, we'd love to."

"That's very nice of you Stevie, and to answer your question, you know we are doing something because *you* haven't been found yet."

James scoffed loudly, "That's hardly to do with you. We haven't been found yet because we went into hiding and we fought off the Whiteflyers that The Controller sent to find us. You and the other rebels were nowhere to be seen"

Deandra rolled her eyes. "That is one opinion, I have another."

James sensed Deandra knew more than she was letting on. "Well, I am sure we are yet to earn your trust, just like you've yet to earn ours, but the only chance of us coming into the fold is if we are completely in the know. Whether you let buzzy Bee here and the others in on your plans is irrelevant to me, but Stevie, Grey and I won't stick around very long for partial stories and direct orders with little knowledge as to why we are doing it. We need to know the end plan," he pushed.

Mack took a step forward, he was obviously not used to his leader being spoken to so directly, but Deandra held out her hand to stop him from getting any closer. She turned to Grey, "Is that right Grey? Do you also agree with what James is saying?"

Grey looked around the room, before taking a long look at James. He then nodded. "He's right Deandra. We can't use our powers to their potential unless we are let in. The gutters are getting more crowded and The Controller is only getting greedier. It's time to let us in on the bigger picture. We can help, I know we can. James in particular. He is one of the best I've ever seen, but I am not going to be dragged around blindfolded and pointed in any given direction anymore, and I sure know he won't be either."

Deandra inhaled a long breath but stayed calm. She didn't seem like the unreasonable type to James, but it was clear she wasn't happy with Grey's change of attitude since he became a Whiteflyer, or more accurately, since he met James and Stevie.

"Well, all I can tell you is that I will think about it and take it to the other rebel leaders. You are aware that it's not my lone choice who can be filled in on what information. For now, why don't you catch me up on where you have been for the last few months and I will catch you up as well as I can on my end?"

James knew Deandra would have preferred to talk to them in private, without Josh, Emmy and Bee's listening ears, but he also knew that she didn't have the final say in the matter. Without another word, he used Air to push the couch he was sitting on to the side, to make room for another he had slowly flying across the room. It would have been quicker to choose the sofa closest to them, which would have only involved a simple shove, but if there was a time to remind Deandra that he was the one with powers, it was now.

"Take a seat," he told her with a grin and an outstretched hand. "Now is as good a time as any to fill in the blanks."

Deandra looked at Josh, Bee and Emmy, who all seemed as though they were ready to jump up and vacate the room at the slightest nod. She decided, however, to go along with James and instead took a seat, motioning for Mack to sit down beside her. "Grey filled me in on your accommodations near Brighton and mentioned you had quite the journey home, why don't you go from there?"

James spent the next while, with help from Stevie

and Grey, recounting the adventures they have had since leaving the cottage. He told Deandra of the fires coming from the gutter, and about what the little boy in the village had told him. He told her of the fight with Matthew, Tim, Roe and Glaze and about the weekly announcement. He didn't mention Stevie's mum, he was pretty sure she would already know of it, so there was no need to pour salt on Stevie's already stinging wound.

Deandra insisted James go over the details in Stevie's uncle's house again and again until every detail was revealed. She didn't care much for the news of the announcement, so James assumed she had people attend it herself. She was most likely already aware of the Whiteflyer's search for the three of them.

"And you had no other encounters with the Whiteflyers since you've been away?" she pushed for what seemed like the hundredth time.

"Well," Grey recalled. "We did have a run in with a man who had been told to keep an eye out for us and report anything suspicious back to The Controller's lackeys, but we got out of there before they had the chance to catch up."

"Got out of where?" Deandra asked.

Grey's eyes shifted to Stevie and back to Deandra again. She turned to Stevie, uncaring of whether she could hurt her feelings or not. "Your mothers?"

Stevie squinted her eyes. "Yes, my mothers."

"And you didn't find her there?" she asked with a blank look on her face.

"You know we didn't," Stevie bit back. "Or you wouldn't have guessed that we had visited her home in the first place."

Deandra nodded. "I am just confirming the story

is all. It's important that none of the details are glossed over. Sometimes, the most important information can be found in the blanks of a story that someone does not think is relevant to tell."

"Well, then I guess you better not leave any out. What has been happening while we have been gone?" James jumped in, half to steer the conversation away from Stevie's mum and half to keep control of the conversation with Deandra.

Deandra stood up and brushed her palms on her tight black trousers, "I think that's enough for one day. We don't want to overload you with information before you have even had time to settle."

James moved to stand up with her, but a hand from Grey stopped him, "Deandra will tell us later, won't you?"

Deandra shrugged, "Maybe later, maybe another time."

James cursed himself for giving so much away without anything in return. He had half a mind to storm out of the hideout altogether, but he was well aware he had nowhere to go if he did. Instead, he watched as Deandra and Mack left the room in hushed whispers.

"You know she's only trying to let you know who is in charge. I knew your play of power with the couches was never going to work. She doesn't respond well to threats."

"I wasn't threatening her, I was letting her know who needs who more."

"Either way, why not try to keep the powers to a minimum? They could use you around here, but that doesn't mean they will."

Stevie grunted, "Stubborn, as well as being very

slow burners. The rebels are really turning out to be a complete disappointment."

"Hey!" Josh scowled. "At least get to know us before you start throwing around insults."

Stevie's cheeks grew pink. "Sorry, I didn't mean you. That whole conversation was just infuriating to say the least."

Bee folded her arms smugly as she pushed her back into the couch. "Well, I think she was right. Who do all of you think you all are making demands of her like that? Don't you have any respect?"

"How about we forget about all of that for now? We have the day to ourselves, so why not make the most of it?" Josh suggested to the room. "I say we break out the board games and steal a few bags of sweets from Deandra's secret stash that we all know she keeps in her office.

Stevie chirped up, "I am in, but only if we can play Articulate, and only if I am not on a team with Grey."

"Ayye, I thought we made up," Grey whined.

"That doesn't mean I think you'd be any good at board games," she chuckled.

For the rest of the afternoon, they all, even Bee, lounged out in the common room of the safe house, playing games and eating rare junk food. They took turns playing on each other's teams and James got to know his new acquaintances.

Bee was, of course, super competitive and she and James made a surprisingly good team. Josh and Grey, who were so similar and who had shared a room for so long, knew each other inside out, so they also made a great pairing.

"This is an inferior super hero who has overrated

abilities, if we can even call them that," Grey rambled at Josh loudly, moving his hand wildly in the air as if it would speed up the answer.

"Batman," Josh screamed back a millisecond before Stevie yelled, "Time."

Grey stuck his hands in the air. "It counts, it counts."

Stevie jumped up. "It certainly does not. I called time before he answered."

"You did not, Josh beat you to it."

"I am going to unfortunately have to side with Grey here," James mediated. "He got there just before you. He wins again"

Stevie hissed at James but conceded and sat back down. "Why do they keep getting to go together? It's not fair, they are too similar."

"Because," Grey smugly explained. "You didn't want to be on a team with me, so I am lending my abilities where they're wanted. Shall we play another game?"

"I'm out," Stevie scoffed. Let's play something else. How about charades?"

"No can do, I am afraid," Josh jumped up followed by Emmy and Bee. "We are on patrol at the headquarters tonight, so we are out."

James joined them as they went to their rooms to get ready, "Cool, I am coming with you."

"Mmm, I don't think Deandra would like that," Grey told him.

"Even better," he smiled and continued on his way to their temporary quarters to grab a notebook and a pencil.

"What are they for?" Stevie asked from over his shoulder.

"I want to take a better note of the Whiteflyers from here. It was information overload when Grey was going through them last time. We need to get to know our enemies."

After some convincing, Bee gave up her complaining and they all made their way to Trafalgar Square in Tartarus. The sun had just gone down, so there was plenty of time to Whiteflyer spot before they lay down for the night.

"So, what brought you here?" James overheard Stevie asking Josh.

"In Tartarus, or here at all?" he inquired.

"Here at all I suppose, who really knows why they end up in which of the Three Worlds?"

"Well, I suppose I do. I am a hacker, well I was a hacker."

Stevie raised her eyebrows. "That is so cool! You are straight out of the movies."

"Well, I wouldn't say it was that glam in real life but I did find out some pretty cool information. Have you ever followed the YouTuber Belle Florence?"

Stevie's eyes grew wide and she eagerly nodded. Belle was known for her impeccable style and her copious amounts of designer belongings back a few years ago but she hadn't been on the scene for some time.

"All of those bags, watches, and whatever else she posts were stolen," Josh revealed.

Stevie gasped, "Surely not? You can't believe anything online nowadays. She really made it out that she was super successful."

"Yes, they sure are. Her ex boyfriend had me hack her computer for proof. He was going to expose her after she left him for some minor football player from up

North."

James smiled as he watched Stevie's reaction to getting the inside scoop. It was nice for her to get some escapism, in whatever form she preferred it.

"So that is why you ended up in Tartarus," she clarified, after getting some more sordid details on Earth's elite. "But how did you end up in the Three Worlds? How did you die?"

"It was about three years ago," Josh recalled. "One of my jobs went ugly. I found out some information about a pretty bad guy and he ended my life for it. Like I said, it wasn't all glitz and glam."

"That's rough! I never knew just how evil the world could be until coming to Tartarus, you all seem to have had such troubled lives."

"Not all of us, but some of us have seen some things alright."

"Where did you grow up?" James asked, interrupting their conversation.

"I grew up in Wales, but I went to university in London which is where I died. The hacking was a side gig for the most part. It paid the bills and kept my stomach warm. I can't deny that I did it for the thrill too though. I always told myself that once I graduated, I would get a job in tech and stop hacking but deep down I don't think I would have. I did it for the fun of it as well as for a job."

Emmy, who had been nearby, spoke. "You never told me that story."

Josh shrugged his shoulders. "You never asked."

Stevie turned to the timid girl. "What about you then?"

Emmy glared at Stevie, didn't reply, and moved up to walk with Bee.

"What was that about?" she turned to Grey, obviously offended.

"Beats me! I guess she just doesn't like you."

"Ha!" Josh smirked.

Stevie looked from Josh to Grey. "Am I missing something?"

"It's nothing," Grey answered, deciding to come clean on what his deal with Emmy was. "We had a little something before I left. I didn't exactly tell her what I was up to and just kind of vanished. She has been acting quite put out since I have come back. I tried to go in and talk to her last night, but she wasn't having any of it. She doesn't seem like it, but she has quite the temper when she wants to."

James studied Stevie's face for any sign of jealousy, but surprisingly, it never came. Instead, she broke out into a fit of laughter, holding her hand against her mouth to avoid angering Emmy any further. "Our Grey with a girlfriend. That's a laugh."

"Hey, I could have a girlfriend. Not that she was mine, but if I wanted a girlfriend I'd have a girlfriend."

James' insides swam in circles. He was nearly sure there was something going on between Stevie and Grey when they were back at the cottage. He had overheard the conversations and he'd seen them getting close, but this conversation threw a complete spanner in the mix.

James moved closer to them. "So, she's the last girl you've been with?" he asked, doing his best effort to act casual.

"Well, it was hardly that long ago. You haven't been with anyone for a few months either," Grey responded, confused about the meaning behind James' question.

James would have scooped into the air, if nobody was around, screamed from the top of the Eiffel Tower. Stevie and Grey hadn't got together after all. As Liza would say, James had once again made a mountain out of a molehill. However, once the joy wore off a pang of guilt rose up inside of him. He'd been acting completely out of sorts and paranoid about the whole Stevie and Grey situation.

"Actually, that explains why she is mad at you but why is she mad at me?" Stevie questioned.

"I suppose she thinks there's something between us," Grey replied.

Once again, Stevie broke into laughter.

Grey was outraged, "What is so funny? If I wanted us to be together, we could be together. I just have never turned my charms on. Unfortunately for you, you're not my type. I prefer brunettes."

This time, Josh and James joined in on Stevie's laughter.

As they came closer to their destination, Josh led them to an abandoned building on the far side of the headquarters. It didn't guard the entrance like the hideout James, Stevie and Grey had stayed in, but it did have a much better view of inside the building.

"Why didn't we stay here before?" Stevie asked Grey as they took a seat on one of the many wooden chairs that occupied the small peach coloured room.

"Well as you can see, it's in constant use by the rebels, so I thought it was best to steer clear of it until we met them on our own terms."

"Or you could have just left us alone forever," Bee chimed in, unwanted as usual.

"Do you ever take a day off?" James bit back.

"Surely it's exhausting being so defensive all of the time."

Bee frowned and took a seat as far from him as she could, before staring out the window pretending as if she was too busy to acknowledge him any further.

For the next few hours, James took notes of everyone who appeared in the windows of the headquarters. They were on the second floor of the abandoned building so they could see into a good few of the rooms. He saw Grey's enemy Rosie and her two lap dogs Danica and Corinne. He was delighted when he spotted Stevie staring at him from the corner of his eye when Rosie, gorgeous as always, appeared. It seemed she was waiting for his reaction. Before he realised he had misjudged the Grey situation he may not have hidden the smile on his face, however, now that it was clear they were nothing more than friends, he pretended to not even notice Rosie. He was aware that Stevie still didn't want to be with him right now, but her odd shows of jealousy gave him hope that there was always a chance in the future. He didn't want to do anything to rupture that.

They also saw Stevie's mum walking through the headquarters hall with Amos. Stevie got up and left the room as soon as she entered, and luckily missed their loving embrace. Grey had been right, there was no chance this was all a ruse on Stevie's mum's part. James watched as he lifted her off the floor and let her feet dangle as he kissed her. James' dad used to call it a bear hug when he was younger. He had named himself dada bear, his mum mama bear and James and Jen baby boy and baby girl bear. He used to wrap them around his neck and stomp up the stairs as a way of getting them to bed. There was pure love in their hugs just like he was witnessing from Stevie's mum and Amos.

"She's gone," James told her as he walked out to the rickety stairs where Stevie was perched.

"I can't believe that's her. How wrong I was about her true intentions all of these years. I often heard my uncle complain about her on the phone to my grandad and various other people before she died. He'd call her selfish and greedy, but I never believed him. I always thought I knew a side to her that others must have missed. Thinking back, I was the only one that missed the real her. I only saw what I wanted to see."

"She's your mum Stevie. I am positive that you didn't miss the real her. If she was going to be her true self around anyone, it would have been you. Your uncle, your grandad, and whoever else, they all had their own relationship with her. Don't let that taint yours. You haven't even spoken to her yet, so until then, please promise me you will remember even some of the good stuff. Even if you just remember the pancakes."

Stevie smiled and looked up at James from the step. "You remembered?" she asked, referring to a story she had told him of her mum making her pancakes when she wasn't drinking.

"Of course I did, so you should too."

Stevie stood up and pulled James towards her. They hadn't held each other just one on one in what seemed like an age. She snuggled her head into his chest and for a fleeting moment, James had an urge to pull her up into a kiss, but the moment passed and she pulled away leaving a wet patch on his jumper, wiping the tears from her eyes.

"Oh, how happy I am to have found you," she told him.

"I do believe I am the one who found you in the

hospital," James disputed.

"True, but I am the one who made you stay."

James couldn't deny that. Something had drawn him to her from the moment she appeared.

"You okay?" Grey asked as they sat back into the room.

"I am now," Stevie smiled back at James.

"Here we go again," Grey joked, which got a deserving slap on the arm from Stevie.

The group packed up and made a move back to the rebel safe house once they were confident everyone had gone to bed in the Whitelfyer headquarters.

"I hate to be the one to say it," James addressed everyone. "But, is that it? Is that all we can expect from a night's work as a so-called rebel? Staring at the Whiteflyers as they brush their teeth and canoodle in the corridors."

Bee grunted and moved up ahead. Evidently she didn't want to hear it anymore.

Josh bowed his head and ran his hand through his hair. "It's not much, but they saved me from that exact mission. The rebels followed the Whiteflyers from the headquarters, who used me as target practice. They saved me before I was too badly hurt."

"It's something," James encouraged him. "However, it's definitely not enough. If we wait for Deandra and the others, we could be waiting a lifetime. I am not saying we do anything right now, but I am asking you to just think about it. He looked from Grey to Emmy and then to Stevie and Grey. We can do much more than that in a night's work. We could go out there and make a real difference."

Josh lifted his head. "Like what?"

"Like go to the gutters. Free those people from that wretched place they've been confined to for starters. Head to the villages and spread the word that we are no longer going to be pushed around, that we all need to fight back and stand up for ourselves."

"We can't ask them to fight back. They'll be tortured, or maybe even worse," Emmy pointed out.

"Even a sprinkle of hope can light a fire too bright to put out," James told her. "Too bright for even a Whiteflyer to extinguish."

CHAPTER 12 -
"THEY ARE DOING
A GUTTER RUN."

The next morning Mack knocked on James, Stevie and Grey's room with a wake up call. Deandra wanted to see them in her quarters once they had got ready. James took this as an opportunity to take an extra longer time to get showered and dressed than usual, after her refusal to share any news the day before.

"What do you think she wants?" Stevie asked Grey, as she sat on the end of her bed tying her boot's laces.

"If I was to guess, she's probably going to give out to us for going to the headquarters yesterday. She likes to know who is where at all times. I am sure Bee let her in on the knowledge that we joined them yesterday by now. I am surprised she didn't go to her before we had the chance to make it out actually."

"Or maybe she's going to tell us what's been happening while we were gone?" Stevie suggested optimistically.

"Doubtful," James said, opening the door to make his way to her office. "She wasn't exactly giving with any information yesterday, that is if she has anything to give at all. The more I learn about these rebels, the less confidence I have that they really know anything at all."

"You should really give her a chance," Grey urged. "She's usually a lot more understanding than she was yesterday. She's a great leader, once you get to know her."

"Once you let her lead," James contradicted.

"Just give her a chance, please?" Grey asked. "For me. If you are not satisfied by the end of the week, I'll personally pack up our bags and we will go somewhere else."

"Is there somewhere else we could go?"

"Well, I am sure we could find somewhere. Maybe we can make our way back to Torpor. They know we are in Tartarus after all, so there's no reason to be here anymore."

James looked to Stevie, she was a big reason they were in Tartarus to begin with, along with being chased out of Arcadius and needing somewhere to hideout.

"Yes, I mean I know where she is and that she's safe, even if she is on the wrong side. I can't exactly ring the doorbell and speak with her, so if we need to go back to Torpor and regroup, I am fine with that."

"See, now we have a plan, so give her a break James and let's all remember that we are on the same side," Grey nudged, as they made their way down the hallway.

Mack opened the door from their knock. "You took your time, didn't you?" he remarked.

Deandra's office was painted a rustic orange and was decorated with bohemian style items including a moon shaped mirror on the wall and a handwoven rug in reds and yellows. A dark wooden table sat in the middle with lighter wooden chairs surrounding it. On top was an old style typewriter that reminded James of his Grandad. He had had a similar one in the same light green that had sat in his always messy office.

"Take a seat please," Deandra gestured, her hand gesturing to the three seats across from her. Mack sat down next to her and the others did as she said.

"I gather you had an interesting night last night, did you?" she asked, looking at each of them individually.

"Not that interesting," James answered nonchalantly. "We didn't do anything productive if that is what you are referring to. We just watched the Whiteflyers go about their daily business."

"Nonetheless, I didn't expect you to leave to visit a safe house on a mission so soon after arriving. We don't usually let outsiders in on our secret hideouts and on the whereabouts of our lookouts around the city." This time Deandra looked straight at Grey, as if he was to blame for revealing their secrets.

"I didn't think it would be an issue, they've seen here, haven't they? And you were fine about the safe house we stayed in before we left London. What does one more matter?"

"Even more reason to keep some of them under wraps. The one you were in when you first got here is no longer usable."

"Well, that wasn't our fault," Stevie jumped in. "We left as soon as we were told to. You must have a rat in the group."

Deandra slowly moved her eye contact away from Grey to the speaker. "I assure you we don't have any spies in this group. However, I'll admit that I cannot be certain about the other rebel teams. Anyway, that is not why I brought you here. I wanted to finish our conversation that we were having yesterday. I have thought about it, and I suppose I can tell you some of what you missed while you were away."

James scooted his seat forward instinctively. "Some of it will do for now, but remember we can always pack our bags and find our own way to put a stop to The Controller," he told her.

Mack snorted, "As if three newbies are a match for the creator of the Three Worlds. If we haven't figured it out by now, then what makes you think you will?"

Fire flashed on James' hand and Mack scowled. "We've got a bit more than secret hideouts and watch outs on our side," he reminded him.

"Enough," Deandra insisted. "I am not saying you will never be completely trusted, but for now, a partial reveal of some information is all we can offer you."

Grey smiled. "We'll take it."

"I'll start from the day you left. As I've just told you, the safe house you were staying in was raided. It was only hours after you left that it was found by the Whiteflyers. You say it didn't come from you, and I believe this to be true. Not because I trust you, but because the same thing has been happening all over the city recently. One by one our safe houses and rebel strongholds are being torched and raided. There have been at least five found by them in the last couple of months. So, as you can imagine, when you ask me to trust you, when I can't even trust the rebels themselves, I find it hard."

James nodded, he knew how hard trust was to earn. "And how do you know it's nobody from this team?"

"That's not something I am willing to divulge, but just believe me when I say, it is not. Everyone here's loyalty has been correctly evaluated. Anyway, it's not just rebel houses that are being torched. The Whiteflyers have been raiding the whole city searching for you while you've been gone. Attacks have multiplied and there aren't enough of us to do something about it all. I've been in talks with the other leaders and we all believe it's bigger than what it seems. Whiteflyers have turned rogue before and The Controller has never taken such a big personal interest in it. Do you have any idea why he might be so eager to find you three?"

James thought back to his first meeting with The Controller and then to the time they were briefed on leading the people of London away from the cities. He remembered the feeling he had gotten when The Controller looked at him and the rage that he had felt when Stevie was summoned to his Palace. He had always thought that there was something more to his hatred, but he had never come up with a credible theory as to what that could be. He shook his head and stuck out his lower lip, he wasn't about to divulge any of that to Deandra, not yet anyway, not until he got to know her better. For all he knew, she was the one sharing the safe house information with the otherside. He couldn't trust her any more than he could trust the rest of them.

Deandra continued when she didn't get an answer, "Stevie and James, you both know Vask. He's in charge of finding you. He's broken the Whiteflyers into task forces. Amos also has some control over Tartarus' search, Madera over Arcadius' and Hatt over Torpor's but your old trainer has been trusted with the bulk of the mission. You bumped into one of his teams at Stevie's uncle's replica house. We were aware they were held up there so if you had come to us first, that run-in could have been avoided. They are now certain that you are still in Tartarus and all of their concentration is being shifted to here."

"How do you know all of this?" James asked.

"We aren't as useless as you might think James. We are always working in the background to build as much information as possible before we strike. Time is of the essence lately," Deandra explained.

"And what about the gutters? What has been happening with them? Do you have a plan in place?"

Deandra sighed, "That brings me to my next point. You told me that you passed a burning gutter yesterday. You were right, there was an uprising there, but unfortunately the whole gutter suffered because of the actions of a few. The Whiteflyers have burnt the place to the ground. They have the instigators strung up by their necks, left to die over and over again until the Whiteflyers in charge decides to take them down."

James could feel himself getting angry, so he settled his nerves. "They have the right to free themselves, to try by any means possible. If we aren't going to help them, the least we can do is not judge them when they help themselves. What would you do if you were in their position?"

"More and more people are being shuttled to the gutters every day. Helping one of them escape doesn't do much for their well being in the long run. We need to go to the root of the cause. The Controller is that root. If we lose people in the meantime on smaller missions, that diminishes our chances of defeating him."

No matter how many times James was told this, it didn't sit right with him. He had seen those people for himself, he'd walked in their shoes for only moments and the horror he felt still haunted him. "And in the meantime, we just leave them to suffer?"

Deandra shook her head and held her forehead. "James, we are going around in circles here. Let's put the gutter conversation to the side or I will have no more to say to you today."

James took a deep breath and nodded. He wanted to hear what else she had to say.

"The news of the weekly meeting was of course not news to me at all. I in fact had been observing it myself. After I heard about your run in, I guessed something like this might happen."

"Any update on how London is reacting to it?" Grey asked.

"Word has spread quickly. The people are divided. Most are staying out of it, minding their own business and staying away from it all. However, there are some who are eager to help you, they know that nothing the Whitflyers say can be trusted. Then again, there are also some who believe that they can become Whiteflyers themselves just by finding you. These people are grouping up and actively looking for you. If you are outside these walls, don't trust anyone and don't draw attention to yourselves. They know that you are travelling as a trio of two boys and a girl, that will be your biggest giveaway."

Grey smiled. "Are you happy for us to leave the hideout then?"

Deandra looked to James. "Well, I don't believe there is much hope of stopping you. I won't be giving you missions yourselves. Not yet anyway, but you are welcome to keep watch on the headquarters while the others are assigned to it."

"How does that work anyway?" Stevie wondered.

"The missions?" Deandra confirmed and continued when Stevie nodded. "We have a wider leadership team that decides what needs to be done for the month and then a schedule is drawn up pinpointing who is doing what. Each team takes turns watching the headquarters, patrolling different areas of the city and going on more covert missions to find out select information."

James absorbed this knowledge. "How big are the rebels overall? How many people are we talking here?"

"That's confidential, but there are a lot more of us than you have seen here. Grey has met some of the other teams for some bigger missions, however, nobody but the leaders really have an accurate picture of our true size."

"And I presume I will get the same answer if I ask where the other teams are based?" James chanced.

"You presume correctly Mr Moore. Now, I think I've answered a lot for today. Was there anything else you urgently wanted to know?"

"Yes," James replied. "What is the bigger plan to take down The Controller?"

Deandra huffed, pulled her fingers through her hair. "Mack, please see these people out, will you?"

Mack grinned, revealing a missing tooth on the right side of his mouth that James hadn't noticed before. "My pleasure."

Stevie lay down on her bed when they got back to their room. "Well at least she told us some bits of information. They seem to have quite a few moles inside the Whiteflyers anyway. How else would they know all of that about the task force?"

"Not necessarily," Grey told her. "They could just have a few lower ranked people on board, or maybe even some of the drudges could be helping."

"Either way I am still disappointed in them all. I can't stand that same answer that I am being fed about why we can't step in when it comes to the gutters."

Grey bowed his head, he'd told James just that same thing on more than one occasion and was looking rather conflicted as to whether he believed it himself after all.

James pat him on the back. "It's not your fault Grey, if you're told something often enough times, you will start to believe it."

Josh, who seemed to have been lingering outside, shouted in to see if he could come in.

"Yes, yes," Grey told him. "We are all decent."

"So spill it. I heard you were in with Deandra, did she tell you anything new?"

"Not really, just filled us in on the safe house raids, and the shuttles to the gutter."

"Yeah I thought I heard that before I came in," Josh replied, before turning bright red. "Not that I had been listening or anything, I was just waiting to knock."

"Sure you were," Stevie grinned. "Are you out on a mission today or tonight? Anything fun that we can join?"

"Emmy and I are patrolling the south of the city, the Clapham area. Did Deandra forbid you from coming with us again?"

"No, just the opposite actually. What time should we be ready?"

"We are meeting in the common room in a couple of hours, but I will knock in before."

James pulled on his boots a while later to get ready for the patrol. He was happy they were doing something more than just keeping an eye on the boring, yet rather raunchy, headquarters. He thrived when he was in the thick of it. Maybe he would even get a chance to kick some

Whiteflyer ass if he was lucky."

Josh knocked on the door. "Emmy's not too happy you're coming Grey. Go out and speak to her, will you? It's awkward for the rest of us, the longer you avoid it. It's going to have to be dealt with sometime, so why not now?"

Grey's eyes widened. "Really, do I have to? I don't think she will take it very well. She didn't last time I tried, she said she wants her space."

Stevie turned to Grey. "When a woman says she wants her space from someone she really likes, she actually wants you to try harder, most of the time anyway. She wants an hour to breathe and then she expects you to be doing everything you can to make it up to her."

Grey shook his head. "That makes no sense."

"And neither does leaving the planet your girlfriend is on without so much as a goodbye or a see you later."

"She was not my girlfriend, we hooked up three times at most."

"It doesn't matter if it was once or one thousand times, it obviously means something to her. Go!" Stevie said the last bit with authority and pointed out the door.

"I am telling you it won't work, but I will try," Grey said as Josh pulled him out the door.

"He's such a dufus," James laughed. "The fact I ever entertained the thought that..."

"That what?" Stevie asked.

James itched his head awkwardly. "Nothing, he's just clueless."

"We can definitely agree on that," Stevie told him.

"How are you?" James asked Stevie now that they

were alone. He'd been wanting a chance to speak with her in private all day.

"I'm good, I mean as good as we all can be in the current situation."

James stared at her. "That's not what I mean. How are you really?"

Stevie nodded her head. "Not great, but I've been thinking about what you said about my mum. I need to see who she is now for myself. It doesn't have to be today or tomorrow, but I eventually want to meet her. I know I said I am willing to go to Torpor, but I would really like the chance to hear her side of things first if possible."

"Of course you do Stevie and you will meet her, sooner rather than later, I promise."

Stevie squeezed his hand and leaned in and kissed him on the cheek.

James' insides exploded and he subconsciously lifted his free hand up to his face to rub the place her lips had just touched. He stared at her and for one fleeting moment he thought she was going to lean in to kiss him on the lips, he was ready to meet her half way.

"Done," Grey exclaimed, skipping into the room. "Oh what's going on here?" he mocked, as Stevie pulled herself a metre from James.

"What's done?" James asked, fuming that his potential chance to kiss Stevie again was interrupted but simultaneously eager to change the subject so as to not complicate the matter further. His mind went to other places as Grey recounted how he made up with Emmy, but he nodded along as he feigned interest. His mind was on Stevie's lips the entire time.

"Come on then," Josh interrupted. "Let's get a move on before the sun comes up preferably."

Emmy seemed a lot more upbeat since she had spoken to Grey, so whatever he had said had evidently worked. James was happy to see another side to the shy standoffish girl that he had met up to this point. While she still didn't seem like a particularly outgoing type, she was at least actively engaging in their conversation and even talking to Stevie as if she hadn't been cold to her before. Stevie, being Stevie, played along as if she was unaware that she had ever been the target of Emmy's jealousy and their walk to Clapham was rather pleasant. James was of course on cloud nine and couldn't think of anything but how he could get Stevie alone again as soon as possible.

"Can't we just fly there?" Josh moaned at Grey. You can carry Emmy and I am sure James could lift my weight."

"Absolutely not," Emmy argued. "I may have forgiven Grey, but we are definitely not going to be hugging in the air all the way across London."

"You'd be too heavy anyway. I would have to take Josh," Grey joked.

Emmy let out a high pitched but quiet giggle that let James know she was aware of Grey's humour and didn't take his words to heart. "Well, we have stolen Deandra's stash twice now. However, I don't believe you mean that. You once told me you could fit me in your pocket."

Grey smiled.

"Get a room," Josh called out, echoing everyone's thoughts.

"Seems all is well in paradise," James whispered to Stevie.

"Yeh, maybe he isn't as clueless as we thought after

all."

"No, I am convinced that he is still a complete and utter moron but for some reason, Emmy doesn't seem to notice or care."

Stevie nodded looking over at the two of them. "You are right and it has to be the latter. It's not exactly a secret after all."

Clapham was quiet when they arrived. Much like the rest of Tartarus, the buildings were derelict and the recreational areas were filled with rubbish. James remembered playing in Clapham Common Park as a kid. One of his mum's favourite Sunday lunch spots, The Horse's Leg, was just across the road. She worked there when she first moved to London, so it was nostalgic as well as delicious. He always insisted on ordering a full beef roast off the adult's menu and never finished it whenever they visited. When the pub closed down a few years back they tried a few places closer to where they lived, however, they had never lived up to her expectations so the weekly tradition had eventually died off.

James stared into the dark park and a shiver went up his spine. It was the antithesis of the fun and bright place he had experienced all those years ago. The green grass was a slush of thick mud and chunks of concrete, the trees he had climbed were nowhere to be found and he could feel, but not see, wide eyes staring at him from the darkest corners.

He then looked over to the pub that had turned into a fancy steak house they had never been able to afford to visit. It was surprisingly not too run down in comparison with some of the other buildings. The glass sat unscratched in the wide windows, the paint wasn't completely peeled off the beige walls, and there was even a light on in one of the rooms upstairs.

"If it looks too good to be true, it always is around here," came a whisper from behind him. "That's a known Whiteflyer station."

James turned to look at Grey who had been watching him take in the building. "Are they in there right now?"

Grey shrugged. "If we knew that, where would the mystery be? We are here to scope out the house and follow anyone inside if they leave."

"Follow them where?" James enquired.

"To wherever, or should I say to whoever, they plan to piss off tonight."

"Yes, so let's lay a bit lower please, so they don't find us before we find them," Josh interrupted, pushing them both to the left of the park by their necks.

Josh directed them a minute down the road to what seemed like a pile of rubble, but like most places, the rebels brought him to, was deceivingly spacious on the inside. There was space for all of them to sit on chair shaped piles of cement, albeit relatively squished together due to the three new additions.

"Impressive, but not as nice as the other places you've brought us to, is it?" Stevie remarked to Grey.

"It's the best we could do. Anything else would be too suspicious, hence the lack of real chairs. We are in a park after all. There's a definite chance people would stumble in here. We once even found someone sleeping on the bench."

Hours passed and James' bum cheeks were really starting to ache. There was no movement inside the house and no sign, other than the light, that anyone was even home. The others were getting noticeably uncomfortable too and it wasn't long after Emmy moaned that her leg had gone dead that Josh called it a night. James was happy to get going, but was once again disappointed at what the rebels referred to as a mission. Staring at buildings and chatting about trivial stuff wasn't exactly helping the greater good. He was going to voice his irritation as they exited the rubble, but something in the window of the house they'd been watching caught his eye. Rosie, Grey's nemesis, was making her way towards the glass to peer outside.

"Can she see us?" he asked Grey, who had noticed her too.

"No," Emmy answered for him when he didn't respond. "It's too dark. She's got a light on."

Moments later, Rosie's two friends, Danica and Corinne, joined her at the window. It was as if they were waiting for something.

"Get back inside," Josh whispered from behind them.

"Emmy said they can't see us," James told him.

"They can't, but they can." Josh was pointing down the road, where two Whiteflyers were gliding towards them.

They scuttered inside quickly and peered through the opening in the pile of wood in front of them.

The two Whiteflyers were holding hands and were slightly familiar to James. He remembered seeing them in the headquarters. The man looked as though he had died in his early thirties. He had jet black hair and white skin that blended into his Whiteflyer robes. When they came to a halt outside the door, he turned to press the woman beside him up against the wall before running his hands through her short blonde hair and pulling her in for a kiss. She seemed to have the Earth age of a woman in her mid twenties. She had sallow skin and deep blue eyes. She wore her Whiteflyer robes loose around her bust, highlighting her curves.

"That's Minnie and Al," Grey confirmed. "They've been on Tartarus as Whiteflyers together for over two hundred years, yet they still act like teenagers who have just hit puberty."

He made a motion as if he was going to get sick forcing Emmy to roll her eyes and scoff. "I think it's cute that some people can be in love and so passionate for so long. You wouldn't know romance if it hit you on the head."

They walked into the building and while James couldn't hear what was being said he could see that there was a commotion happening inside. Rosie's face was red and crinkled and she pointed aggressively at each of them in turn. She then motioned towards a make believe watch on her wrist which led him to believe that Al and Minnie were late for something.

"Get ready," Josh told them. "They're about to leave. Stay well back from them and under no circumstance should you blow your cover by using your powers. That means, if they take to the air, do not follow them. They can't know who you are." He said this directly to James and more sternly than he usually spoke. James just smiled and didn't reply but knew himself that he didn't take orders from any of the rebels, least of all Josh. If needed, he would use his powers to keep up with them or to prevent them from doing anything he deemed to be wrong.

Just as Josh said, Rosie, Corinne, Danica, Al and

Minnie emerged from the building. Rosie led the way with Corinne and Danica just behind her and Al and Minnie a little behind whispering in each other's ears and laughing. Rosie's serious face only highlighted her protuberant cheekbones and gave her an edge.

The rebels followed shortly behind, avoiding talking and treading lightly so that they could hear as much from up ahead as possible. They always stayed close to the shadowed sides and at least five buildings away, going down side streets where possible and only leaving at the last minute to avoid losing their prey. Rosie mentioned something about a house in Balham at one point which James knew to be close enough, so if that was their final destination the walk wouldn't be too long and they'd hopefully avoid flying.

After what seemed like just under half an hour of walking the five Whiteflyers came to an abrupt stop down a small cul de sac. James peered around the corner just as they opened the door to one of the houses. There was a big truck parked outside, the kind that would be used to deliver furniture.

"What now?" Stevie asked Josh. "What's going on here?"

"Those trucks are only used for one thing," he told her. "They're doing a gutter run."

A ball of anger rose inside James. "You mean to say they will be going around London collecting people in that van and bringing them to a gutter?"

"Most likely not," Josh explained further. "My guess is that the people are already held up in the house they just went into."

A small blanket of hope dimmed the disgust in James' stomach. They could still be rescued and even though it was five Whiteflyers against three and two powerless rebels, none of them was a level four like he was.

James went into control mode. "I am going to take the front, Stevie and Grey you go around the back. I am sorry Josh and Emmy, but you're going to have to find somewhere to hide until this is all over. I know you want to help, but it's better this way, trust me."

Stevie and Grey sprang into action and began to take off around the back until Emmy pulled Grey back. "No!" she said firmly. "Those aren't our orders. You heard Deandra, we don't do anything, we need to look at the bigger picture."

"These aren't the gutters," Grey protested. "These people are still in London and they need our help."

"No," James jumped in, surprising Grey and Stevie. "Emmy's right. We do need to look at the bigger picture."

Stevie's face turned to outrage. "How can you say that? What about everything you've been saying until now? Everything you have said since we've been with the rebels?"

"You didn't let me finish. We need to look at the bigger picture, not tomorrow. We need to look at the bigger picture tonight."

Stevie didn't understand so James continued, "If there are people inside going to a gutter, the Whiteflyers will be taking them there. I say we follow them there and free them all once they've left, everyone in the gutter. They will have just visited, so we are guaranteed that none of them will be inside. It's foolproof."

"It's foolish," Emmy corrected. "That is not the bigger picture. You are just looking for something to fan your ego and keep you occupied for the night."

"Well, then it's good that you're not coming. Josh, you can stay behind too if you are too scared to do anything meaningful with your night. I am sure Deandra has more buildings she wants you to stare at."

Josh hesitated, before stepping toward James. "I am in."

CHAPTER 13 - "NO FEAR!"

James was not that surprised that Josh had agreed to go to the gutters with him, Stevie and Grey to free the occupants. He hadn't given off an overly approving vibe whenever the 'bigger picture' was brought up. He was, however, surprised at how adamant Emmy was that they weren't to go. She had come across as so shy at first and had done a complete 180 since she and Grey started talking again. She demanded they come back to the rebel safe house with her and when they refused to, she strode off alone threatening to tell Deandra.

"She won't really," Grey told them, his voice unconvinced. "She's harmless really, she's just very easily persuaded by authority. Her dad was in the military."

James thought about Marcus from training, who had also been in the army, and became more convinced that Emmy would follow through with her threat to tell Deandra. "Let's hope they get a move on then, if they are even going to the gutters tonight. I don't want to give Deandra, Mac, or Bee the chance to catch up with us. Not that it will put a halt in my plans, but it will certainly complicate them and it may end up revealing us before the Whiteflyers leave. I want this plan to be as covert as possible."

"I think we can all agree to that. What exactly is

the plan then?" Josh asked.

"Once the truck departs, we are going to take to the air. I will carry you, well not so much carry as move. We need to stay high and out of sight. When we get there we wait until they leave and we free the people inside. I can raise the ground surrounding the gutter and you guys can direct them out. Hopefully, if all goes to plan, it will be days before the Whiteflyers realise what's happened and the people inside will be long gone."

"That all sounds too easy," Grey voiced. "With us it rarely is, so I have my doubts."

"Who knows, maybe we will catch a break this time?"

"Ha!" Stevie laughed. "Wouldn't that be just splendid?"

"Splendid," Josh mimicked in an accent befit to the queen.

"Don't.." Stevie began before she was cut short by the door opening on the house Rosie and her crew went into.

Al led the way out of it, followed by at least four dozen people, each of them more sullen and scared than the next. The majority of them, like the majority of people on the Three Worlds, were older but there was also a mix of young adults and even children amongst them. They walked in a straight line in a silent march.

The Whiteflyer used air to open the back of the truck and one by one they took a step up into the metal box. One man, with shoulder length hair and a rugged beard, caught James' attention; he didn't have the look of a man who had given up. His eyes moved madly from side to side and when Al turned, to push an old lady who wasn't moving with any speed into the back of the truck, the man took off. His arms flailed at his side as he sped to the left, his eyes on a back gate of the house two doors down. James almost thought he was going to make it unseen, but at the last moment, Rosie made an appearance through the front door.

She scrunched up her nose in anger, and raised her arm. The man flew back with a force James had rarely seen. He lay helpless beneath her feet, the wind taken out of him and his eyes wide in fear.

"I am sorry," he panted, when he managed to catch his breath. "I just…"

However, before James could hear what he was going to say the man's hair blew up in flames, sending his body into convulsions. A woman beside them screamed and her hair too caught fire. The shrieks that followed were deafening but short lived as the man and woman passed out on the floor. The other prisoners held their hands to their mouths, petrified to breath, never mind to scream or run.

"Anybody else want to try something?" she screamed at the crowd. Nobody answered, so she screamed louder. This time heads moved from side to side and there was an odd squeak of 'no'.

James turned to his friends in horror.

"I told you," Grey whispered as quietly as he could. "If The Controller is the devil, she's one of his most loyal demons."

James looked back at the crowd who had now sped up and moved into the truck without hesitation. When they had all piled in Al threw the two unconscious bodies in after them and pulled the door shut. Not a peep came from inside, it was as if nobody was in there at all.

After Rosie, Danica and Corinne piled inside the

front of the rusted Ford Truck and drove off. Al and Minnie turned and made their way on foot directly toward the rebels. They were hidden in a shadow and were not visible from a distance but if the Whiteflyers got any closer their cover would be blown.

James put out his arms to pull Stevie and Josh on his right side and Grey on his left towards the wall. As soon as they touched it, a dead brown vine at their feet began to rise up around them. James moved quickly sprouting leaves and branches. He made sure the plant was dead and a similar colour to the wall to avoid notice.

"Don't move a muscle," he whispered to the group. "It's only covering you where you stand."

The three of them did as they were told and they held their breath as Al and Minnie passed. Minnie rolled her eyes. "Always the dramatics with Rosie," she told Al. Just when it seemed they were free, Josh inhaled a long breath, misplacing the perfectly placed vine at his chest. The bright yellow lightning bolt on his chest came into view. Al moved his head to the right, as though something caught his eye. James got ready to fight. It was three against two, so he was sure they would win, but in the meantime the truck would drive far enough away to get lost on its way out of London. Luckily, just as his eye contact was about to reach Josh, Minnie grabbed Al by the hair and licked the side of his face. Distracted, he picked her up into the air and they flew off after the truck.

"That was close," Grey gasped. "Leave it to you to wear that t-shirt on a mission."

"What's wrong with this t-shirt? We are supposed to blend in as ordinary residents," Josh protested.

"It's a bullseye, that's what's wrong with it," James argued half heartedly, just relieved that they weren't spotted. "However, that's a conversation for another day, let's go." Without prior warning, James scooped Josh into the air, he was used to lifting a weight in the sky for distances after their stay at the cottage. At one point, he'd brought a table through six towns to furnish the house by the sea.

Josh's eyes nearly popped out of his head as he rose in the air. Stevie and Grey jumped into the sky to meet him laughing. James followed, his eyes searching the sky for Al and Minnie and then on the road for the truck. He wasn't surprised to see they weren't going in exactly the same direction. Al and Minnie could cut across London and avoid the roads Rosie would have to drive on. He decided to follow the truck. Even though it would likely take a lot longer, it would avoid an altercation in the sky with Bonnie and Clyde.

When he had set their path in place, James relaxed a little as they followed their target.

"This is so cool," Josh gushed, trying to keep his balance while simultaneously breaking it by flailing his legs in the air. "I can't believe you ever bother to walk."

"Well, I can't say that becoming a Whiteflyer didn't come with its perks," Grey replied.

Josh smiled. "I don't think Deandra is going to be so happy with that after she finds out what we are doing tonight. I am sure Emmy is nearly home by now."

Grey grimaced. " Do you think she will tell her where we are going?"

Josh stuck his lip under his chin and nodded. "Unfortunately I do, at the very least she will tell Bee and we all know what will happen then."

"Who cares if she tells on us?" Stevie chimed in. "We need to start making moves ourselves if they're not going to make them with us."

Grey took a breath. "Yeah, but it's bigger than that. I agree with what you're saying and I think we are doing the right thing, but I've been with the rebels and Deandra since I got to Tartarus. They saved me, it's easier said than done to go against them."

Stevie flew closer to him and squeezed his hand. "They will thank you in the long run. Maybe they will even see how successful this is and work on freeing the rest. This might be the start of something big."

"One can hope," James told her. "I, however, will not be holding my breath. From what little I know about the rebels, they seem to like being in control. They won't be happy that we are taking it from them even if it turns out to be for the best just as we know it will."

Stevie shot him an evil frown and James put his hands up in defence. "Just saying."

"It gets cold up here, doesn't it?" Josh asked, rubbing his shoulders. "How much longer?"

James was also getting a bit restless, it was one thing moving a bed a few towns away but another entirely travelling with a wriggling Josh in tow. He wouldn't say no to going back to solid ground anytime soon.

Grey replied, "Well I can't be sure where they are heading but we've been flying for quite some time, so hopefully it won't be much longer. I can't imagine they would use the Northern gutters, they are usually reserved for people coming from Manchester, Birmingham and the like."

"How many did you say there were?" Stevie asked.

"Well all over the Three Worlds I don't know, but in the UK there are at least a thousand sprinkled around

England, Wales, Scotland and Northern Ireland. A lot of them are in Scotland because there is more room for them due to the population density. The Controller has built a special train for the residents going up there, so it won't be this lot anyway."

"Unless they are bringing us to the train?" James corrected.

Grey went a little white. "Oh yes, I didn't think about that."

As it turned out the Whiteflyers and the truck full of Tartarus residents weren't going to Scotland, so it wasn't long before the vehicle began to slow down. They could see their destination up ahead. It was a gutter James had never seen before. Unlike the ones he had been to, there were no buildings and instead, a mass of people were being locked behind a high wall. There was nowhere for the people to shelter or hide and no way for them to escape with the added security of the drop in the ground metres from the wall. They didn't have so much as a corner of a room to call their own here. The walled off area was only around three acres in size, but the Whiteflyers had crammed at least ten thousand people into it. It looked like sardines in a can from the sky.

"They plan to put more people in there?" Stevie asked dumbfounded.

"They don't care where they are, as long as they are away from anywhere they call home," Grey said. "It's sickening how selfish every last one of them is."

Stevie's cheeks grew hot and Grey, realising what happened, tried to catch himself. "I mean, not all of them I am sure, but The Controller anyway."

"It's fine Grey. You are right, they are all as bad as each other."

As the truck came up to the entrance of the gutter, Al and Minnie, who had been sitting on one of the walls beside the entrance kissing, began to make a move. Danica, who was inside the truck, got out and flew to a forested area on the right side of the gutter. When she came back she was manoeuvring a large floating block of wood. She slotted it over the gap in the ground so the truck could proceed to its destination.

"Interesting," Stevie noted aloud. "Looks like you might not need your powers to get them out at all. We could just put the bridge back when they're gone."

James shook his head. "No way, there are way too many of them. I need to raise the ground at least in parts if we want to ensure it is safe."

Grey moved his hand to his forehead in a salute. "Whatever you say, captain."

When the truck arrived inside the gutter, James prepared for some of the people already in the enclosed prison to try and make a run for it through the open gate, people who wouldn't have known about the mote. However, instead of going towards the entrance when the doors opened, the grim faced prisoners all slowly moved away from it. They were evidently well versed in what would happen if they tried to escape, something the man in the back of the truck probably wished he had learnt earlier and in a much easier fashion.

When the truck door came down they all stepped out one by one, looking around at the open and over populated area surrounding them. Some of their faces showed their shock and others just sadness. They moved away from the five men and women in white and huddled together on the ground, staring out at their new life. The unconscious man and woman were now awake, last to step out into the open air.

Just as easily as they went in, the Whiteflyers departed. With no buildings to reside in, they saw no reason to stick around for any longer than necessary. James foresaw Al and Minnie flying in their direction so made the decision to wait out their exit away from the gutter.

They huddled in the forest, near to where Danica had by now returned the bridge, to discuss their next move.

"We should wait a while," Grey told them. "We need to make sure the Whiteflyers aren't coming back."

"They're still quiet now," James debated, referencing the eerie silence still hanging in the air. "Wouldn't it be better to go into them now to tell them what's happening?"

"I don't know, it just all seems too easy. I thought there would be something more when they arrived. They didn't so much as address the crowd."

"Why would they? Their mission was to drop the new additions off, they had no reason to stay and nobody acted up so there were no lessons to teach."

Grey nodded. "Okay then, what is the plan?"

"I am going to raise up the ground in the area closest to the exit. Once I do that, I need you to go in and make the announcement for them to leave. Stevie, it's your job to open that gate."

"And what about me?" Josh asked, eager to be involved.

"Hmm.. you keep watch."

Josh scoffed, "I can hardly do that amongst these trees."

"Well then you better make your way out of them."

James was the first to take to the sky, landing out in the open, near the mote. He harnessed his power through the earth beneath his feet, searching for the end of the drop. He found it near a mile down and began to work his magic.

Grey stationed himself on the wall near the gate and Stevie at the entrance.

"Don't be scared," Grey told the crowd, his voice amplified across the land using air. "I am not one of them. Yes, I have powers, but I am not here to harm you."

Nobody in the crowd dared speak, afraid they were being tested.

My friends are just on the other side of the wall, we are here to get you out, to set you free. When the gates open you are free to leave. For a while nobody said anything until an old man near the front stepped forward, he had come in on the truck. "Are you one of the people from the announcement? The ones the Whiteflyers warned us to be wary of."

Grey smiled and nodded. "I am, and so are my friends, but we aren't as they say. We are on your side. We are on the side of equality and justice."

James was nearly finished raising the ground, there were only a few metres to go, when he stopped in his tracks. He could feel something weighted on it. There were nearly two dozen fallen bodies on top of it. James stopped himself from hunching over as acid rose in his throat. He had a job to do and vomiting wasn't going to get it done. He braced himself and slowly moved the earth the last few feet.

Men, women and children littered the ground. They weren't decaying as he had thought and if it wasn't for their open horrified eyes some may have looked as though they were just sleeping. Others, however, were bent and disfigured, their arms and legs in unnatural positions.

"What's happening here?" came Josh's voice from behind him. "How long have they been down there?"

James turned to look him in the eyes. "What is happening is The Controller. Actually, I take that back. It's more than one person. It's anyone who doesn't do everything they can to stop it. Worse are those who see evil and standby."

When James turned back, instant panic hit him in the gut, hundreds of people were running towards him. He looked up to see Grey and Stevie sitting on the wall smiling and waving.

James quickly projected his voice at the oncoming people, "No stop running. There are people here. However, this did nothing to slow the stream and in less than a minute the first of the crowd arrived. James tried to remove the bodies as fast as possible without damaging them, but there just wasn't enough time.

A fitter young boy came to a halt first, realising what was lying on the ground in front of him. "Gahhh," he roared, his finger outstretched pointing at one of the more mangled bodies. "They're going to kill us. It's a trick. Run!"

Some others had caught up by now and hastily concluded that what the boy had screamed was true. They ran as far from the bodies as possible in a manic state. A wave of sudden uncontrollable perturbation ran over the entire crowd and without warning, they began to spread out. James' fear about using the bridge to set them free was happening. People sprinted away from the bodies and away from the gutter, towards what they thought was their only chance of freedom, the mile long drop surrounding the walls. The first person to vanish into the lightly covered hole was a young woman of Stevie's age. She tore through the top layer of grassy pretence that the Controller and his followers had used to trick the prisoners into thinking they had a chance for freedom. Dozens tumbled after her, others veered off to the side but landed with the same fate. On the other side of the bodies, the same thing was happening with another group of people. Person after person, falling to their doom.

"What is going on?" Stevie yelled over the crazed mass.

"Put the bodies somewhere safe," James ordered back. "I need to lift the entire ground and fast. Grey, try to control the crowd, use Air, do whatever you have to to get them to stop moving."

Everyone snapped into immediate action, doing as they were ordered. Grey built up a resistance on the densest areas of the crowd, using a trick not unlike Catherine had used on Stevie before to keep her in place. The people began to slow, but some of the more scattered runners were still falling. Josh did his best to run to them to beg them to stop as Grey extended his reach. The crowd behind responded to the people in front of them's hesitation, unaware that it was not out of choice.

Stevie worked as discreetly as possible moving the unconscious people to the side, to give them space and time to heal, without bringing even more attention to their bodies. Their recuperation was happening even as they moved through the air to be laid down at the side of the forest.

All the while this was happening, James was

channelling his powers to seal the hole. The fastest way to do it would be sideways, but it would also bury the fallen. He needed to do it from the bottom up. As he did it, Stevie followed, moving the new bodies with her, some who had just fallen and others who had been down there for unknown lengths of time.

James let out a sigh of relief, as the last of the bodies were uncovered and set aside.

"Now to deal with the crowd," he told himself in a whisper, before jumping into the air to address the bewildered and frightened beneath him.

"Today we have just witnessed the only power that The Controller has at his disposal to keep us in check. To force us to abide by his rules. To let him keep the control he so much desires. Fear. Fear is a power so strong it forces us to forget our morals and throw away our respect. Fear of the unknown and fear of the unthinkable. Without it, The Controller has nothing. Yes he can trap us and he can even torture us, but he certainly cannot kill us. When he knocks us down, know you will always get back up. Look how the people at the edge of the forest slowly come to life. This is the first breath they have taken for minutes, days, weeks, and even years. The time will come when we need to stick together, remember what he's done to you and remember how you have been freed from it, how you can always be free from it. Time is a wonderful thing on Torpor, Arcadius, and Tartarus. The more of us that he attacks, the more that will have the courage and the strength to attack back."

Grey loosened his hold on the prisoners and was the first to throw his fist into the air. "He has nothing without our fear," he roared.

An old woman followed suit, her voice cracking as

she screamed, "No fear."

The throng joined in, the anxiety no longer painted on their faces, as they looked up at James in complete awe and admiration. "No fear! No fear! No fear! No fear!"

When the crowd had finally dispersed, James fell to the floor, looking up at the morning clouds. Grey, Stevie and Josh lay next to him. Stevie reached her arms and legs out in a star shape and the others followed. Nobody said anything for what seemed like forever. They all needed a moment to process what had happened in their own way.

"Well, I still can't decide if that was a success or not," Grey told them as they sat on their honkers.

Stevie raised her eyebrows. "I can. It definitely was not. However, James did kind of half save the day with his bid for president at the end."

James shoved her gently. "That's not what that was. I needed them to leave full of hope or all of this didn't mean much. If they left more scared than when we found them, we may as well have left them where they were. I do think Deandra would have said a big fat 'I told you so' if she was here though."

Josh nodded eagerly. "Oh yes. She definitely would not have been happy with that. She likes order and that was not exactly executed the way we planned. At least you know for next time?"

"Don't you mean at least we know?" James asked him. "You did your part too. We all helped to diffuse what could have continued down an even messier path."

Josh shrugged. "Let's face it. For every one person I stopped from falling down the hole, Grey stopped one thousand. I am not much use to you without powers, and as much as I loved tonight, I belong with the rebels."

James nodded understandingly. He had come to like Josh and he wouldn't have minded him sticking around, but he understood where he was coming from. He would do his part, in his own way, he was sure of that.

"Hate to ruin this moment guys," Stevie told them as she came to her feet. "But we should probably get going. Who knows how often Whiteflyers come by and if the crowd of people coming from this way are spotted, it will be sooner rather than later."

James got up to join her. "As always, you are right. Let's head back to London."

"Back to the rebel safe house?" Grey asked.

"I don't think so, let's head to the safe house where we saw St…" James hesitated, looking at Stevie. "The safe house we were in on the morning of the announcement. We will have to say goodbye once we get to London Josh. We won't be able to travel by Air through the city during the day anyway, but I will carry you to the outskirts."

"You make it sound like you will be carrying me on your back. Like I am a child refusing to walk," Josh laughed.

"Oh sorry, I didn't realise you were willing to walk? We are off so, see you soon I guess."

"Ha, ha, ha, very funny. Leave without me and you're dead to me."

James laughed loudly, lifting Josh into the air with him, Stevie and Grey following. "Up, up we go."

The journey home was a lot more relaxed than the journey there. James felt like a huge weight had been lifted off of his back that he'd been carrying for months. He had finally done something worthwhile. Something that stood up to authority, no matter how small it might have been in the grand scheme of things. It was the start of something big, he could feel it coursing through his body.

They dropped Josh off just outside the city and made their way on foot to their destinations. Josh would be able to get back to the safehouse easily enough from there and deal with the baptism of fire that awaited. It was daylight, so James, Stevie and Grey had to avoid bringing any attention to themselves after Amos' announcement. They separated slightly pretending they weren't together. To begin with, Stevie and James walked side by side with Grey up ahead.

"I have been wanting to talk to you," Stevie began after some idle small talk. "Since that moment in the rebel's house."

"What moment?" James smirked.

"You know what moment Moore. Don't make me say it."

James put his hands up, a huge grin plastered on his face. "I honestly have no idea what moment you're referring to."

Through gritted teeth, Stevie played along with him, "The moment we nearly kissed."

"Ohhh that moment."

"Yes, that moment. Well, I just wanted to say that it wouldn't have been totally dreadful if we weren't interrupted."

Warm chills were making their way up James' chest. "Not totally dreadful? Is that the best I am going to get?"

"The very best, so don't push it."

"Well, in that case, I agree that it would not have been totally dreadful too."

Stevie turned her head to smile and James took

advantage of the moment and moved his hand in to clasp hers. She didn't pull away and they walked in blissful silence until Grey grew bored and demanded someone swap with him.

"Oooo holding hands were we?" Grey asked James when Stevie was out of earshot behind them.

"Could have been," James smiled. "But who knows with Stevie, one minute I think she's into me and the next I've no idea."

"Well if you are referring to when we rescued her in Torpor, you should really talk to her about that. It's not as it seems."

"How would you know?" James asked.

"Because Stevie and I are friends, and friends talk about things that are important to them."

James thought back to the beach house and wondered if that was what Grey was trying to get Stevie to tell him when he overheard their partial conversation.

"Can't you just tell me now?"

"I could, yes, but that doesn't mean I am going to. Friends also don't spill each other's secrets when they are asked not to."

The sun had lowered in the sky when they had arrived at the building that looked over the Whiteflyer headquarters. Their efforts of being inconspicuous had seemed to work and nobody took much notice of them on their journey there. A middle aged, rather dirty man, ran right up to James' face at one point and he nearly knocked him out. However, when he screamed and stuck his tongue out James realised that he was one sandwich short of a picnic. He couldn't blame him of course, if James sat idle for too long in this world his thoughts would also go to strange places.

The former rebel lookout building was the same always and seemed untouched since their last visit, so they settled in the room on the second floor for a well needed nap. James curled up near the stairs to ensure they got no unwanted visitors as they slept and in no time his eyes fell heavy.

As James slept, he dreamt of his time training. He relived the moment that Matthew and Tim pushed his head under the water, this time, however, Vask sat on the sidelines pointing and laughing. Catherine was there too, correcting Matthew on how he was holding James' head in the bath.

"Hold him by the neck," came her shrill voice.

James woke up in a sweat, jumping up from the hard floor and anxiously looking around the now dark room. Grey and Stevie were still sound asleep. He did his best not to wake them as he climbed the stairs to take in the view from the roof.

It was a cloudless night and the moon shone brightly, illuminating the street below. If James was to estimate, there were still a few hours left until the sun came up. Trafalgar Square was completely silent, not in an eerie sort of way, but a completely peaceful one.

James took in a long breath and thought carefully about the night before. If he was to learn anything from Vask in training, it was to always reflect on what you could have done better. He was naive to forget that bodies would appear and should have practised signals with Stevie and Grey to alert them to his readiness. The next time, he wanted to free the people from the first gutter he visited. He had looked those people in the eyes, some he still dreamt about. It was only right that they were prioritised.

Anne was also a focal point of James' nightmares and he felt that it was time they took a trip back to Torpor to check in on her. Stevie wasn't going to leave Tartarus until she spoke to her mum, so that was also something they had to find a way to make happen as soon as possible.

James was pulled out of his thoughts with the sound of a bang below. He jumped into action and stormed down the stairs. Standing not too far away with their backs to him were Grey and Stevie. They were staring at three people across the room, near to where James had been sleeping. It was Deandra, Bee and Josh.

"Sorry," Josh murmured, his face bright red. "I refused to tell them where you were, but they threatened to banish me from the rebels if I didn't."

"I still think we should," Bee snarled.

"Enough," Deandra ordered, her hand up to show she meant business.

"Great to see you all again," Stevie chirped, sarcasm seeping through her words. "I have no idea what could bring you all around here so early. I hope you didn't disrupt your sleep for this visit."

James made a feeble attempt not to laugh, which only angered the newcomers more.

"Emmy told us about your plan," Deandra began. "We were out searching for you all day yesterday, until we got back and found Josh at our hideout with you three nowhere to be found."

"Well, apparently we didn't hide that well," Stevie said. "We do really have to be going don't we James?"

"Yeah now that you say it, we have that appointment. We have missed it once, so it would be rude to be late again."

"Don't leave yet," Deandra told them. "I didn't

come to have a row, I came to show you something. To bring you somewhere."

When nobody replied she whispered a final, "Please."

Grey turned around and nodded at James. Stevie stayed staring at their visitors. Part of James wanted to make a hole in the wall and fly away but the more prominent part was too curious to make an escape.

"Will Bee be there?"

Deandra shook her head. "No, it will just be me and you."

"I won't go anywhere without Stevie and Grey."

"But.."

"It's not up for debate."

Deandra took a deep breath and signalled for them to all follow her before turning to leave.

"I will take that as a yes," Stevie muttered.

CHAPTER 14 - "NICE TO FORMALLY MEET YOU, I AM BRIDGET."

Deandra rushed through the streets of London before the sun came up, such a big group would cause too much suspicion. She dropped Josh and Bee at a junction and told them to continue back to the safe house. There was some reluctance from Josh, so Bee grabbed him by the back of the neck and forced him to go with her. They continued their brisk walk for about a half an hour after that in silence. Finally, as the sun came up, Deandra made a second stop outside what looked like an abandoned garage. It was down a small thin lane with a dead end.

The car garage looked to be attached to a house that's main entrance was nowhere to be seen. Deandra looked from side to side before getting down on her knees. She moved a loose brick from the ground to reveal a rope that was attached to the garage door. James was about to offer to pull it up for her as it looked rather heavy, but she yanked it up with no problem, and revealed an empty cramped dark room with a single hall door on the far side.

Without words, she ushered the three friends into the room and slammed the shutter to a close. "What is this?" James asked. "Where have you taken us?"

"You said you wanted to know more about the rebels, so here we are." Deandra took a key from her pocket and opened the burgundy door as she said this. It led to a grand hall with a pristine marble floor, and high walls. The kind that was too covered in paintings of important people to show much of the mustard coloured wallpaper.

Deandra held her arms out. "Welcome to our own headquarters."

James' mouth hung open, he didn't expect anything as fancy as this when it came to the rebels. This was more like something he would find from the Whiteflyers. The echoey hall reminded James of the house from Mary Poppins.

"Come in," Deandra urged. "They are waiting for us."

James, Stevie and Grey followed Deandra into the house and through the hall. She brought them up a mahogany staircase with a royal blue stair runner. The walls continued on the same pattern up the stairs and were filled with faces of people young and old, nobody who James recognised. He peeked his head into the various rooms they passed on the second floor, all following a similar pattern, screaming importance.

Deandra came to a stop outside the last door before another set of stairs and pushed the gold door knob. The heavy door obeyed.

A dozen faces looked to the door as James and his friends walked through. They all sat around a large oval table on dark wooden chairs with wine coloured upholstered seats.

A woman who appeared in her late 30s, with shoulder length black hair looked from James to Stevie to Grey before addressing Deandra, "Well isn't this a surprise. I thought we agreed that Moore was the only person we were going to invite this morning."

James, not wanting anyone to speak for him, took a step forward. "We decided to extend the invitation at the last moment. Is that a problem?"

The woman narrowed her eyes before smiling. "Of course not, let me summon two more chairs to the table, so everyone can be comfortably accommodated."

To James' surprise, two of the chairs that had been placed up against the right side of the wall moved across the room to gather around the table beside another empty seat on their own accord. He looked back to the woman and she gave an overemphasised wink. She had powers, at least Air anyway.

"You can.." James began.

"You're not the only one here with powers James. Nice to formally meet you, I am Bridget and I am the lead rebel in Tartarus. Please take a seat. You too Stevie and Grey."

Deandra walked around the room and took her place five seats down to Bridget's right and James, Stevie and Grey took a seat opposite her at the end of the table."

Bridget held her hands out to the people around the table, seven women including Deandra and herself, and six men. They were a very eclectic mix of characters. Some of them like Bridget wore a formal style of clothes consisting of a suit and shirt, while others wore t-shirts and jeans, and one younger man even a hoodie. "For the most part, we make up the Tartarus rebel leaders. We have heard a lot about all three of you in the last year, so I know I don't only speak for myself when I say, it is great to finally meet you in person."

"Well, forgive me if I don't share your enthusiasm Bridget. This is the first I have heard of you. Deandra has been quite secretive when it comes to the rebels, much to my frustration," James said.

Bridget smiled. "Yes and for good reason. We are no use to anyone in the hands of the Whiteflyers."

"Why now?" James asked. "Why have you decided to forgo all of the mystery?"

"Well, partly because you decided to take things into your own hands and partly because of someone else."

"The Controller?" James asked.

"No," Bridget answered. "We will get to who in just a moment, but first, please tell me about your escapades in the gutters."

James looked at Grey and Stevie and when there was no objection, he dove into everything from the day before. He wasn't sure why he was so open with this lady, but for some reason he trusted her.

Bridget nodded in parts and grimaced in others, but she never interrupted. The man in the hoodie went to interject when James retold the part of the story about the bodies appearing but stopped when Bridget lifted her index finger to silence him.

"Well, that was a lot more gruesome than we originally thought it may have been, but also it seems quite successful," Bridget said when James had finished.

"I suppose the end was yes, everyone got away."

"No, that is not what I am referring to. While that isn't a bad thing, it isn't very impactful in the grand scheme of things. No, the part I am referring to is your speech. It really seemed to speak to the crowd."

Stevie spoke for the first time, "I will vouch for that. It reminded me of James' performance to become a Whiteflyer."

Bridget nodded. "Yes, that was exactly how I imagined it."

"But you are from Tartarus? How would you have seen my Whiteflyer competition?" James queried.

"And you are from Torpor, but here you are."

James couldn't argue with that, Bridget was becoming more intriguing as the conversation went on and he was starting to think that the rebels might not be as useless as he had originally thought.

"That brings us to your original question, why did we bring you here?" Bridget clarified.

"Yes," James replied. "You said it had something to do with someone."

"Well, I said it partially did. Your decision to free one of the gutters couldn't be ignored. Deandra has told us of your impatience surrounding The Controller. I can't say I am surprised, not with your blood."

"My blood?"

"Yes, your DNA." Bridget looked to the left of the room when she said this.

A marble mantlepiece stood in the centre of the room, topped with four long candles in gold candle sticks. On top of it, another painting. James followed her eyes to the portrait of the man. He had well groomed grey hair and a shaven face. James stared dumbfounded into his familiar blue eyes. "That's my grandad."

"What?" Grey asked. "What's he doing there?"

James shook his head and looked back at Bridget.

"Your grandfather James, or Jim as we often call

him, is one of us. He's a rebel."

James looked around at all the faces again. "That can't be right, my grandad is Irish. He died in Donegal."

"Yes, he is Irish but he spent a lot of his time between here and there because of The Controller's preference for London. He led our last big fight against the Whiteflyers."

James' heart skipped a beat of joy, he'd missed his family more than he dared think about. The thought of meeting his grandad and maybe even his granny too was overwhelming.

"Where is he now? I need to see him. Is he on Tartarus?"

A look of pity washed over Bridget's face. "Unfortunately, he didn't come out of that fight. He hasn't been seen since. He spent a lot of his time on all Three Worlds, although Arcadius was his original residence and Tartarus was where most of the fighting took place, but we aren't completely sure where he is now."

James was horrified. "So, he's missing? What are you doing to find him? How long has it been?"

"I know how this must sound," Deandra told him, stepping in for the first time since they arrived. "But we are doing everything we can to find him and the others."

"The others?"

"Yes, he wasn't the only one that went missing during that time. There are dozens of our best and most passionate men and women unaccounted for," Deandra explained.

James' reignited moment of faith in the rebels passed once more. He stood up, pushing his chair back more aggressively than planned. "So, this is why we haven't been taking action? We lose some of our best soldiers and instead of standing up for what they believe in and what they went missing for, we cower and hide."

Some of the men and women went red with shame, others with anger. Bridget, however, very calmly responded, "We have been regrouping, gathering information and searching for our missing troops."

"And? Where has that got you?"

"It has gotten us a very strong lead."

James wasn't listening and continued on his rant, "I have been wondering what's been going on since Grey brought us to you. You were never the revolutionaries these worlds need. This is all finally making sense."

"Did you hear me James?" Bridget interrupted, unphased by his slightly abusive language. "We think we may have found your grandad and we need you to help us to rescue him."

James' thoughts did a back-flip. His emotions couldn't handle all of this information. He had just found out that his grandad was here, only to have him be pulled away. Now there was a chance to get him back. James sat back into his chair and took a deep breath. "Tell me everything."

"Where do I start," Bridget began. "Your grandad belonged to a very special group of Irish rebels that didn't think taking long periods of time to observe and plan was the way to beat The Controller. I believe the group was started by your great great grandad on your grandmother's side. They used tactics they'd used in wars on Earth where they would launch small scale but fast-moving attacks on the Whiteflyers."

James thought back to his granny's stories of her grandfather, he had never met him of course but from what he'd heard this didn't surprise him at all. His grandad, but probably not his granny, would have joined the cause if they came in contact with the rebels when they died. He was never one to absentmindedly follow authority.

"Your grandad soon became one of their leaders. In Arcadius, of course you can travel between countries easily, so it wasn't hard for him to go back and forth from Ireland, London and even America. After a few years, he decided the only logical next step was to infiltrate the Whiteflyers. Like you, he became a level 4, not that you will find him in their history books. He was one of the strongest and most powerful Whiteflyers since The Controller himself."

James thought back to his first meeting with The Controller. He had stared through him as if they'd met before, as if he knew him. "Did The Controller know he was my grandad?"

"Yes, he did," Bridget told him.

James glared at Deandra, she had once asked him if he knew the reason he took such a special interest in him, when she must have known all along.

"And that is why he hates me?"

"Yes I'm sure that has a lot to do with it. The Controller thought your grandfather was going to help keep the worlds in order. He became closer to him than anyone who had come before. So close that some of the rebels even questioned your grandfather's real intentions. They wondered if he had become power hungry and forgotten his real reason for becoming a Whiteflyer. Until that day, when few would question it again."

Bridget took a moment and stared back up at the picture of James' grandfather but then turned her head to the far corner of the room where another picture hung. It was of a man in his early forties. Someone James had never seen before, but someone that Bridget was obviously very affected by. Her eyes glossed over for a couple of seconds before she turned her head back to James as if the moment never happened.

"That day was supposed to end The Controller's reign. Your grandfather was convinced he knew enough about him to beat him. He insisted we fire then and there, that there was no need to wait any longer. Anyway, that's neither here nor there, there's no point in going through the ins and outs of what transpired and what went wrong. All you need to know is that nearly all of our double crossing agents came out of hiding but within hours, not even a full day, The Controller had rounded up every last one of them including your grandfather and the battle was over before it even began. We lost more than just our men and women that day, we lost our hope. You may look at us and think we aren't trying hard enough and that we can do more but you weren't there then."

A look of guilt gathered itself on James' face. He didn't know what he would have done if he was them, if he could have continued the fight. They'd built up so much hope and it had been knocked down so quickly.

"What's the plan to get him back? Where is he?"

"Not to avoid your questions, they are very valid and will all be answered, but I could really do with a break. Do you mind if we reconvene a bit later to go through all of that?"

James was grateful for a timeout and he was also very happy that Bridget asked him for his input around having one. When Deandra had decided she didn't want to tell him anything else for a while, she wanted to make sure that James knew where he stood and so he had no choice but to take matters into his own hands. Bridget treated him like a team member, and as a result, he wanted to act like one.

James nodded gently. "A break would be good. There has been an awful lot to take in for one afternoon. Not that I am not relieved to finally be included."

"Is there anywhere we can get some air around here?" Grey asked Bridget.

"Yes we have a little hidden courtyard, Andy can you please show them where it is."

The man in the hoodie, Andrew Wilson, stood up and made his way to the door. "I sure can, follow me newbies."

The outside area was just as spectacular as inside the building. It was everything Tartarus wasn't. It was a small space, but different shades of green ivy ran up the four walls and lush grass grew under their feet. A huge tree sat in the middle of the garden with plaited roots as thick as James' body peeping through the ground. A bench was perfectly placed near a granite water fountain to take in the little slice of heaven.

James and Stevie took a seat, and Grey sat opposite them on the grass, pulling it as he spoke. "Well, that was a lot, even for me. How are you feeling buddy?"

"Yeah, it was definitely a lot to take in. I don't really know how I feel, I suppose confused is the best way to describe it," James said. "But also optimistic and proud. My grandad really seemed to be doing something, even if it didn't work out."

"And now you get to see him again," Stevie told him. "Be with your family."

James thought of Stevie's mum and wondered if there was anything he should have asked the rebels about her. "Yeah, I mean hopefully, if everything goes to plan."

Stevie fluffed his hair playfully. "It will."

For the next while James, Stevie and Grey walked around the rebel's headquarters. It was smaller than the Whiteflyer's by a long shot, but it was even more special. The decor in Trafalgar Square was flashy and grand and while here it was definitely expensive, it was tasteful and somehow cosy at the same time. There were no bedrooms at the headquarters which showed that nobody lived there full time, but there were a lot of rooms for relaxation. There were also a good few meeting rooms that fit multiple sized parties. There was only one room they were not allowed to enter, James imagined it housed the files of plans past and future, and maybe even the identities of all of the rebels. It was locked and while James could easily open it he decided to stay on the good side of Bridget. She was including him in the plan to rescue his grandad so he wasn't going to do anything to jeopardise that.

When they settled in a smaller unoccupied room with a few brown leather couches in it and olive green walls a voice came through the door.

"What did you think of Bridget?" asked Deandra

"She's definitely more forthcoming than you were with us anyway," James answered.

"I was only secretive when I had to be. Anyone of us would have been just as tight-lipped until it was approved by the council."

"The council?" Stevie asked.

"Those people in the room. We make up the rebel's council of Tartarus. There are a few missing, for various reasons."

"And Bridget, how does she have powers?"

"She was a Whiteflyer like you at one point, she is also a level 2."

"Are any of the others?"

"Most of us with powers were captured with James' grandad but we still have a few."

"I knew that tunnel to the rebel's house was not man made, it was too perfect. Who are the others? Anybody we know?" James asked.

"I know a couple, but I will wait for her to tell you. I am sure there are others though, it's not only you that is kept in the dark, even I'm not told everything."

"That must be exhausting, working for someone who doesn't trust you."

"It's for very good reason. We believe The Controller was let in on your grandfather's plans hours before they had been executed. Things could have gone very differently if we were more careful back then. If he wasn't prepared for an attack on his Palace, who knows what kind of world we would be living in now. We are definitely not perfect, but we don't make the same mistakes twice. Anyway, here I am babbling on when you are supposed to be taking a break from all of this. Take a breather and I will come and get you before the next meeting, where we will go over the rescue mission."

James looked to Stevie, her face was full of concentration. "Back when I was at The Controller's Palace, I read about your grandad, of course at the time I didn't know it was him. It just came back to me there when Deandra mentioned that the fight took place at the Palace. There were files and files on him and the battle and some of the others that were there with him. I wish I could remember if it said anything else about where they were taken."

"Well, I don't think that will matter now. The rebels seem to know, so we are about to find out either way."

"Yeah I suppose, but maybe there was something else there that I could have taken from it all. There was so much information, I really didn't concentrate too much on anything in particular."

A few hours later, James, Stevie and Grey were back seated in the meeting room on the second floor. The rebels were talking amongst themselves awaiting Bridget's arrival. She had been in the room that was off limits for most of the day. Stevie joked that it wasn't an important room after all and just somewhere she went to take a nap in peace, but her tired face when she came back into the room debunked that idea. James looked at the man in the painting she had looked at earlier. Was she doing all of this for him or had she always been a leader?

Bridget addressed the room, "Thanks for your patience everyone. I know that it has been a long day." She then turned directly to the newcomers. "I hope the garden was to your liking and the rest of the building. It isn't anything like the Whiteflyer's headquarters but it is still beautiful in its own right, wouldn't you agree?"

"I would more than agree," Stevie told her. "I find it even more agreeable, particularly when you consider it is in the middle of Tartarus."

"Yes well, as you probably know by now, Tartarus wasn't always such a wasteland."

James thought the woman seemed to be speaking from experience rather than word of mouth and wondered how long she had been dead for. It was hard to know people's true age when their bodies didn't give the usual tell-tale signs.

Bridget began, "So, as you all know we are gathered here to discuss the rescue of what we hope is all of the rebels that were lost to The Controller in the Battle of the Palace. It goes without saying that nobody outside of this room is permitted to know any of the information shared today. Any rebels that are brought into the fold in order to execute the plan, will only be privy to information on a need to know basis and will be briefed by me and by me alone. James looked around and realised that the others in the room were listening just as intently as he and his friends were. They didn't know the details either and were just as eager to be let in on them.

"It has come to our attention that The Controller has had an island, known as Lundy Heritage Coast on Earth, off the south west of the country warded off for the last few years. This began only weeks after our comrades disappeared and has remained under the radar due to the island's size and its meagre population. The former inhabitants were sent off to the gutters around the same time. We originally believed that the island was being used as a sort of testing centre but we are now quite confident that our people are there."

"Confident why?" James asked.

"From both our own scoping missions, some of which I have been involved in, and from information that has come across our camp."

"Did someone share this information or did we get it ourselves?" James continued.

"That is something I am not privileged to divulge," Bridget answered very matter of factly.

"Privileged or willing?" James asked, pushing his

boundaries slightly.

Bridget smiled. "Both I suppose. I wish it was a privilege, but until then I am certainly not willing."

James could understand this considering that a leak was one of the reason's his grandfather's mission didn't succeed, however, it was still frustrating that he wasn't being let in on all of the secrets.

"They are all in the dark with us," Stevie whispered, reading James' face and pointing out that it wasn't a personal attack on him.

Bridget continued, "Learning from last time, we will not be utilising anyone who is already situated in the enemy camp. However, this will mean that we won't have as many people with powers as we would like." She then turned to James, Stevie and Grey. "This is why you are so valuable. Can we count on you for the mission?"

"Definitely," Grey said first, followed by James.

Stevie didn't say anything and then when nudged by Grey she spoke, "I don't know if you are aware, but my mum is a Whiteflyer."

"Yes we are aware," Bridget told her. "Does that impact your stance?"

"No, however, it's not how I would like to first meet her. Will she be there?"

"I can't promise you for definite that she won't Stevie, but she has never been there when I have been scouting. She is stationed in London, and as this will be a surprise mission, the chances are highly unlikely."

Stevie nodded. "Afterwards, is there any way you could organise a meeting?"

Bridget thought about this for a while. "I couldn't in the traditional sense, but I will keep my ears open for word on her whereabouts. If there is a time that I think it would be safe for you to run into her, I will let you know."

"Safe or not, I am going to find her either way."

"I know you will, but I don't want it to be by my word if I don't think the situation is secure."

Stevie understood this but didn't think any situation with her mum would be hostile, she had to believe that. "Right, I am in."

"Great to hear, so that makes 6 of us, James, Stevie, Grey, Florence, Andy and myself."

James turned to look at the woman Bridget referred to as Florence. She didn't look like the obvious Whiteflyer, she was overweight and had long thin hair. She seemed about sixty or so. "What level did you make it to?"

The woman's voice was a lot deeper than he originally imagined when she answered, "I am like Bridget, a level 2. I was a Whiteflyer way back, but it was too much and I had to get out."

"How did they react to your leaving?"

"Nothing like they have with yours, but then again my grandad is not James McEvoy."

James turned to Andy, the man who had brought them to the garden. "What's your story?"

Andy smiled a toothy grin. "Level 3. I left the Whiteflyers shortly after your grandad Jim was taken. The heat was intense on anyone who they suspected might be double crossing them and I wasn't very good at pretending to be evil or power hungry. They cared that I left, but they figured out pretty soon that it was better I was out than in, even if I still had my powers."

"It's great to be working with all three of you and even better that it is to find my grandad."

"Will you need any of us?" Deandra asked Bridget,

"Or is it solely rebels with powers going on this mission?"

"I will," Bridget told her and the others. "We need distractions in the city and I need a small group to come with us as lookouts. We can reconvene tomorrow on who you think is best suited for the job. Four nights from now is D-Day so until then, we will go over the plan as many times as we can. For now, everyone go back and get some rest, tomorrow is another day."

When the sun went down, James, Stevie and Grey followed Deandra back to their rebel camp. It had been a very long and unexpected day in the end and not much was said as they walked the battered streets of Tartarus. If someone had told him this morning he'd be finally let in on the rebel secrets, and get the chance to meet his grandad again he wouldn't have believed it. It felt right, Bridget, the other rebels and he even saw Deandra in a new light. While she didn't go about it in the right way, all of the secrecy wasn't really her fault. He also supposed the lack of action against The Controller wasn't either. He was just happy that that was coming to an end now. Once he found his grandfather, they would be unstoppable.

When they got back to the underground base, nobody was awake. Grey's bed was still on the floor of the room Stevie and James had been staying in, so they crawled into bed and fell fast asleep. James' dreams were consumed by thoughts of his grandad. He remembered stories he told him of Ireland's struggles against Britain in the early 1900's and how passionate he was about not letting people take advantage of you or your home. His granny was also in and out of his dreams, and when he awoke the next morning he regretted forgetting to ask Bridget about her. She seemed to know a lot about his grandad, so there was a strong chance she knew about his grandmother too. There was even a chance she was in London if his grandad went to and fro and Bridget did not mention her when she told him others were captured too. However, on Earth, when she was alive, it was a rare occasion that she visited her family in England, they usually went to her. James quickly put the hope from his mind, she had said his grandad's base was on Arcadius, so even if she was in London the chances she was in Tartarus were extremely low. Nonetheless, he made a mental note to ask Bridget about it when they were next together in an informal setting.

"Should we go in and face the others?" Grey asked, stretching out on his mattress. "I can't imagine Bee and Emmy will be too happy with everything that has gone on over the last two days."

"Yeah I suppose we should, but I am pre warning you that I won't feel bad blasting her across the room if she so much as looks at me the wrong way."

Stevie laughed, "Sounds like a plan."

When they arrived at the common room, Josh was there alone. He looked tired and anxious and didn't get up straight away to talk to the others.

"Sorry I told Deandra where you were. I had to. They threatened to kick me out."

"Don't worry about it," Stevie told him, patting him on the back. "Surprisingly, it turned out to be a blessing in disguise."

Josh perked up a bit. "Really, what happened? Where did she take you?"

Keeping their promise from the night before they didn't tell him much about what went on in the rebel's headquarters. Bridget was very firm on that and they weren't going to blurt out everything before the mission had even begun.

Grey sighed, "Unfortunately, its rebel business. You know how it goes."

"You can't even tell me?"

Grey looked at James and Stevie who both shook their heads. "Afraid not, but we could tell Deandra how great you did at the gutters. Hopefully, she will let you in," Grey said

"Better you than Bee or Emmy," James added.

"Safe to say they're not pleased," Josh told them. "Emmy hasn't said a word to me since I got back and Bee has been even more obnoxious than usual, and that is saying a lot. She will probably be out soon to give you an earful too."

"Well she better be quick, we are off again today," Grey told him. "Once Deandra is up, we are out."

"Presume you can't tell me where you are going either?"

Grey shook his head. "Sorry mate. You know I would if I could."

It turned out that Bee would have to wait until that night to give James, Stevie and Grey a piece of her mind. Not even twenty minutes later they were all dressed and out the door on their way to see the other rebel leaders.

"Ready for today?" Deandra asked as she lifted the garage door up.

"More prepared than yesterday anyway," Grey chuckled.

"Not that that can be hard to beat," Stevie conceded.

"Yeah it was a lot to spring on you, but Bridget felt the time was right to bring you in. She couldn't risk having you running around the country, risk being caught. You heard how few people we have left with powers."

"Yes, those that aren't undercover anyway," James added slyly, hoping for Deandra to spill something.

"Nice try," she said, opening the main door and walking inside.

James spent the next morning listening to Bridget go over the plans that would take place in two days time. She was sending Florence down a day early to build a map of the area and to familiarise herself with what Whiteflyers were on duty and where. The others were going to follow early the morning before the mission. It would take around a day to get there and then they would need time for Florence to debrief them and rest up.

James was on a complete adrenaline high by the time they cut for a midday break. He loved being in the thick of it. James, Stevie, Grey and Deandra took their rest in the garden. Any chance to feel greenery and smell fresh flowers was one worth taking in Tartarus.

"So, what's your story?" Stevie asked Deandra, never one to shy away from people's business.

"What would you like to know?"

"For starters, where do you come from on Earth? Your accent sounds quite English, but sometimes I get a twang of something more exotic."

Deandra smiled thoughtfully to herself. "For most of my time on Earth, I grew up in Egypt. My parents were quite successful archaeologists, so we didn't spend much time in one place. We went from site to site looking for various tombs and treasure. While I didn't have many friends as a child, I wouldn't change it for the world. I became close to the cook and the maid and the men who my father helped on the sites. While my accent can now be considered more English than anything, in those days it was a complete mix."

"My uncle brought me to Egypt when I was ten," Stevie told them. "It was like another world."

"Well I don't know what it's like now, but when I lived there in the 1920s it was a dream."

"And when did you become a rebel?" James asked.

"That wasn't until a good few years after I arrived at Tartarus. To be honest, I wasn't even aware it was possible. They saved me from a particularly nasty encounter with a Whiteflyer and I signed up immediately and now we are here."

"Does that mean that Bee has been here longer than you? I doubt she's particularly happy she's still a junior?"

"Rightfully, that's not how superiority goes or we would be stuck in the old ages. I have earned my spot at the leader's table, for many reasons Bee has not."

James put his hands in the air in defence. "Oh don't get me wrong, I am 'team anything against Bee' so you don't have to tell me again."

Deandra shook her head. "Speaking of Bee, I know you don't seem to get along with her James, but Bridget has asked me to put someone on the patrol with you. Bee deserves that spot."

James held his tongue from cursing and took a deep breath. "Can't it be Josh or even Emmy?"

Grey joined in, "Josh did work really hard in the gutters. If we want it to go smoothly, I don't think that Bee and James working together is the best idea."

Deandra thought for a while, running her fingers through her hair. "The fact Josh went to the gutters is a reason against him in my opinion. The best rebels do as they're told and don't question it. As loyal as she is, Emmy isn't capable of going on a long mission as important as this. I won't promise anything, but I will think about it for the rest of the day. You do make a compelling argument about having Bee and James working together."

For the rest of the day, the leaders discussed the finer details of the plan. Bridget was no longer the sole speaker and it was interesting watching the dynamics amongst the rebels. There were debates about the best moves and routes to take and Bridget often reversed her opinion and adopted other suggestions she decided would do better. While they weren't exactly a democracy, they were also not a dictatorship.

When they got back to the rebel house that night, Deandra called a meeting with everyone. Bee was less than happy to see James, Stevie and Grey for the first time since they'd come back into the fold, however, she didn't dare say anything with Deandra around. Emmy looked shy and awkward and made sure to sit as far from them as possible. James wondered if she regretted what she did or if she was just too afraid to stand up for her beliefs. He quickly decided that if it was the latter he'd even prefer Bee on the mission over her, at least his rebel adversary had a back bone.

"I know you've all been curious about what's been happening over the last few days and wondering where we have been going and why James, Grey and Stevie are back," Deandra stated when everyone was settled and seated in the common area. "While I do not condone James, Grey and Stevie for what happened on the mission the other night, there are bigger fish to fry and it is not productive to dwell on the past. We all have a common goal and that is what is most important in the here and now. Does anybody still have a problem with what happened? If so, please speak your piece so we can move past it."

Bee, not one to pass an opportunity to scold anyone and everyone, sat forward. "My problem is not with them exactly, I expect nothing less from a rabid dog and his cronies, but I do have an issue with what's been happening over the last few days. Is it true, have they been to see the rebel council? Some of us have been working as rebels since before their parents were born and we haven't had that opportunity. Why is it that they get to skip the queue?"

Deandra looked at Bee sympathetically. James knew there was no such queue from his conversations with Deandra earlier, but Bee evidently had not learned to accept that yet. "Unfortunately, I am not able to divulge where we have been Bee. I know our world can be frustrating at times, but it will all be worth it one day. All the secrets and the hierarchy won't be here forever."

Bee scowled, "It's not the secrets I have a problem with, it's who you are letting in on them."

Deandra brushed her hair back off her face and took a deep breath. "Well I am sorry you feel that way Bee, but that is just not up to you."

Bee rolled her eyes and sat back in defeat.

"Anybody else?" Deandra asked, directing her question towards Emmy, who of course didn't respond. "Very well then, let's get to the reason I have gathered you all here. Bridget has asked me to choose someone from this group to go on a mission in the coming days. You will all have a very important place in it, but only one person, along with one other, will be directly involved. I, myself, will also be staying behind for distraction purposes."

Bee's eyes lit up and she sat forward once more.

"The person I have chosen, and it was a very difficult decision, is Josh."

Bee had no words, she glared at everyone one by one before storming out of the room, unable to listen to anymore.

Josh's broad smile spread up to his eyes when the door slammed behind Bee. "I won't let you down," he promised Deandra.

"You better not," Deandra warned. "You have a lot of making up to do if you want to get back into my good books after your antics the other night."

James went to sleep excited that night. He was over the moon that Bee was annoyed and Josh was coming, but was mostly excited that it wasn't long before he would be able to use his powers to make a difference. He had missed them since leaving the beach house, where how far they could fly away from Tartarus, or how big they could make their fireball, in their daily practice was their biggest worry. They were a part of him now, like walking or talking. Yes, he'd used them sometimes since coming back to London, but since the fight with Matthew and the others, he hadn't been able to push them, to really experiment and see what they could do. This mission was another chance for that, and it was all to save his grandad. He couldn't ask for more than that.

Not surprisingly, the next day none of the others were there to see them off, they'd be camping out at the headquarters that night so they could get an early start the following morning. The rebels wanted to ensure they began their travel out of London while it was still dark. Josh and one other weren't able to fly, so they'd slow down the journey a little.

Bridget was waiting in the hallway when they walked into the house. "Welcome Josh. I am Bridget, master of this mission. I thank you in advance for risking your safety for the greater good. Has Deandra brought you through any of the plans?"

"No I didn't," Deandra answered. "I wasn't sure how much he was going to know."

"Well everything, if this mission is to be a success. Follow me Josh, Tabitha, who is also coming with us is upstairs. I will give you both a debrief."

When James and the others went to follow, Bridget held up her hand. "You won't get much free time until tonight, so I'd take it where I could. I will get Josh to meet you in the garden when he's done. You have heard it all already."

Deandra, who wouldn't be going on the mission, continued into the room but the others obeyed and wandered out into the garden.

"Can you believe the cheek of Bee last night? She's so entitled. She thinks because she died before us she's got the right to be let in on everything," Grey vented.

"Ooo now who is finding her annoying," James teased. "I thought we were to be nice to her because she's had a troubled past."

Grey scoffed, "Well, she's not here to hear me is she? I don't even have the patience for her all the time."

"It did make me wonder," James said. "Just how annoyed she was that she wasn't being let in and we were. She knew there was something big coming. What has her so eager to know all the details? She's never cared before if there were secrets kept."

"Yes, but we have been kept in the dark too, haven't we?" Stevie said.

"I know, but it was the way she went about it. It was all a bit desperate."

"You don't think she had other more sinister reasons for wanting to know?" Stevie asked.

"What are you two talking about? What other reasons?" Grey pushed, his eyebrow arched.

James put his hands up. "All I know is that she was very annoyed when she didn't become a Whiteflyer and that Bridget and Deandra both acknowledged that we have rats amongst us."

Grey, putting it all together, shook his head violently. "No, it can't be. She's one of our most loyal rebels." Then looking at Stevie whose eyes were wide, he started to shake his head less forcefully. "Surely not."

"Let's not say anything to anyone for now anyway. Not unless we find some definitive proof. I can't imagine it will go down too well with Deandra if I blurt out at the next meeting about our suspicions. She seems to like her for some reason and insisted to me before that she was sure that nobody in the group was the one leaking the information. Thankfully, she didn't bring her on the mission anyway. We've got some time to think it through when we get back and do some more digging," James said.

"Your suspicions," Grey corrected. "I know you don't like Bee, but she wouldn't. I know that much."

"You also thought it wasn't a great idea to release the people from the gutters," James reminded him. "Now look at where it's gotten us."

Grey took a deep breath, he looked distressed so Stevie changed the subject. "I wonder what this Tabitha is like, have you ever met her?"

"Yeah I went on a mission with her in the past. I am not surprised she was chosen to come here. She is one of those know it all types. The kind that usually made head girl in school. She's harmless though, she's just very by the book."

A while later Josh and Tabitha walked out to the garden and Stevie and James met her for themselves. She had long poker straight mousey hair pushed back in a hairband that is usually reserved for young kids. She was quite short and wore glasses atop her crooked nose that highlighted how Grey described her. "Nice to meet you all," Tabitha said. "Bridget has just briefed us. It's a pleasure to work with you all and nice to see you again Grey, let's hope this mission is more successful than our last."

When Stevie looked at him Grey explained, "We had to cause a scene in order to distract the Whiteflyers away from the headquarters before, but the flames went out of control and burnt down an entire estate before they were able to extinguish it. Nobody was hurt, but I can't say the same for the houses."

"Oh so the Whiteflyers aren't the only people to blame for the mess that Tartarus is?" James observed.

Tabitha blushed. "It was a rare occurrence." James went red. He had not intended on hurting her feelings.

"Don't mind him," Grey assured her. "He's not being serious, we like to give each other a hard time. It's how we show we care, right James?"

James smiled and pat Grey on the back. "He is like the brother I never had."

The rest of the day was filled with important meetings with the whole team. Bridget went through more potential scenarios than James thought was possible, and definitely more than was probable. She wanted everything covered, including whether The

Controller was there, in which case they would abandon the mission. She also discussed what would happen if they did not find anyone at all, in which case the mission would come to a quick end. James thought that The Controller appearing was highly unlikely. In James' experience missions never went as planned, so sometimes it was best to just wing it. However, he didn't recommend this as a strategy to the rest of the team, who seemed comforted by the preparedness.

That night, everyone that was going on the mission gathered in a room upstairs to get some rest before their trek the following day. The sofas and other furnishings had been cleared for this purpose and replaced with small mattresses strategically positioned on the floor. James was surprised when Bridget entered and took her place on a bed by the door.

"What? You didn't think I was going to get special treatment just because I run this house, did you?" Bridget asked the group as their dumbstruck faces watched her shimmy under her blanket. "No, I start as I mean to go on. Which in this case means as a group. Now, lights out," she ordered, using Air to flick the switch. "We've got a long day of travelling ahead of us tomorrow, and we are up before the sun comes out."

James found it extremely difficult to sleep that night. Even though he found them rather meaningless, he found himself going over the situations again in his head. He kept going back to one in particular, where Bridget had said it was possible that the people that had been taken had been converted to the other side. That they were alive and well, and working for The Controller. She had looked at him when she said it, as if she thought it a possibility that his grandfather had switched sides.

He'd remembered the story Deandra had told, and how she said some people thought that he may have before he was abducted. James knew this not to be true, he knew his grandad through and through, but then he thought of Stevie and her mum and a small bit of doubt started to creep back over him. James brushed it from his mind and settled down to sleep. It would be a long few days, no matter the outcome, and who knew how much rest they would get after tonight?

CHAPTER 15 – "LET'S GET TO THE ISLAND."

"It's time to wake up," Stevie whispered in James' ear, pushing him gently from side to side to wake him up. "We've got to get going."

James opened his eyes and saw a similar situation with Tabitha and Grey to his right. Andy and Bridget were already awake and sitting up on their mattress. Josh's bed was made, but he was nowhere to be seen.

"Anybody seen Josh?" Bridget asked the group. Mumbled nos gave her her answer. "Well, he better not have gone far, we don't have any time to spare if we want to get to the city's border before the sun decides to announce the day."

Josh's whereabouts were uncovered when James came out of the room opposite their temporary bedroom. It was where he had been after getting dressed into his green jumper and black jeans. Josh was standing in the hall, fully dressed, in light grey bootleg trousers and a round neck jumper. "There you are James. We are all ready to go."

"Where have you been?" James asked.

"I've been awake for a while actually, pacing the

house. I am a bit on edge, but please don't tell anyone. I don't want them to think that they were wrong to choose me instead of Bee. I imagine she was a contender."

James smiled. "Your secret is safe with me and try not to worry. We still have a while before we get there and you are just keeping watch when we do. You won't be in the thick of it, however it all goes."

Josh took a deep breath in and nodded, but James suspected from the agitated look on his face that his pep talk might not have worked.

"As we discussed yesterday, we are going to walk out of London and then we will take to the sky, once I give the signal that we are far away from prying eyes. I know it is dark, but it is still suspicious having such a big group travel together. Who knows whom we might run into. Everybody partner up and stay close by, " Bridget instructed. "James, do you mind pairing up with me?"

Although he had originally hoped for some alone time with Stevie, James plastered on a smile. They weren't having the best luck with it lately and he'd jump at any chance he'd get. He supposed he would have to wait until after the mission to really talk either way. "I'd love to," he agreed.

After they'd walked a few streets and Bridget was sure they weren't being followed she relaxed. "I wanted to see how you are doing with all of this? You've been told a lot of information over the last few days and a lot has been expected of you. It's enough to confuse anyone."

"Yes, well I am certainly confused, but mostly I am just excited. The prospect of seeing my grandad again isn't something I ever entertained when I arrived at the Three Worlds. He's dead of course, but I didn't think travelling from country to country would be the easiest task. I wouldn't have any idea of what world he'd be in, even if I did manage it."

"Yes, somehow travelling between the worlds seems normal here but taking a trip across the pond almost seems impossible. Of course it is though, and your grandad definitely took advantage of it. However, he was one of the lucky ones that ended up in Arcadius. It certainly would be a mean feat in Tartarus, and even in Torpor."

"I did have something I wanted to ask you," James remembered. My Granny Mc, have you heard anything about her? I am not sure you knew her but she was married to my grandad, she lived in Donegal with him."

Bridget smiled a very sincere smile. "I did know her, Kathleen, she is a great woman. I met her with your grandad on more than one occasion. She is one of those people that has a knack of brightening up any room."

"That's her," James encouraged. "Would she be with my grandad?"

"No, I am happy to say she is not. She wasn't one for leaving her home country very often, so when everything went down she was still back in Donegal. I checked on her shortly after the mission failed to inform her of what went down and to see if she had heard anything. She was up and well, but of course saddened by the news. She is also in Arcadius. I am afraid I don't know more, I have not made contact since."

A sense of hope filled his stomach, he'd meet her again one day and until then she was safe.

"Thanks Bridget. That is more than enough."

When they'd got out of London, they were given the signal that they could take to the sky. Andy jumped off at speed, followed by Grey and Stevie. James had Josh in tow and Bridget had Tabitha, so they were slightly slower off the mark. However, they gained on their allies once they were in the air. Unlike his first experience in the air, Josh wasn't yelping with joy and taking the air in. He still looked nervous about what was to come and was unusually quiet. James thought about trying to calm him down a bit, but it was never his strong suit. Once they got to the island he would talk to Stevie about taking the lead with it. That was always her expertise. It wouldn't do well for the group if Josh freaked out on the mission and ruined their cover. James began to think that maybe Deandra's first choice of bringing Bee was the better move.

"This is cool," Tabitha announced. "You get to do this whenever you want?"

"Not really," James answered. "We did at one point, but London is well patrolled and we are on the run. If we were to roam freely around the sky it wouldn't be long before we bumped into the wrong kind."

"Well, at least you get to do it sometimes," she told him. "A lot of people would do anything for that chance. I know I would."

"And so they do," Grey said. "They are called Whiteflyers."

Tabitha blushed. "I didn't mean.."

Grey patted her on the back. "I know you didn't, but some do."

When they'd arrived over a particularly gorgeous lake Bridget told them they could have a short break. They took a well needed stretch on the lakeside, skipping stones and going for a swim. James, Grey and Andy dried everyone afterwards, syphoning the droplets off their clothes, skin and hair.

"What was it like?" Tabitha asked.

"Learning to use our powers?" Stevie asked.

"No, meeting The Controller."

Stevie, who knew more than most, took the lead. "At first it was overwhelming and I would even go as far as saying that it was exciting. You learn so much about him in training and when you know what it's like to use your powers, you can't help but wonder about what he can do. He made these worlds after all. However, you quickly realise that it's all an act. Yes, he's powerful, but deep down he's the same as every school teacher that made you feel as if you did something terrible because you were late due to family issues, or every shop's security guard that followed you around because you didn't have time to brush your hair that morning. He's controlling and there's not much more to him at the end of the day."

"Well said," James told her, moving his hand to brush against her arm. "He's a bully, and we don't like bullies, do we?"

"No, so let us do something about it," Bridget encouraged them. "Let's get our people back."

Just before nightfall, James got his first glimpse of the island. It was smaller than he expected, but then again his grandad and his comrades would be unconscious so how much space was really necessary? He hadn't been there on Earth, so was unsure whether it had been altered using powers or if the island was always so enclosed. High cliffs circled the outside that sloped down to the middle revealing an open space. There was only one way into it if you did not have powers and that was through a small gap in the cliffs. It was on the left side where the sea led onto a beach so beautiful you'd expect to find it in Thailand or Mexico.

"There," Bridget told them when they got closer. "Amongst the trees on the far side of the island."

"Is that a building?" Stevie asked.

"Yes, that's the Whiteflyers' stronghold here."

"Is that where they are keeping them?" James asked.

"We believe that's the way in, yes, but we don't know much more than that. Hopefully, Florence was able to gauge something more but I've been up here a few times scoping things out and haven't been able to get inside without being noticed. We are meeting her in the cluster of trees near the beach. Let's wait until the last bit of light goes in before getting any closer."

Half an hour later, all of the rebels lowered themselves into the water. Bridget did not want to risk going by Air so she asked James, Grey and Andy to get everyone there safely by sea.

"Are you sure this is not dangerous?" Josh scuttled, splashing about in the water. "I really think going by Air would be the better option. We are used to that and it's only myself and Tabitha that won't be able to help with the load that way."

"We are more than capable of transporting a few dead weights to the beach Josh," Grey, who was in charge of him, said. "Relax please, all of your splashing isn't helping anything."

Of course Grey was right and it was not long later that seven dry bodies were walking towards their meeting spot with Tabitha.

"You got here safely, and early too," Florence rejoiced as they came towards her.

"We didn't exactly get breaks," Andy told her.

"Excuse you, we had a break at the lake, didn't we?" Bridget corrected him.

Andy rephrased himself, "Okay, let me rephrase that then. We only had one break."

"You must be tired. Luckily I have cleared an area to camp," Florence shared, referring to the open three by three space around them. "There are no Whiteflyers near us so you can unwind a bit, but try not to be too loud all the same."

"Yes and don't stay up too late," Bridget added. "Tomorrow will be a long day and night, who knows when your next chance to sleep will be." Their leader then turned to Florence. "Let me just put this bag down and we can go somewhere private to catch up."

"Anybody want to go down to the beach?" James asked when Bridget and Florence had taken their leave and Andy and Tabitha had crawled up to go to sleep.

"No, we shouldn't. Florence said to be quiet," Josh replied.

"She also said there were no Whiteflyers about. Stevie, Grey?"

"I am up for it," Stevie said.

"Me too," Grey agreed. "It's dark anyway."

"On your own heads be it," Josh groaned and took a seat near a sleeping Tabitha.

"What's with him?" Stevie asked when they'd got out of ear shot.

"He's been like this all day. Don't say I told you, but he's really freaked out about the mission. I was thinking maybe you could try to relax him a bit. I tried to, back in London, but evidently it hasn't worked," James said.

Grey frowned and rubbed his eyebrows. "He's usually quite chill about these things but then again we've never really done anything of too much importance when Whiteflyers were about. At the gutters they were nowhere to be seen, were they?"

Stevie bit her lip. "I suppose we need to remember that he doesn't have powers either. Against any of them, he's dust. I'll have a word with him in the morning if he still seems on edge. I doubt he will get any better though, the closer he gets to it, but it's worth a try."

"He could ruin it for everyone if he's not on his A-game," James warned. "Maybe we should tell Bridget."

"Absolutely not," Grey argued. "He's one of us, we aren't going to rat him out just because he is a little nervous. We all get scared sometimes. I wasn't exactly excited about the prospect of rescuing Stevie at The Controller's Palace, but I came through, just like I am confident that Josh will."

James took a deep breath. "You're right, but let's keep an eye on him."

"That I can do."

The beach on Heritage Island did not disappoint from up close either. The sand was pale and soft and while the water was cold it didn't matter to James. He dipped his feet in and looked out on the bay. It was like something from a movie. It was hard to imagine that such horrible things could be happening in such a beautiful place.

"The calm before the storm," Grey predicted as they watched the waves coming in.

"No matter what happens tomorrow, we all stick together," James promised.

"Agreed," the two others chimed in. "Nobody gets left behind."

The next morning began with a debriefing from

Florence.

"So, you mean to say they have all left?" Stevie asked in shock. It has just been revealed that a couple of hours before they had arrived the previous night, half a dozen Whiteflyers made their exit from the island.

"No, I don't know that, but any that I had seen throughout the day did. Someone came in and they all left together. There are most likely still some Whiteflyers inside the wooden house."

"What does that mean?" Grey asked Bridget. "Are James' grandfather and the others still here too?"

Bridget shrugged. "I know as much as you do, but if they are, we have definitely caught a bit of luck. Wouldn't you say? Six Whiteflyers down is a good thing, maybe we won't be outnumbered by whoever might be inside."

"But it doesn't make sense," Stevie contemplated. "Where have they all gone?"

"There must be an emergency requiring their attention on the mainland, however, we can't worry about what that might or might not be until we get back. For the moment let's just be grateful that we have less of them to deal with."

"I did think it was awfully quiet last night," Tabitha told them. "It wasn't what I was expecting anyway."

"Well, what is the plan then?" James asked. "We didn't exactly anticipate this when we went through the hundred and one different scenarios."

"The plan stays the same more or less. We still need to be on guard in case we come across anyone. However, I am not sure the distraction that Tabitha and Josh were going to be in charge of is necessary any longer. If there are no Whiteflyers outside the building it might do more harm than good."

"Then what should we do if not that?" Tabitha asked, slightly annoyed that her part in everything was being dismissed so easily.

"Nothing, I am afraid. You will have to wait here until we get back."

"And if you don't come back?" she asked, slightly horrified.

"There will be a search party looking for us over the next week if we don't make it back, but let's not think negatively please Ms Laveen."

Tabitha blushed. "Sorry, I didn't mean it like that."

James looked to Josh who seemed to perk up a good deal with the news that he wouldn't have to do much after all. It was for the best really that he wasn't involved. James was delighted that he didn't have to tell Bridget about Josh after all, but if he was paired with him for anything important in the future, he was afraid he'd have to refuse. Josh's nerves were even throwing James off a bit and he had to be at his best if they were all going to come out of this mission healthy and well, and with a few more passengers in tow.

"Right, for the rest of the day I need patrols around the island," Bridget ordered. We need to confirm what Florence saw and suss out whether or not there are any others to be found. There is also always the chance that the Whiteflyers who left will be back before nightfall, so we still need to stay alert. Josh and Tabitha, you two can take this area. The rest of you pair up and ship out. Report back here when the sun is at its highest in the sky."

James decided to partner up with Andy for the morning's escapades. For one, he wanted to get to know him better, but he also didn't want Grey to feel left out if he was planning to make another move on Stevie after all of this was over. He wanted to make sure he still felt very much a part of the trio. Not that it was all going to be finished with after tonight, but at least the chapter of saving his grandfather would be over. Then he could concentrate a little more of his efforts on making Stevie fall for him.

"Level 4 aye? How does that feel?" Andy asked as they made their way through the forest behind the beach, towards the building the Whiteflyers were supposedly occupying.

"I mean you know for the most part, you are a level 3. It's just that with a little more," James told him.

"I don't know about that. I heard about you before you arrived on Tartarus and definitely before Deandra brought you to see the rebel leaders. If the rumours are to be believed, you are pretty darn powerful."

James shrugged awkwardly. He thought himself to be more powerful than some of the level 4s he had come across in Torpor, but it wasn't something he liked to discuss with anyone. He wasn't any different and he certainly wasn't special.

"What's your story anyway?" James asked, deflecting the conversation away from himself. "You don't seem like the other rebel leaders."

"What do you mean by that?" Andy asked.

"You are very chill for one, Deandra, Bridget and the others are fine and all, but they are definitely a little wound up. "

"Yeah, I mean I get that, but really we are all quite different if you get to know us. We wouldn't exactly be mates on Earth, however, we all have a common goal that unites us more than what TV series we watched or what bar we liked to visit on the weekend. By now, we are a family."

"Yeah, I suppose when you put it like that I know exactly what you mean." James wasn't sure why, but he felt at ease with Andy, like he could tell him anything.

When they got to the building, Florence's debrief was proven to be true. The building was made completely of wood, with only small glass windows that were fogged and could not be looked through. Tall, wide trees and bushes surrounded the fortress, and somehow made it look like it was always meant to be there. Like it was not man-made at all, but a part of nature. Of course, James knew this to be false, and decided instead that it was the work of a particularly creative level 4 Whiteflyer, maybe even The Controller himself.

"Should we go in?" James asked Andy, aware that he was considered his superior even if James could beat him in battle.

"No, we can't risk messing up tonight's mission. We will have to have patience if we want everything to run smoothly. Bridget wouldn't forgive me if we blew it."

James pursed his lips and nodded. "I wouldn't forgive myself. Let's report back then and wait until tonight."

The others had come to the same conclusion as James and Andy. The island was empty unless there were Whiteflyers inside the wooden base. James worried that this meant they'd missed their shot and that the building was vacant too, but there was no point in dwelling on what might happen. In a few hours, they'd find out exactly what they needed to know.

CHAPTER 16 - "IS SHE DEAD?"

James walked down to the beach as everyone else tried to fit in a small nap before everything kicked off. They did not know when they would get a chance to sleep again, but he couldn't rest, not when he was so close to possibly seeing his grandad again. His family felt so far away from him since coming to Tartarus. In Torpor, the resemblance to Earth made it possible to trick his mind into thinking he was only on holiday. That he'd see them once again sometime soon. However, in Tartarus, that illusion was all too brittle. His grandad on the other hand had possibly sat on this beach, he'd talked with his own allies and most importantly he'd tried to make a difference.

He thought of how his mum would react to seeing them reunited. She was always extremely close to her dad and always thought that he could fix anything. If a fuse went out in the house or if she was having a problem at work, he was the first person on the other end of the phone. Even when he passed away from cancer, she prayed to him whenever she had a problem and if it was resolved, she'd whisper a short thank you.

Memories of his grandad fluttered through James' mind for the rest of the afternoon, with his granny and grandad's relationship taking the lead. While his parents loved each other very much, nothing could beat how his grandparents felt about one another. It was only in recent months, since meeting Stevie, that James knew how they must feel. "Maybe one day," he mumbled under his breath.

"Wakey, wakey," James whispered to Stevie a while later.

"Is it time to go? Did I sleep in?" Stevie asked, her eyes wide and her mouth open as she frantically looked around their small camp.

"No, no you didn't. There's still a little bit to go before we embark. I just wanted to have a word with you before we do."

Stevie rolled to a seating position and rubbed her eyes. "Yes, sure of course. I'd say you're anxious to see your grandad, are you?"

"No it's not that, I wonder if we could go for a walk?"

Stevie looked at him strangely but stretched out and stood up to follow him out of the enclosure.

"Have I ever told you how much you mean to me?" James asked.

"Well, I don't know if you've said it in words exactly, but you don't need to. We are best friends, family really. I feel what you feel."

James took a deep breath and started to pick at his fingers, "No I don't mean like that. I mean have I ever really told you how I feel about you?"

Stevie stared at him in silence and came to a stop, her eyes glazing over.

"I love you Stevie Miller. I have since the day you followed me around the hospital, telling me wild tales of your childhood. I love every hair on your stubborn little head, every finger on your gentle and caring hands, and every toe on your determined, and well rather lanky, feet. I know you might not feel the same, but I was sitting on the beach and I realised that it didn't matter. Before we go into the unexpected, I wanted you to know. I love you and I probably always will."

Tears fell from Stevie's eyes, so James wiped them away. "In Torpor, you spent so much time looking for Liza. You got so mad when anyone even suggested we may be anything other than friends," Stevie gushed. "I didn't dare let myself believe that you thought of me in a romantic way. Then once you found out she was on Earth, you kissed me. At first, I thought I must have been wrong, that you loved me all along. However, then I thought about it, all of those feelings for Liza, they can't have gone away in a second just because she wasn't dead. I convinced myself that I was second best, that if Liza was ever to die, that we'd be over."

"No Stevie, don't you see. It's always been you. If I was angry it was because I knew it to be true. My search for Liza was out of guilt, not love. Not the love that I feel for you anyway, this is like something I can't describe. It's all-consuming. Of course she will always be a part of me, but just like Jen is or my mum or dad. You are the one I really want, the person I belong with."

Stevie's tears streamed even faster down her puffy cheeks as she sniffled. She released a great big smile and James, taking his queue, leaned in for their second kiss. He grabbed the arch in her back and pulled her in closer. She ran her hands through his hair and down his arms, squeezing as she got to the well defined muscle. James lifted her up as she simultaneously wrapped her legs around his waist. He felt like they were the only two in the world.

When Stevie finally came back to ground and they pulled away, James couldn't help but let out a gentle laugh. It had finally come true, she was his and he was hers.

"What are you laughing at silly?" Stevie asked, playfully hitting him on the chest.

"Nothing, I am just happy is all."

"Well, we could have been happy a lot sooner if you'd just have told me all of this earlier. I suppose you're not all to blame though, I should have too. Grey told me to on more than one occasion, but of course I didn't listen."

"Grey told you?" James asked, laughing even harder. "I have to admit, I did think there was something going on between you two at one stage."

"Me and Grey? Absolutely not, that is completely delusional. Although, I did confide in him a lot about everything. He's a great comfort and an even better friend."

James smiled, nodding in agreement.

When Stevie and James walked back into the clearing hand in hand, Grey, who was now awake with the others, stood up in applause. "The prodigal son and his fair maiden, at last."

James blushed and Stevie rolled her eyes. "Very funny, I thought you'd be happy. I finally told him everything."

"So, does that mean there are no more secrets between us?"

"No more secrets."

"Isn't that a relief? Just before we go into battle too."

"I don't know if anybody is going into battle tonight," Bridget revealed. "There is still no sign of any Whiteflyers on the island. Nonetheless, we go in prepared as if the place is flooded with our enemy. I know we planned to wait until midnight, but due to the circumstances I think we can and we should leave as soon as everyone is ready.

"But, there's still no need for us?" Josh asked jittery.

"No, I am afraid not," Bridget answered, not picking up the hope in his voice. "You two will wait here until we either return or until the rescue party comes for you in a few days."

"I can still help," Tabitha, who actually wanted in on the action, pleaded. "If there are no signs of Whiteflyers there's no need for us to wait back here. We can do something useful if we come."

Bridget gave her a pitiful look and shook her head. "Not this time Tabitha. I am sorry."

"Right, is everyone ready?" Bridget asked when everything was packed and hidden and her recruits were dressed and standing. "We enter as we planned. First myself and Andy, then Florence will come in with everyone else once she gets given the signal. We take it room by room and everyone sticks together. Under no circumstance is anyone to think they are too big for the mission and to go off on their own. This needs to run as smoothly and as seamlessly as possible."

When everyone reassured Bridget that they knew the plan back to front and inside out and the sun began to set, they said goodbye to Josh and Tabitha and set off towards the wooden cabin. It wasn't too long a distance because the island was small. However, there were trees and debris in the way so by the time their destination was in view they all breathed a sigh of relief.

"This is it," Bridget told them. "Remember, nobody

is to come forward until the door swings gently open."

James watched intently as Andy and the rebel leader walked towards the building. It was dark, and there were no lights switched on inside, but the moon was full and lit up their path. The building looked especially spectacular in the night's light and some of the flowers growing up the walls sparkled. Then he saw it, the front door opened gently, with what seemed like the result of a strong breeze.

"Now," Florence said motioning onwards. James followed behind, with Stevie and Grey in tow. As they got closer, James could see a shadow in the window to the right of the door. His guard shot up and he was ready to attack. However, when he stepped up the two wooden steps and inside the doorframe, it proved to be Andy keeping watch out the window.

The room they walked into was just as beautiful as the exterior of the building. Flowers of all colours hung from the ceiling and vines grew through the cracks in the floor and up the walls. However, one thing stood out across the room, something that didn't blend in with nature or seem like it belonged. It was a large metal door, sealed shut with no handle to get inside.

"Everybody prepare yourself," Bridget whispered. "I am going to try and get it open with Air."

James was sure she wouldn't be able to, with no access to the other side of the door and with no handle for leverage, but stopping her would be a bigger fuss than waiting it out. When the door wouldn't budge, Bridget looked to James. He'd already decided that the best way to get it open would be to loosen the door frame surrounding it and use air to remove it completely. Within seconds, the door was quietly on its back and the dark room on the other side was waiting.

Bridget was the first through the door, and one by one the others followed. Once again the room was empty, however, very differently decorated than the first. There was nothing fairy-like about the thick grey brick walls. It felt more like a prison than anything else. The focal point of the bare room was not the low ceilings, or the lack of windows, but the hole in the centre of the room that held stairs leading underground.

"Stay alert," Bridget reminded them as they took their mission underground.

James didn't think it possible, but he almost felt like the absence of any Whiteflyers heightened his nerves. Balls of fire and gusts of wind he could take, but the anticipation of the unknown was the scariest feeling of all.

The long cavern downstairs was too dark to see into, so following the lead from Bridget, small flames appeared on the hands of each rebel, illuminating the way. The dungeon smelled damp. The floor dipped in areas, filling James' boots with water, and drips from the ceiling threatened to extinguish his flame with every step.

"It's too quiet," Andy said to Bridget in hushed tones. "There can't be anyone here. They've moved them, it's an ambush."

"Or they are unconscious and unable to make a sound," Bridget suggested. "We keep moving until we've covered the whole ground, we've come too far to turn back."

"And if it's a trap? If they know we are coming?"

"We all knew the risks when we agreed to come. Don't give up on me now Andy."

"I would never," he said frustrated and offended that she thought his words were due to nerves. "I just know this has to be on our terms, and right now I am not getting the feeling that we are in control."

"What do the rest of you think?" Bridget asked.

Florence was the first to answer, "I am with you Bridget. We see it through."

"We go on," James reiterated.

"I third that," Stevie added.

"I don't know," Grey said, "It all seems too perfect if they are here, but I suppose it doesn't matter what I think if it is two against four."

Bridget inhaled through her nose, nodded and turned back around.

James wasn't sure how long they had been walking down the underground lane for before the scenery finally changed, but it was safe to say they were nowhere near the wooden building anymore.

"What's that up ahead?" Stevie asked. "I see a light."

"I think there's a light on the wall. It's a flame torch."

"There's loads of them," James noted as his vision got used to the light. "I think we are coming close to something."

"Or someone," Stevie proposed.

"Let's hope it's the right 'someone' if so," Andy said, still unconvinced that moving forward was the right idea.

As they moved down the concrete tunnel, and got closer to the lights. James started to make out a similar hole in the floor to that in the wooden house. At first he thought their journey was to be continued on a lower level, but the closer they got the louder he could hear familiar swishing sounds. It wasn't a hollow passageway at all. Instead, it made itself known as a watering hole.

"What is it?" Stevie asked Bridget. "Are we supposed to go down there?"

"No," Bridget told her, as they stared into blackness, only broken up by lightly moving water. "Nobody is going swimming into a dark hole. That is where I cross the line. I am afraid you were right Andy. We need to turn around and regroup. This is an unforeseen event we have not planned for."

"No," James said, louder than he should have, his voice echoing back where they came from. "Have you forgotten? We have powers and Water happens to be one of mine."

"James, you have nowhere to clear the water away to. You will flood us up here if you drain it from down there."

"She's right James," Andy agreed.

"No I won't, because I can not only control the water from the hole but also the ground you are walking on and even more useful, the ground above our heads."

"Won't that cause a scene?" Grey worried.

"Well, as luck would have it there are no Whiteflyers on the island, so there is nobody to witness my 'scene'."

"James, we have no idea who is up there now, we haven't seen light in well over an hour."

"I am not turning back, my grandad could be down there."

Bridget looked back into the hole and back at James, before scrunching her eyes closed. "Make a scene."

James' eyes lit up as he flashed his pearly teeth.

"Stand back."

Nobody had to be asked twice and they made their way back down the tunnel.

To begin, James needed light, so with a flick of his eyes to the surrounding lanterns, each of them magnified threefold. Next he looked up at the thick concrete above him. He channelled his power source through his feet and up the walls to meet his gaze and within seconds anything above him was obliterated to nothing. Concrete and mud rained into the distance.

"Well, I guess we aren't going down the subtle route," Grey shouted down to him.

"Nope, we are going down the fast lane," James shouted back.

James looked into the basin of dark water. He could feel, using Earth, that it was deeper even than it looked. There was a lot of water to get rid of and he needed to be able to see up above if he was going to disperse it safely. So, with one jump he was up in the air dangling above the hole a stream of water following him. The sea was quite far away, but he could easily make the distance, so with a swish of his hand, he willed the salty water back home.

When James was satisfied the hole was empty, he made his way back into the hole and peered downwards into the empty abyss.

"I can take it from here," Bridget said, lighting up the unknown with one hundred controlled tiny flames shooting out of her hand.

"There," Stevie pointed, peering down from beside James. "What are those black boxes towards the bottom?"

James immediately jumped in to find out and made his way towards the most central box. It was damp and cold, but James barely noticed. His adrenaline was pumping and his sole concern was in front of him.

James slowed as he got closer to the box, he couldn't believe what he was seeing. Surely it wasn't what it looked like.

"What are they?" Bridget shouted down.

He had by now landed on his feet and was crouched over the long box. "It's a... I think they are coffins."

One by one the rebels removed all sixteen coffins from the underground prison. They wanted to be out in the open, unrestricted when they opened them. Anything could be waiting inside and Bridget insisted they were in the best position possible when they found out. James' heart and stomach couldn't stand the wait. He was sure you couldn't die here, but then what was the need for a coffin? How much could they all really know about the Three Worlds when their creator was The Controller?

"Whatever we find here, we stick to the plan. Nobody goes missing, we go back to London together. Is everybody clear?" Bridget confirmed as they circled around the coffins.

When everybody agreed, she stepped forward and made her way toward the first one. James held his breath as she used Air to open the lock and push the lid open. He was almost expecting The Controller himself to jump out of the box. When nothing happened, he moved closer to look inside.

"Is that?" Florence asked, getting a view inside the coffin before him. He moved forward quickly, the anticipation unbearable. His stomach dropped. A dark woman was lying motionless inside. She was sopping wet, her skin rubbery and prune like.

Bridget's face depicted a mix of shock, disgust and

also a slight bit of relief. "Yes, that's Margot."

"Is she dead?" Stevie asked from behind.

Bridget knelt down to feel for a pulse and within seconds her face brightened. "She's just unconscious."

One by one the rebels opened the coffins, acknowledging each person inside. Bridget insisted they took special care with each one, aware that any of them could be a trap. James waited with bated breath for his grandad, but ten coffins, then twelve were open and there was no sign of him. Bridget also looked worried, for his grandad, who was a dear friend and a valuable asset to the rebels, but also it seemed for someone else. She was having an unspoken conversation with Florence after every person was revealed.

"One left," Stevie told him, squeezing his hand as they stood over the last black coffin. With a small gust of air the lid was blown off, James quickly shut his eyes, he wasn't ready for the disappointment just yet. Bridget yelped and dropped to the floor and for one moment James' heart stopped. He opened his eyes. He was lying there. Not his grandad, but the man hanging on Bridget's wall. The one she looked to when she went over the night of their disappearance.

Everybody watched as she held his body close, tears falling into his already wet hair. "Harry," she whispered. "I thought I had lost you."

James sank to the ground, how could this have happened? They'd come so far, found so many, but he'd trade them all back for a moment with his Grandad. His stomach clenched as the realisation of the selfishness of his thoughts set in.

"I'm sorry James," Stevie tried to comfort him. "We won't stop until we find him. We found these people, we can find him too. I am sure of it.

"I am sorry too James, for getting your hopes up, only to have them be shot down," Bridget acknowledged. "But Harry and the others, they might know something. They were there that night. As soon as they wake up…" As if on cue, one of the men began to move. His eyes opened slightly, but came back to a close.

Florence rushed to him. "Joseph, can you hear me?" she said clearly. "It's Florence, Bridget and Andy are with me too. Are you there?"

The grey haired man's eyes opened again, this time staying ajar. Andy held his back up from the hard wooden coffin. "Of course, you'd be the first one to awaken. You are hard as nails. You'll never let us forget this," he laughed, relief flooding his voice.

Just then, another body began to move, and then another, and another. Before it had really sunk in that his grandad was not, after all, amongst them, everybody was up and about, being told about what had happened by a very elated Bridget.

"Where is James?" a younger man asked, looking around the group when Bridget had finished a rundown of their whereabouts. For a second James thought he was referring to him before realising that his grandad was their true hero.

Bridget looked at James. "James, or Jim as most of us know him, was not with you. He's the only one from that mission who is still missing." Looking at the faces of these men and women, James realised that some were angry.

"It's no wonder," Joseph shouted, his fist tightly clenched. "What a coincidence, that The Controller's best friend wasn't left to rot with the rest of us."

Confusion flooded James' brain, surely this man didn't think the reason his grandad wasn't here was because he wasn't on their side after all.

"I knew it," another raged.

"We told you, you wouldn't listen," came another.

James looked frantically through their faces, some angry, some sad, and some still in shock.

"SILENCE," came the loudest voice of all, coming from the man Bridget had called Harry. "I will not have his name tarnished when he is not here to defend it. How many of you were with him when everything went down? Beside him, when The Controller arrived and reigned down hell? Because I was and not for one second did he falter in our plan, did he hesitate against the most powerful man in history. If he is not here, it's because he is suffering a fate worse than ours for crimes the ruler of these worlds sees far outweighs ours."

The ball of anxiety that had been building in James' stomach started to shrink as the mumbles of traitor subsided.

Bridget looked to James in reassurance and when he nodded she turned back to the crowd. "Debriefs of that day will have to wait until we get back to a safe location. As you can see there are no Whiteflyers on guard. Only yesterday this was not the case. We need to leave as..." Once again Bridget was cut off. She was staring at someone running towards her from the bushes screaming.

"They're coming!" Tabitha screamed. "He told them we were here."

James searched the bushes behind her for Josh, but when he was nowhere to be seen all of the pieces from the last few days fell into place. His delight at flying the first time James had taken him into the air, refusing to leave with Emmy and going to the gutters with them, his disappearance the other morning before they left, his out of character nervousness. Josh was the rat.

CHAPTER 17 - "SO, WE MEET AGAIN."

"He can't have told the Whiteflyers on us. It's Josh, that's not him," Grey pleaded with Tabitha as she was giving Bridget a run down about what had happened since they had left.

"Grey, there's no doubt, he's fighting for the other side," Tabitha assured him. "As soon as you all left he started to pack up and was marching around the area we camped in panicked circles. He kept mumbling about how they were coming, and wondering whether he'd done the right thing and saying that it was too late to go back now. I told him to sit down and take a breath and that we'd signed up for it. I told him you'd all be fine and in a week from now we would be toasting our success back at the headquarters. However, he wasn't even listening, it was as if I wasn't even there."

"And is that when he left? Did he say who was coming?" Bridget asked, looking at the sky frantically.

"No, he stayed for a bit longer, but was on edge staring into the bushes and looking out to the mainland. When he went to leave, he finally acknowledged me with a warning."

"What did he say?" Harry asked, his face white.

"To hide, that the Whiteflyers were coming, that they knew we were here and that anyone they found would suffer a fate worse than death. Then he ran into the bushes and that's when I came straight here."

"Did he say when they were coming?" Bridget urged.

"No, but if I was to guess it would be at midnight. That's the time you were supposed to start the mission, that's the time he would have told them."

"I think so too," Bridget agreed, before turning to Harry. "Do any of you still have your powers?"

Harry shook his head gravely, "No, they were taken from us when we were captured. We have no powers.."

"Do you mind me asking how?" James asked, he knew it wasn't the time but if the Whiteflyers were on their way it may be valuable information if he was to be captured.

"I've no idea," Harry told him. "It wasn't through our blood anyway, like we always thought. When I was in his presence, I felt them being slowly drained, it was a pull like I can't describe. Within moments they were gone. We could never have won against him, we were powerless, quite literally. Your grandfather held onto his for quite some time, I have no idea how, but in the end The Controller got what he wanted. He always will."

"Not while I am here," James protested. "If my grandad held onto his powers for even a moment longer than you could, there must be a way to prevent him from taking them."

"Well, if he's on his way with the Whiteflyers, and if they're here by midnight, unfortunately you don't have very long to find out."

"Harry, you can't be here when he comes, none of you can," Bridget announced. "You have been through enough, you need to get out of here. The rebels need you back at home. I need you."

"You can't fight them alone," Harry urged her. "You need to go, everyone who can fly. Take one person with you. The rest of us can hide."

"I don't think there's time for escaping," came a shaky Grey from behind. James turned to see him pointing into the sky. "They're here."

"Run," Bridget screamed at them. "You are useless to us here. Hide where you can, we will hold them off. There is a rebel search party coming here in a few days, they'll get you out."

"I am not leaving you," Harry insisted. "Look at what happened last time we failed to stick together."

"Harry, you will only slow me down, give me something to worry about and end up distracting me"

"She's right," James told him. "You all need to leave and let us do our job. You will weigh us down if you don't."

Harry looked to the group of desperate people behind him. It was obvious they needed him more than Bridget. "Come back to me," he mouthed to Bridget before running off, with the people they had just rescued, following in his wake through the dense trees.

"Is everybody with us?" Bridget asked James, Stevie, Grey, Andy and Florence. "Anybody who isn't, follow Harry now."

The troops looked at one another before looking back to Bridget and nodding. "Oh, we are in this," James said. "Let's cook us up some Whiteflyer scrambled eggs."

They got into formation, James at the front ready. Nearly ten Whiteflyers were zooming through the sky. Their destination was focused on the beach, but at the last minute they turned towards the cabin. James wondered if Josh was signalling them in this direction or if they had been spotted.

"Can anybody see The Controller? Bridget asked, her eyes squinted towards the sky.

"I can't see him," Andy said. "Maybe he's not coming after all."

"If he knows James is here, he's coming. It all depends on how much information that weasel shared with them."

Grey cringed at her words.

"Matthew's with them," Stevie told James and Grey. "However, I can't make out Rowe or Tim."

"That's Glaze on the very right and Rosie next to him," Grey noted. "I'll handle them."

"No, I will take Rosie," Stevie decided. "She's been pissing me off since I first heard her name and I've never even met her. That's not Watson, is it James, the blonde beside Matthew?"

James knew it was as soon as she said it. Watson was someone he had actually admired from back in Torpor and seeing him fly towards him was like a punch in the stomach. "Yep, it sure is. Him and Matthew are mine."

"I'll take Edith, that's the woman beside Watson," Bridget declared as the Whiteflyers gained speed and neared them. "Andy you go between everyone as you are needed and Florence you take Baz."

"You know Watson?" Stevie asked.

"I know everyone," Bridget smiled. "James, don't pay too much attention to him. Concentrate on Matthew."

"What is that supposed to mean?"

"No time to explain," Bridget answered, just as the Whiteflyers feet touched the ground.

James felt an anger bubble inside him as he

stared across the clearing. With a swift movement of her arm the woman Bridget had called Edith swept away the coffins littered on the ground. Matthew cracked his knuckles and Watson stared intently toward the rebel leader. James looked to her to see why, but there was no obvious reason painted on her face.

"Well, well we meet again," Matthew said directly to James.

"Looks like it," James replied. "You got out of the hole you were in last time then did you? I promise I won't make it so easy to get free from the one you will end up in tonight."

Matthew scrunched up his nose and spat on the ground, ready to spring into action albeit Watson held his shoulder. "Relax Avery, that's an order."

"I see you released our prisoners," Watson addressed the group. "Did they all get away?"

"Yes, some time ago. They are clear of this island," Bridget informed him.

"Oh, but you just thought you'd stick around did you?" Edith asked sarcastically.

"No, we thought we'd stay back and search for clues as to where James' grandfather is, he was not with the others after all."

Watson's eyes narrowed as she said this and James had an instinctive feeling that Bridget was sending him some sort of a message.

"Well, you can ask The Controller yourself very soon, he's on his way," Watson shared.

At that moment, the back of James' neck tingled. Was Watson sending them a warning? He didn't dare presume he was on their side, he had to still be on guard, but everything was pointing in his favour. Shaking these thoughts from his head, the gravity of what Watson had told them kicked in and James jumped into protective mode, he had to get Stevie off the island.

"No point in waiting for the grass to grow", James announced to the gathering, sending a huge gust of wind towards the Whiteflyers. Edith fell backwards almost immediately, knocked out with the sheer force. Baz and Glaze lost their footing, but put up enough of a block just in time so that they weren't out of the game just yet. Matthew, Rosie and Watson were still standing untouched.

"Not this time Moore," Matthew roared, sending a stream of fireballs his way. James blew each of them out before they'd even passed the halfway mark. Meanwhile, Stevie had jumped into the air above Rosie, trying to flatten her from the top down and Grey had summoned the last of the water from the coffin's hideout and aimed it at Glazes' head. Each of the rebels was doing their part to rid themselves of the Whiteflyers before The Controller arrived. James decided that it was best to do as Bridget had said and put all his attention on Matthew. He tried to keep his promise and bury him again, however, Matthew knowing this was coming dodged it at every turn. Fireballs flew across the yard, with gusts of wind coming just as quickly.

"Afraid Catherine will give you a spanking if you are not successful this time?" James asked, trying to cause a distraction. "Or maybe it's your dad that you are looking to impress?"

Matthew's face went raw red which gave James the small opportunity he needed. He opened the ground behind his feet and with one last push of wind, sent him backwards before closing the earth neatly on top of him.

James turned to the others, but he was seconds too late. A stream of fire was engulfing Florence. She let out a sharp piercing cry before falling to the ground. James turned on Baz, anger flaring from up his body and did the exact same thing back to him. Baz, too stubborn to admit pain, quietly submitted to his fate.

James turned to Stevie, with help from Andy she was doing a pretty good job of keeping on top of Rosie and he couldn't help but feel a bubble of pride for how far she had come since their first week in training. Not long after, Rosie was lying motionless in a tree. With only Glaze, and possibly Watson left, everyone turned on Glaze at once. In no time, he had joined Rosie in the tree. James then moved to take down Watson, however, before he had time to even heat up his fingertips Bridget put her hand up to block him. "No James, he is one of us," she revealed.

A warm feeling shuddered up James' back. There was nobody in Torpor that he would rather hear this news about.

"Ahh so you're the one that has been giving the inside scoop to the rebels?" Stevie asked, her smile revealing that she was just as happy as James felt.

"No time to go into details I am afraid, Miss Miller. It's not over that easy," Watson said, his eyes wide at the sky. "Bridget, unless you think I can help by revealing myself, I think it is best you knock me out." Bridget didn't have to be asked twice, within seconds Watson was on his back.

James watched as four people flew towards them. The Controller in the middle, Vask on one side and Amos and Stevie's mum on the other.

Stevie held her breath. "It's her."

"Don't let her fool you Stevie, she's not with us, she

never has been," Bridget petitioned. "It's not the time to get to know her again or to see if there is any good left in her."

James' head was spinning."Or maybe it is just the time for that. Promise me Stevie, that you will do what you need to do to get out of here in one piece. I need to know you're safe if this goes pear shaped."

Stevie shook her head in shock. "Absolutely not, I won't leave you. We have just.."

"You can't help us if you're seen to be a rebel with us. Please do this. You will have Watson."

Stevie didn't say anything else, but her face told James enough, she wasn't going to go with her mum if the opportunity arose.

"Prepare for the worst," Bridget whispered. "This is it."

James watched in disgust as The Controller's feet touched down on the island only metres in front of them. He was looking immaculately groomed as always, not a brown hair out of place in his perfectly kept black suit. Vask's face was unreadable standing strong beside him in his Whiteflyer robes. He was avoiding eye contact with James altogether. Stevie's mum was smiling at her daughter, clutching onto Amos' hand.

"We meet again, James Moore. You have been causing quite the disturbance since we last met, haven't you? And my beautiful Stevie, how nice it will be to have you back in my palace." He then turned to Stevie's mum, "I believe you know Monica here. Come and embrace her." Stevie's mum loosened her grip on Amos and stepped forward, but Stevie didn't move.

"Stevie, I know it's been a while. I can't quite believe it myself. You are so grown up" her mum gushed.

"It's okay, you will be safe with me, your mum."

Stevie scrunched up her nose and squinted her eyes. "I have no mum. I didn't have one on Earth and as it turns out, I don't have one here."

"I am not the same woman I was back then. I know I did not bring you up as I should have. We didn't have anything, but now we have the Three Worlds at our feet. Come and enjoy it with me. Everything I've done here is for you, so we can finally have a better life together."

"Funny you say that, everything I have done since I got here was for you too, or so I thought," Stevie replied. "I thought you'd need my help. That Tartarus would destroy you, that you didn't deserve to be here because of an addiction on Earth, but it turns out that the addiction did not change you, you always were a bad person. The addiction just weakened you, so I was unable to see your true colours."

"Stevie, I am your family, I know what's best for you, even if you don't see it now. These people are trouble."

Stevie motioned to Grey and James. "These people are my family, you on the other hand mean nothing to me."

Stevie's mum looked confused. It seemed she really did think Stevie would be on her side once she was found.

"That was not a request, show your mum the respect she deserves," The Controller insisted calmly. Before James had time to do anything, Stevie was being pulled at an unnatural speed toward the woman. James saw red, The Controller's smirk in his direction only heightening it.

"Let go of her," he roared, simultaneously using Air to pull Stevie back.

"Ahhh, please stop James, you are hurting me" Stevie screamed, as she was throttled in every direction. James loosened his hold on her and instead aimed his powers at The Controller. Fire came pouring out of his fingers towards his adversary. It was pushed to the side and set Amos alight. Monica's attention was immediately pulled away from her only child as her lover's skin flayed and he rocked on the ground.

The Controller screamed in anger. He was furious that one of his soldiers was already down. James imagined it had nothing to do with Amos himself and everything to do with his own power trip. "ENOUGH," he yelled, putting James' flames out instantly. Grey stepped forward, realising what was about to happen and with all his might he attempted to blow The Controller off his feet. His clothes didn't even sway in the wind, but his attention did shift. He stared at Grey intently with narrow eyes.

"What's happening?" Grey yelped anxiously.

James couldn't see how he was being harmed, but the look of sheer horror on his friend's face confirmed that something bad was happening. Stevie, realising the same thing, jumped in.

"Get back," Monica screamed. "You are my daughter. I will not let you interfere with the master of the Three Worlds."

Stevie scowled at the woman she barely recognised. "Be with your lover," she mumbled, and within seconds Monica was burning fire.

James turned back to Grey, he was staring at the palms of his hands. "My powers, they're gone," he mumbled.

Remembering what Harry had said, James realised

what was happening. Before the end of the night, The Controller intended for each of them to share Grey's distress.

"Get into formation," he screamed at the other rebels.

The Controller, thinking this was beyond him, turned to Vask. "Deal with them," he ordered. He was one of the most powerful Whiteflyer's James knew, probably even stronger than Hatt and Catherine. James instinctively put an Air guard up, blocking his friends. It would do little long term, but it would give them a few seconds to prepare. Vask looked from The Controller and then back to the line of rebels. James waited for the attack, but time went by and it never came. "I said, deal with them," The Controller commanded again, this time with an edge to his voice. Vask listened and jumped into the air. He looked out at sea, and with a few hand movements, a ball of water the size of a small house was making its way towards them. James went to jump into the air after him, to stop it before it got close, but a pull on his arm stopped him. It was Andy, he was shaking his head gently at him.

When the water ball neared, Vask took one more look at the rebels, this time settling on Bridget, James watched closely and swore he saw a little nod.

"What are you waiting for?" The Controller asked, outraged at Vask's impotence.

"This," Vask replied before turning his aim towards his leader. The Controller splashed around furiously as the water enclosed him. James looked on in shock in realisation that another one of the Whiteflyers made their true side known.

"Everybody, to the air," Bridget ordered. "We need

to weaken him."

"Bring him towards the sea," Vask instructed.

James and the others didn't have to be asked twice. Grey, powerless, and Florence who was unconscious, were the only two left behind. The Controller was lifted into the air, trapped in the ball of water. The Water rebels helped Vask to control the water as best they could, but they hadn't even flown two metres towards the sea when the bubble was broken from the inside out and The Controller was set free. His face was furious, but he needed to catch his breath before he could reign down the hell that he was no doubt planning. "Again," Vask called out, summoning the water droplets that had broken free back together. James and Andy assisted him, but it was too slow and their enemy too fast. A massive tornado came crashing towards them, demanding their attention. All of them pushed on the wind, determined to use it against its master. Its pace slowed but it came forward all the same. James made a rash decision, he needed to go rogue. He released himself from his current task and roughly landed near Grey. Earth was the only chance they really had, if they had any at all.

"Stay back," he shouted to Grey as the Earth beneath them started to rumble. The other rebels followed suit and stayed back in the air. Vask, however, realising what James was doing, landed near to him. Together they drilled a crater in the island, deeper than even the motes surrounding the gutters. The Controller came swooping down to the land furious.

"You think you can beat me here, on my land," he said with an air of lunacy. "I fertilised this ground, I grew those trees, this land is me." With that, the Earth went against James' will and began to close. James felt Vask give in and let go, but he couldn't. He closed his eyes, numbing himself as he had done the day he first used his powers. He pulled on the land with everything he had, and slowly, to his disbelief, it began to obey him. The Controller was outraged and Vask just as shocked. "I said, this is my land!" The Controller roared again, as if he was attempting to command the very earth they stood on, but still the land continued to split. All James needed was to keep it open long enough, to produce enough Air to force The Controller down. Just as Vask had attempted with the sea, with the right amount of pressure, he'd suffocate before he made his way to the top. He was sure it was not a permanent solution, but it would give them time to get free from the island or better, find a way to defeat him once and for all.

Just then, James felt it. He could no longer feel his power source buzzing around his head. It then disappeared from his neck and then from his shoulders. He looked at The Controller and the smirk on his face confirmed it. As he had done with Grey, The Controller was pulling his powers from him from the head down. The gap in the ground started to close again, as the earth was enriching and James was weakening.

"What's happening?" Vask asked, noticing the difference.

"He's draining my powers," James told him in a panic.

"Remember what Harry said," Bridget shouted to him. "Your grandfather held him off, so you can too."

The Controller's words rang in James' head. He specifically said that this was his land. "Vask, cover for me," James demanded. He looked to the floor and felt it. The Controller was pulling his powers out using his connection to the planet. Just as someone needed to be grounded in order to use Earth, James wondered if he had to be touching the soil in order for The Controller to take his powers. He had no choice but to try, so he lifted himself from the ground.

Instantly, the crater in the island closed and James' power source began to buzz around his body once more.

"Get out of here now," Vask shouted, streams of fire flowing from his body as he tried to hold off The Controller with help from the other rebels. "You are useless to us with no powers."

James' head was scrambled, he couldn't just leave them. "Now James," came Bridget from just behind him. "The Whiteflyers, they're waking up."

James looked to the ground to see Edith stirring. "I can't leave you in this mess."

"You can and you will," Bridget told him reassuringly. "Your powers just now were like nothing I have ever seen. I now see the truth in what Vask has been telling me since your training. You're our only hope if we want to defeat him."

"But I can't, my powers, they are his for the taking if he can get me on solid ground."

"Find your grandad, he will know what to do."

James took a deep breath. Once Bridget mentioned his grandad, the decision was made for him. He swooped back down towards the ground, making sure to avoid touching the Earth and grabbed Grey. "Stevie, we need to leave, and fast."

Stevie didn't hesitate and in no time at all, before Edith even had time to open her eyes, they were off the edge of the island.

CHAPTER 18 - "HOW DO YOU ALL FEEL ABOUT A TRIP TO ARCADIUS?"

James and Stevie flew as fast as they could, with Grey in tow, until the sun came up. They needed to get as far away from the island as possible before they could even think about taking a break. The Controller would be well out of the predicament he was in by now and he could be on their heels. James couldn't help but feel entirely guilty about the rebels they had to leave behind. They'd no doubt be tortured for information or just for punishment. He did, however, get satisfaction from thinking about how Matthew would react when he was rescued and realised that James and his friends had gotten away again.

As soon as they landed, Stevie ran to James and held him in an embrace. He kissed her all over her face before pulling her back into a hug. For one moment, James forgot all of his worries and remembered about their conversation from before the Whiteflyers arrived. The island had been bitter sweet for him. "Get over here," Stevie yelled to Grey, tears streaming down her face as she motioned for him to join in on their hug.

Grey didn't move and continued to stare into space. "It's over for me," he said sullenly, sitting on the floor outside the old barn they intended to rest up in. "I feel empty. Without my powers I am useless and to make matters even worse, it's all Josh's fault. I trusted him with my life. If it wasn't for me, he wouldn't even have been involved in the mission."

James had some idea of how he felt, when he had thought he was going to lose his own powers, his body went into full panic mode. His face almost felt numb when the power source left it. "Don't be so ridiculous, none of us could have known. We all begged for Josh to replace Bee. If there was a rat amongst us, she was who I was putting my money on. Also, about your powers, I am going to get them back for you very soon," James promised, walking over to sit next to him. "If The Controller can take them as he pleases, I am sure I can find a way to give them back."

"I guess it's safe to say all of those vials of blood and getting rid of your powers by draining the body are a load of codswallop. It must be what he says to get people off his scent," Stevie guessed.

James nodded. "I reckon so, it doesn't add up, there's something bigger at play here. Didn't Catherine once say that he travelled the Worlds before making sure only those he could trust had powers? He must have to be in their presence himself. I can't decide if that is a good thing or a bad thing."

"Well, I don't think she used those exact words, but yes something like that."

"Another thing, the ground," James remembered. "It was getting greener and the grass was growing, as my powers were sucked under."

Grey looked at him in thought, "Now that I think about it, I am sure it was the same for me. It almost felt like it was being nurtured by them."

"If he is the key to our powers, he must have been there the day we got them. It's a wonder Vask never knew about it all. I am still on a high that he was on our side, and Watson, I can't forget about him. Hopefully, he will be spared at least."

"Maybe Vask did know?" Stevie asked.

"No, he would have told Bridget and the others. They were clueless about how he took people's powers from them."

"I guess he never really trusts anyone."

"Nobody, except I have my suspicions that at one time, he may just have trusted one person enough to let him on everything," James told her. "And, we are going to find him. How do you all feel about a trip to Arcadius? I think it's about time we give our lordship's house another visit. I believe you said there was some interesting reading we should catch up on while we are there Stevie."

Stevie smiled, "Yes, I believe I did."

ABOUT THE AUTHOR

Kieva Mclaughlin

Kieva McLaughlin was born in Dublin, Ireland. She studied Journalism at University and later when on to get an MSc in Marketing. From an early age, Kieva was drawn to books that didn't reflect normal everyday life. Fantasy books, stories set in a different era and war novels have always been amongst her favourites.

After waking from a vivid night of dreaming, Kieva jotted down what memories she had left of a sleep filled with afterlives, flying soldiers, fire throwers and love. Two years later, The Three Worlds series was born.

BOOKS IN THIS SERIES

The Three Worlds

Torpor